IN TOO DEEP

THE BLACKHAWK BOYS, BOOK 5

IN TOO DEEP

THE BLACKHAWK BOYS, BOOK 5

New York Times Bestselling Author

LEXI RYAN

Interior design and formatting by:

E.M. TIPPETTS BOOK DESIGNS

www.emtippettsbookdesigns.com

For Stef

About
IN TOO DEEP

New York Times bestselling author Lexi Ryan brings readers a sexy NFL player who's pulled out all the stops for one more chance with the love of his life.

I have four months to make my wife fall in love with me or let her go forever.

I loved Bailey Green long before she watched her loser ex take his last breaths. I held her while they lowered his coffin into the ground, stilled her shaking hands when the nightmares would tear her from sleep. I waited for her through her grief. But while she was always willing to let me in her bed, she refused to let me in the one place I longed to be—her heart.

Tired of playing second string to a dead man, I let her go. I moved to Florida to begin my NFL career and tried to pretend my perfect life didn't leave me empty. I'd almost given up. Until one drunken night in Vegas, we stumbled down the aisle and said, "I do."

In exchange for the divorce she wants so badly, she's agreed to remain my wife until the end of the year. She has no idea the favors I've called in or the lies I've told to get her here, but if I succeed, none of that matters.

My secrets always seemed justified, but Bailey has her own—

secrets that explain why she always pushed me away, secrets that make me wonder if I should have let her. Now we're in too deep and I might lose the only girl I've ever loved and the best friend I've ever had.

IN TOO DEEP is a sexy and emotional novel intended for mature readers. It's the fifth book in the world of the Blackhawk Boys, but can be enjoyed as a standalone.

Football. Secrets. Lies. Passion. These boys don't play fair. Which Blackhawk Boy will steal your heart?

Book 1 - SPINNING OUT (Arrow's story)
Book 2 - RUSHING IN (Christopher's story)
Book 3 - GOING UNDER (Sebastian's story)
Book 4 - FALLING HARD (Keegan's story)
Book 5 - IN TOO DEEP (Mason's story)

kisses turn to little nibbles. He slides a hand up my bare stomach to cup my breast, and my mind latches on to the possibility of this as my new life—of feeling Mason's tender kisses every morning, of getting to talk to him after a bad day, of sleeping in his bed and waking in his arms. I've spent years coming to terms with that life being some other girl's reality. I never let myself imagine it could be mine.

With a hand on my shoulder, he guides me to my back, and his gorgeous green eyes lock on mine as he positions himself on top of me. "You know how long I've been lying here waiting for you to wake up?"

A moan escapes my lips at the weight of him right where I want him, but I force myself to focus. I press my hands to his chest before he can lower his mouth to mine. "*Why* is there a ring on my finger?" But my brain has been lulled into submission by the feel of his body, and all logic must have abandoned me, because I don't sound the least bit panicked. My words are soft and low, almost flirty.

"I'm pretty sure we got married." His eyes crinkle in the corners. He is so goddamned good-looking that it makes me want to forget the panic I should be feeling. Behind that smile is a man who dated me when I was still a stripper and treated me like I was precious. This is the guy who wiped my tears and held me through my sobs as I grieved for another man. This is the man who waited and fought for me even when I didn't deserve it.

If a girl is going to wake up in Vegas, surprise-married to someone, she couldn't do much better than Mason Dahl.

"We can't be married." I mentally catalogue last night: dinner, burlesque show, dancing, and too many drinks at every stop. I'm trying really hard to concentrate on finding rational Bailey somewhere beneath all this lust and longing, but she's hiding. *Coward.*

Maybe I'm still a little drunk. When we were drinking last night, I figured we'd end up sleeping together. I *hoped.* I wanted him . . . just one more time. I still do.

My legs part instinctively, letting him settle between them. His face softens, and his eyes float closed as he exhales. "Fuck, I've missed this."

Me too. God, have I missed it. He feels so damn good—hot skin and hard muscle, like he woke up ready to touch me, thinking *only* of touching me. His eyes open again and lock on mine, and I know his thoughts haven't strayed off course.

Sleeping with Mason is one thing. But *marrying* him? Maybe this is a dream; maybe I don't have to be logical about anything and can just *enjoy.* Panic fights its way to the surface of my consciousness, but I push it away and draw my knees up to his waist. We can deal with these pesky rings later, can't we? I want to relish this moment.

I can't. The ache in my heart won't let me. No matter how good he feels here. No matter how much I've missed him.

His gaze drops to my breasts, his lips twisted in raw hunger. I take his face in my hands, guiding him to meet my gaze. "Focus."

"I'm pretty damn focused."

Dear God. I didn't even realize how much I missed that husky rumble of his voice. Goosebumps dance across my skin, and my thighs clench instinctively. I long for the feel of his breath against my ear as he slides inside me.

He dips his head and presses a kiss to the top of one breast and then the other. I arch into him, because *that mouth* . . . "Was there somewhere in particular you wanted me to focus? I aim to please."

I don't want to protest. I want to sink into the pleasure of his tongue flattening against my nipple and the gentle pressure of his hand cupping my breast. "Focus on the rings we're wearing," I say weakly.

"But they're not nearly as interesting as your body." He pauses a beat and lifts his head to meet my gaze. "Unless they mean I get to taste you every morning."

Every morning. "No." Now the panic surges, more powerful, bringing a wave of nausea with it. "This is a disaster."

He rolls off me and sits on the side of the bed, scraping a hand over his face. "Not the way I hoped to start our first day as husband and wife."

I gape. "You can't be serious."

He tosses a glance at me over his shoulder. "We're fucking great together." He swallows. "Or we were. Once. Is it really the worst thing that could have happened?"

No. The worst is knowing I have to undo it. The worst is knowing I have what I want in my hands and a past that requires me to give it back. This isn't the worst. *This* is just a ripple in the pond of my mediocre life. *This* is just fate teasing me with what I can't have. "We can't be married."

"Of course. Because you don't want me unless you're drunk or I'm offering a no-strings night in my bed."

I don't flinch. Other girls might, but not me. Why flinch when it's true?

My phone buzzes, and the sound of Mia's ringtone makes me wilt. My sole job for the next two weeks is to not fuck up Mia's perfect day. We're in Vegas for her bachelorette party, and in two weeks it will be her wedding. I want to go to her and tell her I woke up married. I want to beg her to help me fix it. Mia is a fixer, and when she can't fix, she listens. But telling her would open a whole can of worms I'm not prepared to deal with, so I ignore the phone.

"We really got married?" I sound weak. Helpless.

Mason stands, and I can't help but watch as he swaggers toward the minibar and pulls out a bottle of water. He unscrews the cap and drains half of it in one long pull before replying, "We did."

"Wh-*why*?" How drunk was I that I thought that was a good idea? How drunk was I that I believed I was someone else—someone good enough for him, someone who hasn't made promises that can't be broken?

He winces then grabs a second bottle of water and brings it to me. "Drink this."

I sit up in bed and take a sip. My stomach rolls in protest. I have to fix this, and fast. "Can we keep this quiet?"

"What exactly are we keeping quiet?"

I hold up my hand. “This marriage? This ring? Oh my God.” I yank it off my finger, grab his hand, and press it into his open palm. “The media is going to go crazy if they catch wind.”

He searches my face. “It would make an okay story, but not an outrageous one. NFL player marries old friend in Vegas?” He shrugs, as if the idea of our mistake flashing in headlines is of no consequence to him.

Shit, fuck, damn. What have I done?

He got the headline wrong. It would read, *NFL player marries* stripper *in Vegas.* And he's wrong about the other part, too. The media would love this story. They'd make it out to be outrageous and dig for dirt on me—not that it would be hard to get something juicy. The stripper thing isn't exactly a secret, and it would probably satisfy them enough that they wouldn't bother to dig deeper. *Please, God, don't let them dig deeper.*

There are other people who wouldn't love the story of our impulsive marriage, people who'd be quick to remind me I've made promises.

“We can't let that happen. Mia and Arrow—their wedding,” I stammer. There's a special place in Best Friend Hell where I'll burn for using Mia as an excuse to keep this mistake quiet. “We can't have the media hounding us for a story when the next two weeks should be about *them.* The last thing Mia needs right now is me stealing the show with my drama.” My phone rings again, and again the ringtone tells me it's her. She's probably wondering where I am. I can't avoid her much longer. “Can we just keep this quiet and figure it out on our own?”

“Sure thing.” His jaw is hard as he digs my phone from my purse and tosses it on the bed. “It’ll be our secret.” Then he walks to the bathroom and shuts the door behind him, his anger rolling off him in waves and making me feel like a world-class bitch.

CHAPTER 1

MASON

Bill McCombs smacks me between the shoulder blades so hard that I choke on the water going down my throat. "How you doing there, son?" he asks, his voice too loud, too jovial.

Coughing, I pull my water bottle from my lips and wipe at my mouth with the back of my hand. I stayed after practice to run more routes with Dre, and now I'm sweaty and exhausted and in desperate need of an ice bath. "Good to see you, Bill," I say between coughs.

"Have you talked to my daughter recently?"

Oh, fuck. The Florida sun is beating down on me, but at the mention of Bill's daughter, a chill goes up my spine as if I were already in the ice bath waiting for me in the locker room. Bill McCombs is the owner of the Gulf Gators, the NFL franchise that signed me for two years after I graduated from Blackhawk

Hills University. Last spring, I made the biggest mistake of my adult life when I took his daughter—my former girlfriend, Lindy—home with me. I've been waiting for it to come back and bite me in the ass.

He chuckles a little too loudly. "She's coming to town after training camp, and she'll be right in your backyard all regular season."

I clear my throat. "I saw her when she was here for spring break. I think she mentioned it then." *Tread carefully, Mason.* "She's coming for an internship. Is that right?"

"That's right. My baby girl's gonna be a marketing mastermind." He rubs his hands together. "But more importantly, you two can be reunited."

I try to get a read on his features. What does he know? Does he mean reunited for the first time since we dated in high school, or reunited for the first time since April?

"I didn't know you met up with her in April, you old dog." He smacks my shoulder. "My girl still talks about you all the time. She admires you and what you've made of yourself so much. To be honest, Mrs. McCombs and I are pretty proud of you too. We've always seen you as a son."

"Thank you." This time my smile is sincere. The McCombs are old family friends. They were practically a second set of parents to me when I was growing up. I appreciate everything they've done for me over the years, even if I'd rather they lay off on the whole matchmaking thing.

"You'll make sure you're around for her welcome-home

party? The whole team's invited, of course. We need to celebrate the start of her real career. My girl's gonna do big things. Can't wait."

"Of course. I wouldn't miss it." I hope this is the end of the conversation, but I'm worried it's just the beginning of the mess I've made for myself.

Hayden Owen catches my eye from where he's standing a few feet away on the sideline. He arches a brow before sticking his tongue in the side of his mouth in a lewd miming of a blowjob. I know he's telling me to suck up to Bill, but he has no idea that my relationship with Bill is far more complicated than that of the typical player and team owner. I've never told Owen about Lindy.

"I'll see you at the party," Bill says, and he heads over to talk to the coach.

What did Bill say to me after drafting me in the second round? *"I'm just looking out for my family. I wouldn't want your career in anyone else's hands."*

I thought he meant "family" in the metaphorical sense, but now I have a sick ache in my gut that tells me he was looking out for Lindy by giving me a job, and now he's ready to see his plans come to fruition.

BAILEY

That son of a bitch is dodging my calls.

Alone in my car with the sun beating down on me through the windshield, I scowl at my phone as if it alone is responsible for putting me in this situation. When I woke up in Vegas with Mason's ring on my finger, my biggest concern was keeping it quiet. After he agreed to that, I assumed the divorce part would come easily. The marriage was a mistake for both of us, so ending it was the obvious solution. Right?

But no, two months later and we're still married. He's making it impossible for me to make arrangements to change that. I've called him half a dozen times since Arrow and Mia's wedding, and he either doesn't answer or is too busy to talk. If we stay married for much longer, someone's going to find out about it. And if one person does, someone else will, and eventually it will get back to the wrong people.

After shoving my phone into my purse, I sling it over my shoulder and head into the bank. I'm half grateful for my irritation with Mason, if only because it helps me forget the nerves slithering in my belly like a pit of snakes.

When I push from the hot sidewalk in through the glass doors, the cool air washes over me and cools my face. *God bless modern conveniences.* The guy at the reception desk smiles brightly when I step inside. "Can I help you?"

"I have an appointment with Jim Brewer?" It comes out like a question, and I feel like an idiot. I don't know why I'm even here. I already know the odds of me getting this loan are slightly worse than Satan needing a fleece coat in hell.

"He's expecting you," the man says. He has a vaguely familiar round baby face, an eager-to-please smile, and eyes that study me just a little too long. I wonder if he knows just by looking at me that I don't belong here.

"Thank you." I squeeze my purse strap in my hand and follow him into a dark-paneled hallway.

When we reach the last door at the end of the hall, he takes the knob in his hand but stops before opening the door. He turns toward me. "I don't know if you remember me." He clears his throat and looks over my shoulder to make sure no one has followed us. Seemingly satisfied that we're alone, he says, "It's been a couple of years now, but I used to see you . . ." His cheeks turn red. "A *lot*."

It clicks—why he looks familiar. *Awesome.* I'm at the bank for the most intimidating meeting of my life, and the man leading the way is an old regular. At least this guy was respectful and kind, which I can't say for all the patrons at the Pretty Kitty. However, if memory serves, he was a shitty tipper, and I wasn't a dancer because I found it personally gratifying.

I force a smile. "Right, I thought I recognized you. Was it . . ." He's not wearing a nametag. Damn. "Steve?"

"Ron," he says.

"Oh, right. Sorry!" I couldn't have told you this dude's name if you'd offered me a million in cash. If this makes me the worst, so be it. "Good to see you again." *Not really.*

"Yes. Really turned my day around." His gaze drops to my tits as if he expects them to be bare instead of modestly covered by my purple shirt. I can practically see the movie reel in his mind replaying every lap dance he ever got from me, and hear his mental soundtrack cataloguing every song I ever shook my ass to. "So good to be reunited." His hand is still on the doorknob but not turning, so I guess he wants to play catchup. *Shoot me now.*

I could brush him off, but since he's standing between me and an important meeting, I don't really want to be a bitch. *Small talk it is.* "How have you been?"

He lifts his gaze back to mine and gives a helpless shrug. "Okay. Finally cleaned up my act for the old lady, but I still have the same old problems."

"Oh, I'm sorry to hear that." I have no idea what problems he's talking about. None.

"She just shuts me out, you know?" His eyes flick down the hall again, but unfortunately, we're still alone. He lowers his voice. "She puts out, like, maybe twice a year if I'm lucky. And then she has the nerve to get pissed about the money I spend at the Kitty."

"Oh, that's rough." *Turn the knob, Ron. Turn. It.*

So, okay, maybe I'm the worst *ever*. That's fine by me. Lonely dudes told me their problems all the time when I danced. I pretended to care because it was part of my job, but I got through those hours by turning off all emotion. That included empathy.

"Do you ever think about going back?" Ron asks. "The Kitty isn't the same without you." Oh, great. His gaze has returned to my tits, and the memory reel has started turning again.

"I've moved on. It's just not the scene for me anymore." I clear my throat and wave toward the door. "I don't want to keep Mr. Brewer waiting, but it was so great to catch up."

I'm the worst *and* a liar, but he's opening the door, so all's well that ends well.

"Stop by the front on your way out if you would," Ron says to me before turning to the man sitting behind the polished walnut desk. "Bailey Green here for you, sir." He flashes me a grin. "She's an old friend, so treat her well."

"Thanks, Ron," Mr. Brewer says.

Three steps and the click of a door later, I'm free of my adoring fan. I approach the desk and offer my hand. "Thank you for meeting with me."

Mr. Brewer stands and gives my hand a firm shake before retaking his seat. "Please, make yourself at home. How do you know my assistant?"

"Oh, you know, around town." *Awkward.* "Have you had the chance to look at my application?" I sink into the upholstered chair in front of his desk, and he taps his pen on the file in front of him. Before he speaks, I know his answer.

"Ms. Green," he begins, his tone saccharine. "The good news is that the bar looks like it's a sound business, and I believe it would be a great investment. You should be proud for seeing that for yourself and exploring the opportunity before the local investors get wind of the owners wanting to sell."

I swallow. "The bad news?"

He grimaces, but it looks more practiced than sincere. "The bad news is that I can't give you a loan without someone cosigning for you. The business isn't the problem; it's your credit score and already profound debt-to-income ratio. Either would make our underwriters take pause, but together . . ." He shakes his head.

"I'm working on that." I force a smile I don't feel. "I've developed a side business in photography, so as that picks up, I'll have more income to start paying down my debt. I don't plan on giving myself a raise once the bar's mine, and I'll continue to work there, so the bar's cash flow will be better than it is now." I swallow to stop myself from rambling. This was all included in my business proposal. "I just know my friends want to sell it so they can move on, and I don't want to end up working for"—I cut myself off before saying *some asshole*—"just anyone."

"I fully understand that. Have you thought about turning your photography business into a full-time job? As opposed to the bar, something like photography doesn't take much capital to get started. You already have the equipment, and you wouldn't need to have a studio right away. If all businesses were so cheap to start up, I'd be out of work." He chuckles, as if the prospect is hilarious.

"I don't think there's enough interest for my niche, honestly." My shoulders sag. It's not that I don't love the idea of making my side gig my primary source of income. The opposite, really. I found a passion for taking boudoir shots by accident, but it's so fulfilling. Unlike stripping, this little risky business venture is something I *do* find personally gratifying. Women deserve to know they're beautiful and desirable, and how rad that I can use a camera and some simple props to make them believe it. I just don't think it's possible to turn that into something that pays the bills.

I don't know why I bothered coming here. Keegan's been offering to sell me the bar since he was picked up by the Gators, and I always told him no because I knew exactly how this meeting would go. Now that he and Arrow are serious about offloading the responsibility of ownership, I had to try.

"Our background check shows that you're married," Mr. Brewer says, and *that* gets my attention.

Shit. I didn't even think of that. Just because Mason and I haven't acted like husband and wife doesn't mean it's not legally so. "Sorry. I didn't think to include that."

"You should have. It could benefit you, actually," the banker says. "I didn't run your husband's credit because you didn't include him on the application, but I couldn't help but notice his name, and if that's the Mason Dahl I think it is, we should get him on here." He looks to me expectantly.

"No, thank you. If I buy the business, it will be under my name only. I don't want my . . . husband involved." *My husband.* Wow. That's the first time I've used those words together, and it feels ridiculous, as if I'm a little girl who's pretending to be married to her celebrity crush.

"You understand that having his name on the application could get you the loan, right?"

"I'm doing this without him." He probably thinks I'm insane. Who marries an NFL player and then takes her shitty-ass credit score to try to buy an established business along with all of its equipment and inventory?

"Okay. I just wanted to bring it up. You don't have anyone

who can cosign for you? A parent or sibling? Maybe a good friend who wants to be a silent partner?"

I shake my head. Mom might be the only one in town with credit worse than mine, and all my good friends have settled elsewhere. Whether they say it out loud or not, they're all ready to cut ties with Blackhawk Valley and move on with their lives. *Thus, the need for this miserably embarrassing meeting.* "No one."

"I wish I had better news for you." He takes the thick manila folder off the table and offers it to me. It holds more details about my finances than anyone in my life knows. "Good luck, Ms. Green."

I stand and take the folder. "Thank you. Sorry I wasted your time."

He stands, and we do an awkward repeat of our introduction as he shakes my hand. "You didn't waste my time at all. I hope you're able to work something out." He comes around to my side of the desk, then looks to the door and hesitates a beat before turning back to me. "I don't mean to pry, but if your husband is in Florida, why are you hoping to buy a business in Blackhawk Valley?"

As if it's not bad enough that this man knows the dirty details of my financial situation, now I have to tell him my other embarrassing secret. I could choose not to say anything, but he might talk to people about my marriage, and that would be a disaster. I swallow what's left of my pride. "We aren't going to stay married. We're old friends. When we were in Vegas together, apparently we thought saying vows would be a blast." I clutch the folder to my chest. "We're getting an annulment. It just hasn't processed yet." *Hasn't processed* is stretching the truth, but it'll do. "If you could keep this between us, I'd appreciate it. We've managed to keep our elopement from the press, and I'd like to keep it that way."

"Right. Yes. Of course. I won't tell anyone." He smirks. "Too bad you can't really be married to an NFL player, am I right? Then you'd be able to kiss all that debt goodbye *and* have your bar." He chuckles and lowers his voice to add, "Though you probably wouldn't need to run a business if you were his wife, huh? You wouldn't need to make investments in anything more stressful than beach houses and designer purses."

I flinch, but Mr. Brewer misses it. Is that the best I can hope for? Some rich husband who can make my debt disappear?

He opens the door for me and smiles. "Good luck with everything. I hope you'll come back to see me someday when I can give you better news."

I thank him again, put my head down, and head straight for the exit.

When I open the door, the heat smacks me in the face, and I'm suddenly so jealous of all my friends and their glamourous lives. If they were faced with a day this hot, they'd go swim in their private pools or take a day at the beach. They definitely wouldn't spend it getting rejected for a loan for a business they're not really sure they want or talking to a desperate married guy who's too well acquainted with their personal anatomy.

CHAPTER 2

MASON

"Why don't you just marry his hot, totally fuckable daughter? Sounds like if you did, he'd trip over himself to give you a new contract the second you're eligible." On that note, Hayden Owen drains the rest of his whiskey and gives me a proud smile that says, *I just solved all your problems. You're welcome.* "Seriously, it's almost unfair. Cardinal rule of football is to never fuck with the daughters—not the owner's, not the coaches', not the GM's. Hands off the daughters, no matter how hot. But in your case, you get to. Fuck her, marry her, hell, give that old man some grandkids and he'll probably hand you one hell of a signing bonus."

I narrow my eyes at Owen. "You know I can't do that."

"Oh. Right." He tips his head back and laughs. "Because you're already married to the chick who's hounding you for a divorce. I forgot. Damn, and I thought my love life was a mess."

"I wish I'd never told you," I say, and he smirks. *Asshole.* Aside from my current marital status, I can't marry Lindy McCombs because I'd rather have my balls ripped off than spend my life with her. But those aren't words a guy says out loud when said guy needs to be in the good graces of Bill McCombs. "Lindy doesn't interest me."

Owen cocks a brow. "I've met her, and I wouldn't throw her out of bed for eating crackers."

I scratch my jaw and study him. "You are one shallow son of a bitch, know that?"

He shrugs, unoffended. "You're the one who slept with her when you don't even like her."

I groan. "Don't remind me. Not one of my finer moments."

"Okay then, think of your career."

"I am thinking about my career. That's why I'm worried." I rub the back of my neck, where tension has been gathering every day since my conversation with Bill. I signed a two-year contract, so it's not as if I'm in danger of losing my spot this year, but if the Gators' hands-on owner is pissed at me and won't let the coach take me off the bench, I can kiss a new contract goodbye.

I take a deep breath. I'm being paranoid. I shouldn't assume the worst. "I don't want to talk about Lindy."

"Bill does, though," Owen says. "I overheard you two tonight, and he seemed *very interested* in talking about his daughter. And you. And how much she *admires* you. Tell me, are you looking forward to reuniting with your high school sweetheart? Because you told him you were, but my lie detector said that answer was *bullshit.*"

"Didn't your mama ever teach you that it's rude to eavesdrop?"

Owen smacks the table and laughs, but I know, beneath his ribbing, he's starting to worry about my fate on the team. He knows as well as I do that with another capable receiver on the field, he won't be buried in double coverage, and he might actually get the chance to score. We're better off if we're both playing.

"It'll be fine," I say. "Lindy is reasonable, and when I tell her—again—that what happened in April was a mistake, she'll understand. She's matured too much to run to her dad and demand I be punished for leading her on."

"Are you trying to convince me or yourself?"

I don't need to answer that question. "I wish she didn't have this damn internship here. Our parents will spend the entire season pushing us together, and though I regularly remind them that arranged marriages aren't a thing in twenty-first-century America, I don't want it to mess with my career."

My phone buzzes with a call and rattles against the tabletop. Bailey's face appears on the screen. Her blond hair is piled into a messy knot on the top of her head, and she's sticking her tongue out and crossing her eyes. I snapped the picture while we were at the pool in Vegas, and every time I see it I smile. As always, my happiness at seeing her face is immediately followed by that sick pull in my gut that reminds me I can't postpone the inevitable much longer. She doesn't want me, and it's time to let her go.

Owen grabs the phone from my hand and grunts. "This the one who's got you all tied up in knots?"

I take it back and swipe left to decline the call. It's been more than two months since our drunken wedding vows. I promised her we'd get our marriage annulled after Arrow and Mia's wedding, but their wedding came and went, and I'm afraid that if I let Bailey go now, she'll be out of my life forever.

She wants to end our marriage. It needs to be done, but it can wait. A divorce just feels so damn . . . final.

"Why don't you just tell Bill and Lindy the truth about Bailey?"

A handful of *truths* about Bailey come to mind, but I know he's referring to our marriage. "Why would I want him to know?" I'm not sure what's more embarrassing—that we did it to begin with or that I woke up thinking she would finally give us a chance just because we'd exchanged rings and signed some papers.

Owen taps my phone. "If Bill knew about your wife, he wouldn't pressure you into making babies with his daughter. I mean, he might not like it at first, but it could go a long way to keep the peace. Bill can't blame you for shirking his daughter's affections when you're already married."

"I guess. In theory." I shrug. "It's a moot point. The only part of this marriage that interests Bailey is how we end it."

"Didn't you say she wants to be friends? Maybe she'd let it drag out a couple more months—just to get you through the princess daughter's visit."

I take a sip of my whiskey and process his words. It makes

a lot of sense and it might work, but not without serious complications. For one, Bailey would have to agree to tell people about our marriage—something she's been totally against to date—*and* move in with me. Two, I'd have to live with Bailey for a whole season knowing she's not really mine, and at the end of it I'd have to let her go. That sounds like a special kind of hell I'm not keen on inviting into my life.

"It'll work out." Owen stands and tosses a couple of bills on the table before smacking me between the shoulder blades. "One way or another, it always does. You coming to my place for the cookout?"

"I can't," I say. "I promised my parents I'd drive home for the meeting with their event coordinator. They're planning their thirtieth anniversary party."

Owen's lips curl into the charming smile that landed him on the cover of *GQ* last year. "Thirty years, no shit?"

"No shit."

"Which puts your mom in her fifties?"

I sigh, knowing where this is going. When she was younger, Mom was a model for a high-end lingerie company, and she's remained an icon for the brand. "Yeah."

"Damn. She's still got it. Send her my regards."

I grunt as I push out of my side of the booth. "You wish."

My phone buzzes with a text.

Bailey: *You'd better be dead in a ditch somewhere, you call-dodging asshole.*

BAILEY

It's ninety-five degrees in Blackhawk Valley tonight, and the air is thick and sticky with humidity—not so different to what I imagine it'd be like to live in a giant, sweaty armpit. If hell is a dry heat, I could go for a visit about now. Instead, I'm scrubbing tables on the patio of The End Zone because no matter how hot it is, the smokers want a place to drink where they can also provide carcinogens with the most direct path to their lungs.

The bar is quiet and will remain that way until BHU is back in session in the fall, but it'll pick up a little with the after-work crowd. I want to have the patio ready so I can help Tia behind the bar if she needs it. I toss my rag in my bucket, and I'm reaching for my broom when my phone buzzes in my pocket. I pull it out to check it and my jaw drops in surprise.

Sweet baby Jesus, it's a miracle. Mason answered my text. I lean against the side of the building and unlock my screen to read his message. I'm so used to him ignoring me, I'm almost too shocked to be annoyed by his response.

Mason: *Not dead or in a ditch. Just busy.*

I'm sure he's busy—busy enjoying the beach or busy spending his money. Busy living a charmed life while I'm sweeping up cigarette butts and melting in the heat. I narrow my eyes as my thumbs fly across the screen to type my reply.

> ***Me:*** *In that case, I'm going to have to come down there and kill you myself.*
> ***Mason:*** *Perfect. When can I expect you?*

Yes. I'm definitely going to kill him. I'm heading to Seaside tomorrow to do a last-minute session with a friend and hopefully see my sister, but it looks like a visit to my accidental husband remains on the list. I type a series of expletives in the reply field then force myself to delete them and shut off my screen. I'll see him in the flesh soon enough, and those words are more effective when delivered in person.

"Bailey!"

The sound of the familiar voice behind me makes me pause before turning. He taps my shoulder, and I turn to face him. *Shit.*

It's Ron, the assistant from the bank who remembered me from the Pretty Kitty. I've never seen him at The End Zone before—probably because he prefers establishments where the servers aren't fully clothed. I'd like to think he's here for a drink, but judging by the way he's eyeing my tits, I'd guess today's reunion gave him ideas. *Joy.*

"Hi, Rob." I know it's Ron, but I'm a bitch, and I don't love that he came here looking for me.

"Ron," he corrects with a smile. "You forgot to stop on your way out today." His face is flushed and he's breathing hard, as if he ran here from the bank.

"Sorry about that." *Not sorry.*

"I looked up your workplace on your loan application. I hope that's okay."

I stiffen. *It's not.*

"I wanted to give you something." He holds out a business card. "My cell's on there. Since you're not working at the Pretty Kitty anymore, I can finally take you out for that dinner we always talked about."

We? In our many "conversations," I'm pretty sure Ron's the only one who ever talked about us doing dinner. I just offered the excuses. I stare at the card before blinking up at his bright pink face. Sweat is rolling down his cheeks, and he wipes at it with the back of his hand. "You're *married*, Ron."

"Does it really matter?" His grin is probably supposed to be mischievous, but he just looks like another douchebag in a long line of douches I've met in my life. Seriously, the world is full of assholes. Even if it makes me a hypocrite, since I used to strip in front of *this* asshole, I feel really bad for Ron's wife.

"Yeah," I say. "It matters. I'm not interested in going out with any man who's spent *years* as a regular at the Pretty Kitty, but I wouldn't be interested in a married man regardless of how desperate he is for attention."

He pulls back. "So you can rub your ass against my dick and take my money, but you're too good to eat a meal with me?" He rubs his sweaty pink chin. "Do you know what that makes you? But don't worry. I can pay."

I put my hand on his chest, and his sneer drops away as his

lips part and his eyes dilate. *Too easy.*

Smiling, I tug on his tie to pull him down as I bring my mouth to his ear. "It makes me a woman who knew how to play you when I needed cash," I whisper, and when he tries to yank away, I tighten my grip on his tie. "And it makes you a pathetic schmuck who can't even score with his wife because he doesn't see her as anything more than a walking pussy who can cook."

He yanks away, and I release his tie at the same moment, making him stumble back a few steps then fall on his ass between two tables. "What turned you into such a bitch?"

I shake my head. "I was always a bitch. But I am sorry I rubbed my ass against your dick. I didn't mean to. It's just so small I didn't realize it was there."

Tia pokes her head out the back door. "Are you okay?"

"I'm fine," Ron says, standing and smoothing his tailored pants.

She sneers at him. "I wasn't talking to you."

I wave her off. "I'm fine. *Rob* was just leaving." Then I grab my broom and bucket and head through the staff door into the kitchen. I stick my shaking hands under hot water as if I could wash away the film of disgust that meeting left on my skin.

I can't believe any girl would settle for marrying a guy like that, and here I am, married to Mason Dahl—best guy I've ever known—and doing backflips for a divorce.

CHAPTER 3

MASON

I thrum my fingers against my thigh as the event coordinator pulls the catering books off the table and replaces them with binders of information about florists.

"I don't remember it being this overwhelming when I was planning my wedding," Mom says.

Dad nudges her. "Oh, I remember. You obsessed over every little decision. You made Bridezilla look like a puppy."

"Hey!" She laughs and turns to the event coordinator. "I was a gentle bride. Full of grace. It was my mother who was intolerable."

I'm glad that my parents are happy, and since things like elaborate celebrations add to that happiness, I'm behind them having this anniversary party. But I'm not thrilled that they want me in on the plans. Big, fancy parties aren't my thing. *Drunken nuptials in Vegas, anyone?*

If I were celebrating thirty years of marriage, I'd want my wife to myself on a quiet little island somewhere. I instantly picture Bailey, a little older, a little softer, laid out on a beach in Fiji, her skin golden from the sun, her fingers twined with mine. *That's* a celebration.

"Listen," Greta, the event coordinator, says. "I have another appointment in twenty minutes."

Thank you, God. It's over.

Mom looks at her watch. "Greta, I am so sorry. I didn't realize we'd been here so long!"

"It's been my pleasure," Greta says. "How about I send these binders with you, and we'll meet again on Monday? We'll carpool to the venues so you can see them before you make your choice."

"Sounds great," Mom says.

"Will you be available as well?" Greta asks me.

I shake my head. I leave for training camp on Sunday. "I'm sorry. I'm unavailable." *Spoiler alert: I'm not actually sorry.*

"Oh, that's too bad." She gives a tight smile, and I feel as if I'm being judged and coming up short.

"But I was hoping you could help us choose a location, Mason," Mom says. "You sure you can't show up to camp a day late?"

I smile. "I'm sure Greta will be very helpful. You won't need me."

Mom stands and swings her purse over her shoulder. It's a Louis Vuitton. I know because I bought it for her for Christmas. She loves it, but you could feed a small country for what it cost. "Well, we will see you Monday, then," she says, shaking Greta's hand. "I'm so excited to pin down the details. I want it to be perfect."

"It will be," Greta promises, and as we head to our cars, my shoulders relax.

"Lindy called us last night," Mom says. And just like that, I'm as anxious to get away from my parents as I was to get out of that meeting. "She's really looking forward to her internship. Think how much time you two will have together."

It's not just the Gators' owner who sees wedding bells when he thinks of me and Lindy. If my parents had a choice in the matter, Lindy and I would have entered into an arranged marriage upon our college graduation. My father's been doing business with Lindy's father since I was a kid. They're both investors with their hands in a lot of domestic and international ventures. When Lindy and I were growing up, our parents always joked we'd end up married, and for a while, when we were dating in high school, the joke seemed more like a reality. After Lindy and I went our separate ways, the joke wasn't funny anymore.

"She says she ran into you back in the spring," Mom says.

I freeze at that unwelcome reminder of my big-ass mistake. Why has Lindy been gabbing to our parents about that night? "Lindy's a nice girl," I tell Mom, "but as I've told you before, there's no future for us."

"We should talk about that," Dad says. "I think I could make it worth your while if you'd give that young girl a chance. Together, you two would have an empire."

"What are we doing here? Bartering cattle?" I frown at him.

"Because it sounds like you're trying to butter me up for the sale."

"Stop that, Mason." Mom's perfectly arched brows draw together with her frown. "Your father just means that you two are compatible, and it might benefit both of our families if you didn't dismiss her so carelessly. She likes you, you know. And you used to like her. Before."

I bite my tongue, because I want to tell them about Bailey. Maybe Owen is right. Maybe if they knew I was married, they'd back the fuck off about me and Lindy. "I have to go."

"Have a great time at training camp," Mom says with a smile.

Dad stays silent, but his eyes are hard, and I know he's unhappy with me. I don't care. I'm so over them meddling in my life and trying to control me—been there, done that, got the emotional baggage.

On a good day, it's a little over five hours between my parents' home in St. Augustine and mine in Seaside, but the highway is riddled with construction, making the traffic worse than usual, and the matter of Lindy's temporary move to Seaside looms heavily in my mind.

When I bumped into her in April, I was in my favorite Seaside bar, drunk on whiskey and self-pity. There I was, living my dream life, and nearly a year after leaving Blackhawk Valley, I still thought about Bailey every single day. That day, Bailey had posted a video of herself on Instagram stumbling around on the bar at The End Zone and captioned it, *What you really look like when you're drunk and trying to dance sexy on the bar.*

It was goofy and hilarious and so Bailey that it made me

miss her with an intensity I hadn't felt in months. I was desperate to stop thinking about the blond, curvy heartbreaker, and then Lindy appeared. We talked about old times—the good ones, at least—and she told me about her graduate program and her plans for after graduation. After nearly four years of being shut down by Bailey, my ego loved her attention. It felt good to have someone next to me, laughing at my jokes, leaning closer at every opportunity. After a few more whiskeys and more laughs, we climbed into a cab together and went back to my house.

I let things go too far. I was hoping to feel something—*anything*—with someone who hadn't spent the better part of the last four years pushing me away. It didn't work, and it complicated the fuck out of my relationship with Lindy—a relationship I closed the door on five years ago.

By the time I pull through the gates of my subdivision, it's dark, and I just want a shower and a drink. Hell, I might skip the drink and fantasize about keeping Bailey as my wife instead. Some good old Bailey fantasies are just as intoxicating as bourbon and less likely to screw with tomorrow's training.

Maybe Owen's right. Maybe going public with our marriage could solve my problems. Bailey's life in Blackhawk Valley isn't exactly glamorous, and the collection notices with her name that have started to show up in my mailbox tell me she has problems of her own. Maybe we could make an arrangement that would help us both.

When I turn into the drive, my lights flash on the front of the house and I see a woman sitting on the porch swing, sipping a glass of wine. I wish I could say I was surprised, but Lindy is who she is. She goes after what she wants, and after five years apart, she's decided she still wants me.

I don't bother pulling in to the garage. I stop in the driveway, cut the engine, and climb out. "What are you doing here?" I ask. Lindy's dark hair is down around her shoulders, and her porcelain skin glows in the porchlight.

Her wine-stained lips stretch into a smile. "Is that any way to greet your lover?"

I rub the back of my neck, irritated that she's made herself at home but trying not to show it. "We're not lovers."

She takes another drink of her wine and flashes me a mischievous grin. "That's not what it looked like a few months ago."

"I've told you, that night was a mistake." Such a big fucking mistake. I thought if Lindy and I reconnected, maybe I'd feel something—maybe I could move on from Bailey. "Everything between us is history. There is no future."

Lindy looks away and wraps her arms around her waist. "If I were pregnant, you wouldn't be turning me away right now."

I scrape a hand over my face. I was in Vegas when Lindy texted me to tell me she wasn't pregnant.

I know it was silly to hope. I just thought a baby could bring us back together.

It hadn't even occurred to me that she might be until she'd sent that, and then I spent the rest of the trip thanking my lucky stars Lindy wasn't pregnant with my child. *That* would have been a disaster.

I draw in a breath. She's always been emotional, and since I fucked up enough to sleep with her, the least I can do is attempt to be patient. "Lindy . . ."

"You know it's true. If I were carrying your baby, you'd be happy to have me here. We would make this work."

"You're not pregnant and we're not a couple, so there's nothing to make work."

My phone buzzes in my pocket, and I pull it out and stare at the screen to see Bailey's face.

"I think it's time I talk to my father about you," Lindy says. Her voice rises an octave, and her words pick up speed. "You wouldn't be *anyone* if it weren't for him. If he knows you used me for sex, you can kiss another contract goodbye."

I stiffen. I can practically feel my career teetering on the edge of the hysteria in her voice. Maybe I took a deal with the devil when Bill McCombs got his people to draft me, but at the time, Lindy was seriously involved with someone else. It seemed safe.

"Why would you do that?" Even after hearing her say it, I don't want to believe it. Once, we were friends. Once, we banded together against our parents' attempts to manipulate us and control our lives, and now she's trying to control me.

"You toy with me. I thought you'd grown up, but look at you now. Pushing me away again." She shakes her head. "Do you have any idea how used and dirty that makes me feel?"

"I'm really sorry," I say, and I have to be entering into the triple digits of apologies.

“Can you give me one good reason we can’t be together?”

Hell, I could give her a laundry list of reasons, but she doesn’t want to hear any of those. In fact, there’s only one reason that might make her dial back the crazy.

I draw in a long breath, trying to stop myself from breaking my promise, making myself take one more beat before beginning to unravel the plan that’s been hatching since Arrow and Mia’s wedding. My hesitation is nothing more than a formality. I made my decision weeks ago when I started dodging Bailey’s calls and ignoring the texts that read, *You. Me. A romantic divorce? When are we going to do this thing?*

“There is someone else.” I wait for Lindy’s gaze to meet mine and say a prayer that I can talk Bailey into going along with this. “Lindy, I’m married.”

CHAPTER 4

BAILEY

The airport waiting area is filling up, but it'll be another half-hour before they start boarding our plane. I dial my sister and cross my fingers while I wait for her to answer.

"Hello?"

I grin at the sound of her voice. I haven't seen her in months and suddenly, I can't wait to be down there. "Sarah!"

"Hi, Bailey, how are you?"

"I'm good. I'm at the airport, heading your way soon!"

"Oh." I can practically hear the smile fall from her face. "You are? Like, without any notice?"

Can't wait to see you either, sis. "I have a job in Seaside. I'm doing a little photography on the side these days, and my friend decided at the last minute that she wanted me to take some pictures for her." *And I need to get my husband to divorce me.* But my sister already thinks I'm impulsive, careless, and irresponsible. No need to give her ammunition for those conclusions. "I thought I could swing by and see you and Faith."

Sarah lives near Rock Hill, about thirty minutes from where Keegan, Emma, and Mason live in Seaside. Since she never comes home to visit, I only get to see her and Faith when I go down there.

"Sure. Give us a call when you're down here, and we'll see if we can make it work. The summer's really busy. Faith has day camp while I'm at work and then nights are dance, gymnastics, and swimming."

"I know you two are busy. I'm flexible." I'm determined to keep the cheer in my voice. "I'm going straight to my photoshoot off the plane, but I could come by after."

"Tonight's not good, Bailey. Call tomorrow, okay?"

I bite my lip as my throat goes thick. "Sure thing." I'm not going to let her get to me. I don't need my family drama hanging over my head right now. I have enough on my plate.

We say goodbye, and I end the call. I have thirty minutes until I get to board the plane that'll take me to my husband. I might as well get some work done.

I focus my attention on the set of photos I'm editing on my laptop. The girl from this shoot was exceptionally nervous. She lost a bunch of weight while her husband was deployed and wanted to surprise him with boudoir photos when he returned home. The upside of spending a couple of years stripping is that I can be clinical about body parts, so it doesn't feel overly intimate to take pictures of women in lingerie. I did it for a friend of a friend a few months ago, and then word spread, and now I've done almost a dozen boudoir sessions and have another four on the books. Most women have no idea how beautiful they are, so I use lighting and shadows to show them. Watching a woman who's afraid to look at her pictures fall in love with the images on the screen is the best thing ever. I think this one is going to love hers. There's a whole series where she's wearing one of his camo jackets and a scrappy lace thong with a stripe of black paint under each eye. If *she* doesn't love them, I know *he* will.

I apply a filter to soften an image of her standing in knee-high grass at sunset, and my phone buzzes. I grab it with one hand and tilt my head to study the finished product on the screen. Only when I'm convinced it's the perfect blend of sexy and cute to add to the set do I look at the text that came through. I don't recognize the number, but as soon as I read the words, I know the message is from Ron from the bank.

> *A slut like you would be lucky to have a chance with a man like me.*

MASON

"I want a divorce."

A thousand times I've imagined Bailey Green showing up at

my front door, and those were *almost* the words I hoped would come out of her mouth. In countless fantasies, her sentences started with "I want."

I want you.

I want your mouth . . . hands . . . body.

I want us to try to make this work.

All that. But never *I want a divorce.*

Even so, this isn't unexpected. The timing is, however, pretty damn inconvenient.

"Good to see you too."

She groans and stomps inside my house. "Jesus." She spins around the foyer and gapes as she takes in the open-concept kitchen and living room. "What did you do? Fuck an interior designer? A bachelor pad isn't supposed to look like this."

"I'm not a bachelor," I say.

Her eyes widen and her cheeks blaze pink. I'm not sure I'll ever tire of reminding her of our drunken Vegas nuptials.

I drag my eyes from the roots of her blond hair down to the tips of her toes. I'm still waiting for the day that looking at her doesn't punch me in the gut with need. I'm not sure it will ever come. She's dressed for the Florida heat in cutoffs and a tank. Those curves would make a godless man believe. I want to drop to my knees and give thanks in every way I know how, starting with the strip of soft skin exposed between her shirt and her shorts. Instead, I kick the door closed behind me and tuck my hands into my pockets, where they can't get me into trouble.

God, I've missed her, and there's not much I want to do right now more than hold her face in my hands and kiss her. Just a kiss. Then another. Would that be what I need to let her go?

When I moved down here to play for the Gators, I'd given up on her. I did everything I could think of to get my mind off her, to move on from the girl who'd give me her body but refused to give me her heart.

And then, a month after I stupidly slept with Lindy, Bailey and I were in Vegas with our friends. One drink made the next seem like a good idea, and the third made dancing and touching seem like a good idea, and then more drinks made for more touching. We capped off the night with our best idea of all: a visit to the wedding chapel down the Strip.

I knew she was drunk and I was taking advantage of her at a weak moment, but the fact of the matter is, when Bailey's guard was down, she said "I do" with tears in her eyes and her hands gripping mine like she was afraid I might run away.

"We agreed we'd deal with this after Mia and Arrow's wedding. Their wedding is over." She swallows. "Let's deal with it."

"About that . . ." I wander into the kitchen and lean against the center island. "I changed my mind."

She blinks at me. "Changed your mind about what?"

"I don't want a divorce."

"You . . . don't want . . . a div—" She shakes her head. "No. Do you *want* to make my life difficult? You don't get to put me off for weeks only to stand there and tell me you don't want one."

"But I don't. My circumstances have changed."

She bites her bottom lip. "I didn't *mean* to marry you."

I grunt. "Yeah, you did."

"I was drunk."

"You were sober enough to walk into that chapel and down the aisle. Sober enough to repeat the words." My gaze flicks to her hand and to her bare ring finger. I came home from Vegas with two rings and no wife. "You were sober enough to make me promise that I wouldn't let our impulsive marriage ruin my life."

"That does sound like me." She frowns. "You know I don't need you to end this, right? I *can* get a divorce without you."

I draw in a breath through my teeth. "Yeah, but contested divorces are a whole lot harder to get."

"So that's your plan?" she asks. "You're going to stay married to a woman who doesn't want to be married to you until I'm willing to go through some ugly divorce?" She stares at me, as if she's waiting for me to come to my senses. "Why are you doing this?"

"Like I said, my circumstances changed. I need a wife, and conveniently, I already have one."

She combs a hand through her hair. "You're a sexy NFL receiver."

I grin. "Thanks. You're not so bad to look at yourself."

She groans and tugs her bottom lip between her teeth. I have to avert my eyes to block out the raw sensuality of the image. There's no denying that this woman gets to me on every level. She's my kryptonite. "My point is, if you're so desperate to have a *Mrs. Dahl*, there are lines of women who would happily take up the position."

I don't want them. "Why would I go to that trouble when I already have you?"

She backs away from me as if I'm a wild animal and she's trying to escape without moving too fast. "You really want word to get out that you married the stripper?"

"Stop it. You're not a stripper anymore."

"The trailer trash." She lifts her chin and swallows hard. "The broke bitch gold-digger."

I flinch. "Stop." Those are labels my snobby parents would throw around. I don't like hearing Bailey talk about herself that way.

"Do I need to continue with the things they'll say about me if this reaches the media?"

"Four months," I say. "That's all I'm asking."

She shakes her head. "For what?"

"I have to leave for training camp Sunday, but I'm asking you to move in when I come back."

"Move *in*?"

"Temporarily. Live here through the regular season—that's through the end of the year. I'll pay you well to act like my wife, to *be* my wife for those four months." I draw in a breath. This is the hard part—the part I have to promise myself I'll stick to, no matter how much it sucks. "If you do me this favor, come January, I'll take care of all the legalities of ending our marriage." *I'll let you go, no matter how much it hurts.* "And you'll be thirty thousand dollars richer."

She sputters. "Thirty thou— You're offering to pay me *thirty thousand dollars* to be your wife?"

I shrug. "Yeah."

"For *four months*?"

"If you move in right after training camp, it's technically four and a half." I fold my arms. "It's better than what you'd make managing The End Zone in that time."

"No shit. You're insane. Completely insane." She screws up her face as she studies me, as if she's never seen me before and is trying to figure me out. "Is this about sex? Are you offering me money to warm your bed for four months? Is that what you think of me?"

I cock my head and wait a beat before stepping forward and cupping her face in one hand. I can't help myself. When she's close, I want to touch her. "You and I both know you've always been happy to come to my bed." My gaze drops to her lips before my thumb sweeps over them. "But right now, I need more than that from you."

"I can't give you more." Her voice trembles. Is that regret? Sadness? I might know if she'd let me in. But she's kept her walls up for four years. I'm not holding my breath that she's going to let them down now. "I have nothing to offer you."

"That's where you're wrong. You're already my wife. It'd be a favor, Bailey. A favor that just might save my career."

CHAPTER 5

BAILEY

I blink at him, half delirious under the spell of his touch. His hand feels so good against my skin—warm and reassuring and *right*. Even though he's only touching my face, every cell in my body takes notice. "What does our marriage have to do with your career?"

He drops his hand and steps back. I want to follow him and ask him to touch me again, because I feel so much stronger when his heat is on my skin. Instead, I lean against the counter and remind myself why I'm here. "The owner of the Gulf Gators has a daughter," he says. "A beautiful, young daughter he thinks walks on water. Our families are friends, and they've always had this idea that we'd end up together." He cuts his eyes away. "When she was visiting in the spring, I slept with her."

Jealousy is a dull blade sawing through my lungs. The daughter of an NFL franchise owner is exactly the kind of woman a guy like Mason should end up with. And the exact opposite of everything I am. And the idea that he *slept* with her? Fuck, why bother with the small talk? Why not grab the knife from the butcher block and carve out my heart?

I have no right to be hurt—I have no claim on Mason, and after years of pushing him away, I'm a hypocrite for feeling jealous at all—but that doesn't change the fact that I am.

"She's doing an internship with the Gators this season," Mason continues. "And when she wasn't taking the hint that I'm not interested in making our night together into something more, I told her I'm married."

"I'm not following how this is going to help with your career. What does your relationship with her have to do with your job?"

"It shouldn't have anything to do with it, but Bill McCombs is a very powerful man who likes to give his children exactly what they want. Right now, Lindy wants me. If I'm married and uninterested, I'm faithful. If I'm unmarried and uninterested, I'm an asshole."

"You want a fake wife so you can fend off some rich bitch?"

"She's the owner's daughter, and I'm just trying to keep the peace." He studies me, his eyes soft. "My career is on the line, and our accidental marriage might be the best thing to save it."

"Mason, what do you make after endorsement deals? Seven figures a year?"

He shrugs. "It's not all guaranteed money, but it's definitely enough to compensate you for your time."

"Seven figures a year, and on top of that, I bet you have a trust fund."

"Why are you bringing up money?" His expression is guarded, but I see in his eyes that I'm right. Of course I am. His mom was some sort of model and his family is rolling in money.

"I'm bringing up money because you have all that net worth, and you married me in Vegas without a prenup. Regardless of whether or not an *heiress* is pursuing you, you should be *jumping* at the opportunity to end this with no strings."

"Now I'm supposed to believe you married me to swindle me out of my trust fund?" He folds his arms, making his biceps strain across the soft fabric of his T-shirt. *Sweet Lord, he's fun to look at.* "You and I both know I could write you a check right now for everything I have and you wouldn't take it."

"You don't know that." But it feels good that he believes it—the bittersweet ache of someone believing you're better than you are. "You're sure this is just about your career? Four months of a pretend relationship, and then I go back to my life?"

He's silent for a beat too long, his jaw hard, his eyes studying my face. "Like you said, why would I want to be married to a woman who doesn't want to be married to me?"

That crushes me, because this isn't about what I want. It's about the promises I've made. But I can't tell him that. "Let me think about it."

"What's there to think about? We're already married."

"Oh, I don't know, how about my job or my life back in Blackhawk Valley? How about how I'm going to explain this to our friends?" I stare at him, looking into his eyes and wishing

I could say yes. I want to do this for him, but it's so damn complicated. "I'm not taking your money."

"You have bills to pay." He casts me a sideways glance. "And clearly your job at The End Zone isn't cutting it."

I frown. "How do you know that?"

He shrugs. "There's a pile of collection notices in the office addressed to you. They started showing up a couple of weeks ago. Someone's really determined to get the money you owe them."

I flinch, feeling confused and exposed. "That's private."

He holds up a hand. "I didn't open them. I'm just saying you could make better money working down here than Keegan can pay you to run that bar. That's in addition to what I'd give you, and obviously, you need it. Is my offer too low? Name your price."

"I don't want your *money.*" My phone buzzes, and I reach for it, thinking it might be my sister.

He shoves his hands into his pockets.

I take my cell from my pocket and unlock the screen to open the last text message. A single swipe of the screen, and I'm eye to eye with some asshole's cock.

> *You won't think my dick is small when I shove it down your throat.*

I gasp, as if it isn't just a picture, as if Ron is actually in front of me and whipping it out.

Mason takes the phone from my hand. "What in the actual fuck?" His eyes go wide and his jaw hardens before he looks back to me. "Who is this asshole?"

Maybe it shouldn't matter, but I'm glad I didn't get that text while I was alone. My skin is crawling, and I feel a little dizzy with the implied threat in the message. "I don't know for sure, but I think it's probably from a guy I ran into at the bank yesterday."

He stares at me, dumbfounded. "This is *normal behavior* for guys you run into at the bank?"

"No, obviously not. I . . ." Why is this so embarrassing? How can I be so grateful that he's here, seeing what this ass sent, and at the same time wish he'd never found out about it? How can I want to tell him everything about my interaction with Ron while simultaneously wishing I could keep it a secret? "Ron was a regular when I worked at the Pretty Kitty, and he didn't take it too well when I declined his invitation to take me to dinner."

Mason scrolls up and reads the text Ron sent me when I was at the airport last night. His nostrils flare as he grips the phone tighter. "What's his last name?"

"What? Why?"

"Because I think I need to visit Blackhawk Valley and pay this asshole a visit."

"I don't know, and it doesn't matter." I shake my head. "He's just mad that he got rejected. I'll have his number blocked, and it will be over. Don't go looking for trouble."

He draws in a breath, and I can see that he's struggling to remain calm. "Do you get this shit a lot?"

Honestly, it comes with the territory of being a stripper—even a *former* stripper—in a small town. "I keep my number pretty private, and that helps. He found my workplace from my account at the bank, so I'm guessing he snagged my number while he was at it."

"Sounds like his boss needs a call at the very least." He steps closer and puts the phone on the counter behind me, then cages me in with a hand on either side of me. When he looks down into my eyes, it feels as if he's washing away all the ugliness Ron's message made me feel. "I really want to kick his ass, Bailey." His voice is low and simmers with something volatile, and I feel guilty for loving it, for finding a sense of security in his rage.

"I know you do. And . . . thanks."

Guys like Ron are a dime a dozen. They think that because they could pay to look at me once, I remain their property on some level. They're the reason I stopped dancing even when my debt was still piling up. They're the reason I was so happy to have my friend Sebastian be my roommate in college.

But guys like Mason are one of a kind. He never treated me like a piece of property or made me feel like my most important qualities were physical ones. Not once.

I lift my hand to his face, and his gaze drops to my mouth. Before I can overthink it, I push onto my toes and brush my lips against his. The kiss is soft and brief, and it seems to take him by surprise, because he draws in a sharp breath. I pull away, just an inch, my hand still on his jaw, and the room goes too quiet. I don't think either of us breathes for several seconds.

"What was that for?" he asks.

"For being you." I shrug as if it's nothing, as if he hasn't been the rock holding me up during the last four years. Again and again, when it seems as if my entire world is crumbling beneath my feet, Mason is solid.

"Does that mean you'll be my wife?"

The emotions swirl and battle in my chest, and I laugh outright. "It means I'll think about it."

Four years ago . . .

The Pretty Kitty was packed tonight. When I change into my street clothes, I'm exhausted, but I'm leaving with a purse full of cash and the knowledge that my sister will be able to pay the rent for one more month.

I don't officially work here. Gary can't pay me because this club serves alcohol, and therefore I can't *legally* be an employee until I'm twenty-one. But if he's not paying me, then he can pretend I'm just a customer who likes to get on stage. It's not his fault my fake ID is so convincing.

Not that anyone's checking up on him. Blackhawk Valley isn't that strait-laced. Hell, some of my regulars have badges tucked into their back pockets.

Usually, I'll let Hammer walk me to my car, and I leave the dressing room to look for him. Sometimes, assholes think that just because they paid for a lap dance and bought a girl a few drinks, they're entitled to something more. We keep Hammer around for the ones who like to wait outside and ask for their "money's worth" for their tips. Hammer isn't really his name. They just call him that because rumor has it that Hammer's fist feels worse than a sledgehammer to the skull.

I spot him talking to Gary and decide I'm too anxious to leave to wait for an escort. I walk out the back door, find a man leaning against my car, and immediately regret my decision to come out here alone.

But when I see the man with his slow, stoned smile and the greed in his gaze, I don't turn around and get Hammer. I know this guy from before Nic went to prison. Clarence Houston is more powerful in this town than anyone realizes. People think the Woodisons have all the power because they have the flashy kind of wealth. They own Woodison Farms and the Woodison Pork factory, and employ half the people who live in Blackhawk Valley. But anyone who was raised on the other side of the trailer park fence knows that money doesn't always come packaged in fancy houses and luxurious Caribbean vacations. Sometimes money comes packaged in expensive habits that go up your nose or straight into your bloodstream. Sometimes it comes as expensive women who've been paid to fulfill your dirtiest desires.

As much as I want to get Hammer, if Clarence is here looking for me, there's a reason. And if that reason is Nic, I need to know what he has to say. I keep my distance, staying within reach of the back door. "You need something?"

His grin is slow and slimy as his gaze slides over me. If I wasn't already in the habit of showering this place off me the second I got home, I'd be doing it tonight to wash away how his eyes make me feel. "I need a lot of things," he says. He steps forward. "Mostly, though, I want my money from Nic Mendez."

I arch a brow. "Your money?"

"Punk owes me fifteen grand."

The number is a punch to the gut, but I don't let anything show on my face. "And you think *I* have it?" I'm impressed my tone doesn't reveal how nervous I am. The sound of Nic's name alone still makes my stomach shimmy. But pair that name with someone as powerful as Clarence saying he's owed fifteen grand, and I'm scared. I'm scared for Nic, and I'm scared for me.

"I heard you're his girl," he says.

"Really? You think that just because I slept with him, that makes me *his girl*?" I usually don't mind this game, don't mind pretending to be the slut who gets around. But when the man in question is Nic, I want to be more than that. Pretending that I was nothing more than Nic's piece on the side feels a little like selling my soul. "I'm not Nic's girl."

"Who you belong to, then?"

I fold my arms and mentally correct his grammar before answering. "I don't belong to anyone but myself."

"You sure you're not his girl?"

"I'm positive."

"I guess I'll have to find my money somewhere else, then." He takes another step closer, and I notice the two guys standing in the shadows by Clarence's jacked-up pickup. I've been able to recognize that car and the man who drives it since before Nic went to prison. *"Stay away from him,"* Nic would say, pointing out

Clarence's car. *"And never let him know you're my girl."*

"Guess you will." I'm outnumbered in a big way here. *Please come out back to check on me, Hammer.*

"Sweet girl like you shouldn't be dancing to pay the bills," Clarence says, skimming that greedy gaze over me. "You need a man who can take care of you."

There is no way in hell I'd sign on to let Clarence "take care" of me, but I'm not dumb enough to laugh in his face. Like I said, Clarence is powerful around here. "I don't need anyone."

His lips twist into a crooked smirk. "Sure you don't. But just so you know"—his tongue darts out to wet his lip—"if you *were* Nic's girl or if you just wanted to help him out, you and me could work something out." He skims the tip of his index finger down my cheek. "You might even like it."

I step back. "Like I said, I'm not his girl."

He shrugs and tucks his hands into his pockets. "My offer stands. For now." Then he and the two goons behind him pile into the truck and pull away in a puff of exhaust.

When I climb into my car, I can't lock the doors fast enough. I'm shaking. Shaking because I didn't know Nic owed Clarence money, and that spells trouble. Shaking because I'm smart enough to be scared of Clarence.

CHAPTER 6

MASON

Present day . . .

After getting up early for practices most of my life, I usually love mornings. But this morning, I'm dragging ass. I spent my entire night and this morning's run worrying about Bailey. The picture and message she got last night only reinforced my opinion that Blackhawk Valley is toxic for her, and I've been racking my brain trying to come up with something I can offer her so she'll take my proposal.

She needs money, but she's always refused to take mine. She needs a better job, but despite all her bluster, she has the self-esteem of a backward, pimple-faced teenager, and won't pursue one. She needs to let go of the past—including Nic Mendez—and give herself permission to live her life. But for some reason, she buried her heart with her first love, and there's not a damn thing I can do about that.

I've played by Bailey's rules for four years, and if I were to keep playing by them, I'd make this easy and end our marriage. Telling Lindy about Bailey was selfish—the easiest way to convince her there's no future for us. But suddenly getting Bailey to agree to move in isn't only about Lindy or my career. It's about Bailey.

I grab a protein shake from the fridge and sink into the couch, no closer to an answer than I was when I walked her to her car last night.

I pick up my phone and open the file with my pictures from Vegas. The whole weekend is catalogued here in one form or another—the first night when we went to Rain, our lazy day at the pool, Arrow, Mia, Bailey, me, and the rest of the crew piled into the party bus. As I scroll through the pictures, they transition from pictures of the group to just pictures of Bailey, and of Bailey and me together.

I stop at a photo we took of ourselves in front of the Bellagio fountain on our last night there. The rest of our group had paired off and disappeared back to their rooms, and we were the last ones standing. She was clinging to me as we watched the lights and water, reminding me how much I wanted *more.*

"Will you *ever* touch me again?" she asked.

Grinning, I tightened my grip on her hips. "I'm touching you now."

"You know what I mean." She turned into me and pressed her hand flat against my chest. "What do I have to do to convince you to take me to your bed, Mason?"

"Marry me."

She laughed so hard, like it was the most ridiculous idea. "What, now you're some born-again virgin who needs to be married to have sex?" I answered with a shrug, and she propped her hand on her hip. "Fine. I'm calling your bluff. Let's do it."

The wise thing would have been to say no, to point out that she was too drunk to make a decision like that, or to simply remind myself that she'd been pushing me away for nearly four years and one night in Vegas couldn't change that. But my heart wasn't interested in wisdom when Bailey was at my fingertips, daring me to take exactly what I'd wanted for years.

I scroll past the pictures of us at the fountains and hesitate when I see the play icon on the video from our next stop.

She's made it clear where we stand, and despite the chaste kiss we shared in my kitchen last night, I know better than to believe she's going to change her mind about our chances as a couple. But that doesn't mean that there's no chance for the life she'd inevitably build here between now and the end of the season. What's waiting for her back in Blackhawk Valley? Debt, obviously. A job she's not passionate about. And assholes like *Ron*, who send her dick pics captioned with thinly veiled threats. Fuck that. She deserves better than that life, whether she knows it or not. If she's not brave enough to move away from her hometown and start fresh, I need to help her. Maybe I can't have her, but I don't have to watch her throw her life away.

That means I can't play by her rules anymore.

I pull up my contact list and call my agent.

He answers on the first ring—probably because he's a

workaholic who never leaves his desk. "Mason! How's it going, bud?"

"Good, thanks." I swallow hard. "Listen, I'm going to send you something, and I need your help releasing it to the press."

BAILEY

The restaurant is fancier than I'd choose, but Emma made the reservation, so here I am. "Vodka martini with a twist," I tell the server. Normally, I avoid drinks like martinis just because of the price tag, but tonight I need the double dose of booze.

When the waiter leaves, I decide to try my sister's cell again. Emma is meeting me for an early dinner so I can show her the pictures from yesterday's shoot. I'm early and waiting in our booth until my friend arrives.

I dial Sarah and hold my breath while I wait for her to answer.

"Hi, Bailey," she says. She sounds tired, and I'm sure she is. Her days are long. She gets Faith ready in the morning and then works all day until she has to pick her up. She makes a healthy dinner and then rushes from one activity to the next, returning home in time for a bath before bed, and she does it all again the next day. The responsibilities of a single mom are no joke, and Sarah takes every one of them very seriously. "I have five minutes before we have to leave for gymnastics. Sorry I didn't call you back last night."

She sounds sincere, so I swallow back my insecurity. "It's okay. I was wondering if you and Faith would like to do breakfast tomorrow? I remember that sweet little café down the street from your house."

"Can't." Her voice goes muffled, and I imagine her covering it with her hand as she tells Faith to get changed. "I have an early meeting, and I don't want to disrupt Faith's routine. It's hard enough to get that girl out the door. How about I call you when we get home from dance tomorrow night?"

I rub my arms and wish I'd brought a sweater into the restaurant. "Yeah. Sure, that'd be great. I don't want to hassle you, but I miss you both."

"I miss you too, Bailey. If I'd had some warning you were coming, we could have cleared our schedule. Our days are pretty busy."

"I know. I'm sorry." I bite my lip. "So, I'll talk to you tomorrow."

"Yep. Thanks. Have fun tonight, whatever you're doing. But be safe, okay?"

I flinch. I'm sure Sarah imagines me clubbing all night long, and hell, right now that sounds pretty good. That's not my regular night out, and I hate that she thinks it is, but I don't have the energy to explain that it's not like that. "I will. I promise."

We say our goodbyes, and when I end the call I'm left feeling tired and lonely. Last night, after Mason's ridiculous proposal, I went to a coffee shop by my motel and worked on the shoot I'd done with Emma Rothschild when I arrived in Seaside. Since Emma and her boyfriend, Keegan, are both good friends of mine, it's really important to me that these pictures wow—not that it was hard, given how gorgeous Emma is.

It was easy to lose myself in my work until it was time to check into my motel and get some sleep. Unfortunately, once tucked into my dingy discount room, I couldn't turn off my brain, and my thoughts have been scattered ever since. What am I going to do about Mason? I can't be his wife, not for real, but could I play the part for a few months?

It's been twenty-four hours since I kissed him in his kitchen, and I'm no closer to an answer now than I was then.

"Hello, hello," Emma says, taking a seat across from me in the booth. She looks like something out of a magazine—fucking beautiful and *glowing* with happiness. Then again, that might just be sleep deprivation talking. I feel gross by comparison after missing my shower this morning (no way was I bathing in the disgusting space the motel was trying to pass off as a shower stall), but she seems especially radiant today. She's grinning, and her curly red hair is down around her bare shoulders. "Someone needs a drink."

I slide my phone back into my purse so I can give Emma my full attention. "You have no idea."

"The divorce request didn't go as well as you anticipated?"

I sigh. "He wants me to move in with him after training camp and act like his wife until the end of the year. Apparently, he needs a wife because he screwed up and slept with Bill McCombs's daughter." I shake my head. It sounds so dumb when I spell it out. I can see how telling the woman about me would help Mason, but surely we could find a way to do this without living together for the whole season.

"I've tried really hard not to pry into your business," Emma says, her tone cautious, "but do you want to tell me why you won't just be with Mason?"

I lean back in my seat at those words. Where is our server? I could really use that drink. "You're hilarious."

"What's so funny about that? You obviously love him."

"It doesn't matter how I feel about Mason. He's not a choice for me."

She holds my gaze and waits for an explanation. When I don't offer one, she says, "Spill."

"I care about Mason, but I respect myself too much to try to have a real relationship with him when I will never fit into his world."

"Oh, Bailey, that's not true. Look at me and Keegan."

"I see you two, but it's not the same with Mason and me." I don't expect her to understand, but I draw in a deep breath and try my best. "Before I was born, my mom was a stripper. She met my father at work and they had a relationship." I drop my gaze to my hands. To this day, the story fills me with shame. Mom thought they were in love, but I don't think my father cared about anything but getting off. Everything that came after was no more than a consequence he had to deal with. "He wasn't a rich man by normal standards, but he was by Mom's, and when she got pregnant, they tried to make it work. They eloped before I was born, and she gave up her apartment so she and my sister could move in with him. I was only a few months old when he died unexpectedly of a heart attack."

"Bailey, I'm so sorry."

I shake my head. "Don't be. I never knew him."

"But that doesn't mean you didn't lose him."

Emma's so sweet to understand that. I don't grieve for my father, but there's no denying I've always had a void in that role. "His family made Mom's life miserable before he died, and hell after. They wanted nothing to do with her. He'd lived above his means, and anything left was used to pay off his debts, but they thought she'd blown through it all."

"That's terrible," Emma says. "She was grieving, and they were focused on the money."

"My mom still loves my father." I think about my words then shake my head. "No, she still *idolizes* him. But the short time between moving in with him and his death was terrible for her. His family hated her. They thought she was beneath him and let it be known. It was terrible for them both, and to this day she blames his heart attack on the stress they caused. Marriage isn't just about two people. We don't live in isolation. We marry someone and their family comes with them."

Her forehead wrinkles as she studies me. "Mason's parents have been unkind to you?"

I laugh, but the sound comes out like a helpless squeak. "They have made it clear that they don't want me in his life." It's not the full truth, but it's enough. "I respect myself too much to endure their disapproval and care about Mason too much to put him through that."

"What are you going to do?" Her eyes are full of sympathy.

"I don't know. I guess I'm considering it because I want to help him. If it's only temporary, maybe it will be okay. I mean, he's going to be so busy with football anyway, and I really think this is all about appearances and getting the girl off his back."

"Oh, so he needs a pretend wife?"

I laugh. "I guess you'd know something about that." We stop talking when the server returns with my martini, and Emma orders one for herself.

"I think my situation with Zachary was a little different than yours with Mason," Emma says when we're alone again. "But I'm all for it. Live with him for a few months. *Enjoy yourself.* Maybe by the end of it, his parents will have changed their tune and you two can give it a go."

Her naivety is almost adorable. "Except Keegan would kill me." I bring my martini to my lips and force myself to take a small sip when I want to chug. "I can't just leave the bar."

"Sure you can." She waves her hand. "I'll make sure he doesn't give you any grief about it. Tia can handle it while you're gone, don't you think?"

I groan. "Why can't you rationalize all the reasons to get a divorce, huh? I thought you were supposed to be my friend."

"I am your friend." She smiles, steals my martini out of my hand, and takes a drink. "That's why I want you to move to Florida. Mason's place is great and right on the beach. Enjoy yourself. You deserve the break, and I get to see you more. Win-win."

Spoken like someone who could afford not to work another day of her life if that was what she wanted.

"Is it about the money?" she asks, because apparently, she's a fucking mind reader.

I sigh. "A little bit."

"You know, Keegan and I are more than comfortable. Let us help with whatever you would need to take time off. When was the last time you took more than a few days off work? Doesn't everyone deserve a vacation?"

"I don't want your—" That's when it happens. Emma folds her hands on the table, and I gasp. "There's a big-ass rock on your finger, Emma!"

Her grin is wide and immediate. "I know!"

"On your *ring* finger."

"I know!"

"You got engaged and didn't tell me?"

"I was going to tell you tonight, but you looked worried when I got here. I didn't want it to all be about me."

I jump out of my chair and rush around the table to hug her. I wasn't very easy on Emma when she first came into Keegan's life, but I couldn't be happier to know she's staying there. "Congratulations!"

"Thank you. I'm so happy." She squeezes me back, hard, and I admit, I'm a little choked up. My throat is thick, and my eyes burn as I blink away tears. When I sit back down, I have to take a few breaths to make sure I'm not going to cry like some sap. "Will you be one of my bridesmaids?" she asks, and then my eyes well up again.

"Bitch, you're making me cry." I wipe away the tears that escape. "I would love to."

She claps her hands, positively glowing in her joy. "I absolutely hated everything about planning my wedding to Zachary, but this is going to be so much fun. We're going to have a beach wedding, and Jazzy is going to be my flower girl, and it could pour down rain and the caterer could forget to show up and it would still be the best day of my life."

"You're disgusting in your happiness, you know that, right?" I make a face, wrinkling my nose. "Oh, crap, you and Keegan are probably going to want to have a bachelor and bachelorette thing in Vegas like Mia and Arrow did, aren't you?"

She nods. "Oh, yeah. And Keegan's going to ask Mason to be a groomsman. Are you going to be okay with that?"

Last time we were in Vegas with our group, Mason and I ended up married. I should be worried about all the time this wedding will push me and Mason together, but instead I'm relieved. It sucks being the only one left living in Blackhawk Valley, and I miss Mason more than I miss anyone else. "It'll be fine."

She bites her lip and looks away before turning back to me. "I know you just explained your situation with Mason's parents, but is Mia's brother part of the reason you won't be with Mason? Is this about Nic?"

Emma didn't come into our lives until after the awful accident that took the life of Mia's brother, Nic, and our friend Brogan, but I know she's been given the basic details. I shrug. "Maybe on some level, everything in my life is about Nic."

CHAPTER 7

BAILEY

Four years ago . . .

I spend my Saturday mornings at the federal prison in Terre Haute, and with every trip, I have too much time to think, too much time to worry. Today, my worries are heavier than ever because of what Clarence said last night, but I haven't decided what to do about it yet.

I park and head to the facility's main building, beginning the long process of working my way through security. After two years, a lot of the corrections officers recognize me and ask how I am, but even though I'm more comfortable with the process, I'll never be comfortable in this space. It's not meant for comfort. It's meant for punishment—no matter what anyone might feed you about efforts to "rehabilitate" criminals. This isn't where they send you if they think you can change. This is where you go when society has given up on you. But I refuse to give up on the boy I've loved since I was nine years old.

I'll never forget the day I fell for Nic. I wrecked my bike outside the trailer park, and my knees and chin were busted open. There was so much blood that I was frozen in panic, just sitting there in the ditch beside Old Grotto Road, silently crying. Nic, my neighbor and best friend's big brother, found me, scooped me into his arms, and carried me home.

It was a hero-worship kind of love that got way more complicated a few years later when I watched him repair the roof on his trailer. He was shirtless, his skin dark from the summer sun, his hair shaggy around his jaw. At thirteen, I thought he was the most beautiful thing I'd ever seen. His dark, broody eyes, the way he'd mumble to himself in Spanish, and that massive chip on his shoulder.

By the time Mia and I were in high school, my secret was out. I loved my best friend's big brother, and she knew it.

Nic was a *bad boy,* and I'm not talking about what uppity bitches mean when they say those words. Nic wasn't just some young punk who liked leather jackets and tattoos and wasn't afraid to drop F-bombs. That's an amateur bad boy; Nic was a professional. He was the kind of guy who didn't give a shit that he was breaking the rules. If he thought breaking the rules was the only way he could get on even ground, he'd break them twice.

He ended up in prison because his family needed money, and he did what he had to do to get it. Nic's problem was that he thought he was smarter than the guys he was working with, and they didn't like his ego. They knew he wasn't loyal and were happy to see him go down. But guys like that always expect their money back.

Nic has spent the last two years in this place, and he'll spend the rest of his life here if he makes the same mistake when he gets out. This isn't some rich white kid who got caught selling coke to his friends. This is a Mexican-American guy from a trailer park who's spent his whole life having people decide he was trouble after just one glance.

The first time I visited here, I expected to talk to Nic on the telephone through a Plexiglas panel, like in the movies. But the visiting room is made up of rows and rows of chairs. There are officers all around, cameras everywhere, and not even the illusion of privacy.

When I see him today, it's like someone reaching into my chest and bringing my heart out into the fresh air. He's in his typical neon-green jumpsuit and slip-on shoes. His dark hair is wet, as if he just got out of the shower. Every time I visit, he looks more tired than the last. Not even after his mom left did he look this rundown. It's like this place sucks the soul out of him, and I don't like to imagine what he'll become if he doesn't get parole at his next hearing.

"Bailey," he says softly. He draws me in for the first of two hugs we're allowed—one at the beginning of the visit, and one at the end. "Why the fuck are you wasting another day visiting me?"

The thing about bad boys is they tend to be real assholes. Nic is no exception.

"Nothing better to do, I guess." We do this dance with every visit. He pretends he doesn't want me here, and I pretend my visit is no more inconvenient than stopping for a gallon of milk on my way home. We both know better.

We separate and take our seats, and I study his face, memorizing the hard line of his lips and the broody darkness of his eyes.

"Now I'm here, so I guess you're going to have to talk to me, unless you want to walk away and make my drive over here for nothing."

He shakes his head, but his eyes soften as his gaze drops to my mouth for a beat. The attention makes my stomach flip in anticipation, even though my brain knows his gaze is the only thing that's touched my mouth since he was sentenced. Along with our allotted hug at the beginning and end of our visit, we're allowed one kiss at each of those times. But Nic never kisses me. It's as if he's determined to push me away now more than ever. "How's college? You keeping up with all those rich kids?"

"It's fine."

His jaw hardens. "I heard a rumor that you're dancing at the Pretty Kitty. Please tell me that's not fucking true."

I lift a shoulder in a halfhearted shrug, trying to play it off as if it's nothing, like I don't care what he thinks about me shaking my ass for strange men.

"Christ, Bailey. The fuckers who spend their time there aren't good enough to look at you."

"*You* always liked going there."

He arches a brow. "Like I said. Not good enough to look at

you."

Why does he have to say that shit? My chest hurts. "Gotta pay for college somehow." It's the excuse I've used with everyone, and Nic seems to buy it just like everyone else did. I want to tell him the truth about why I need the money. He's the only one I could tell, but he still wouldn't like it. "Your old boy came around last night." I know better than to speak his name here, where there are too many curious ears, but Nic knows who I mean. "He was waiting for me when my shift ended."

His jaw goes tight, and every muscle in his body tenses and he sits a couple inches taller. "What'd he say to you?"

"He said you owe him money. Wanted to know if I have it," I say. When he lifts his chin ever so slightly, I know it's true. He owes those assholes money. "The goods the police found in your trunk . . . those weren't yours, were they?"

"A cut would have been mine, but they weren't paid for."

"He wants his money. Where are you going to come up with that kind of cash?"

He looks away.

I draw in a ragged breath. "You know, he's a regular at the Pretty Kitty." Nic doesn't meet my eyes. I swallow. "Last night he offered to let me pay off your debt."

His head whips around. He's not slow or naïve. He knows exactly what Clarence was offering. "Is that what you want?"

"Are you kidding me? I don't *want* his hands anywhere near me." *And I'm not a whore.* It's one thing to take off my clothes and shake my ass, to shimmy up a pole so some drunken idiots will hand over the cash in their wallet. It's another thing altogether to spread my legs and let a man inside me. I swallow hard and lower my voice. "This isn't about what I *want*, it's about making sure you can start fresh and stay clean when you get out of here." He deserves *someone* who'll make a sacrifice for him, and considering how he got here, that someone should be me. "If you had a way of saving *me* from having a shit life, you'd do it."

"I don't need you to save me from anything."

"You're going to get parole. I just know it. The last thing you need is to get out of here already in debt."

"I'll figure it out." His voice is as hard as his jaw now, and he's not looking at me. "It's *my* problem, not yours, so back off."

"Maybe I can find another way to get the money. Or maybe you just don't come back to Blackhawk Valley. Go somewhere else, start a new life." I reach out to touch his hand. "I'll come with you."

He yanks his hand away and sneers. Finally, he's looking at me, but those brown eyes aren't kind. "Listen, Bailey," he says. "Whatever little-girl fantasies you're carrying around about us ending up together, you need to get rid of them right now. Move on with your life. Stop trying to play my hero, and stop trying to be my girl. That's not what I want."

It's impressive how hard he can hit without touching me. I want to be tough and hide how much it hurts, but I'm failing. My vision blurs with tears.

His shoulders sag. "I never should have gotten involved with you. You get too attached."

But you did. “I’ll find a way to pay him back.” Someone has to. I won’t let myself think about what will happen if Nic has to work off what he owes Clarence. It’s not an option.

“No, you won’t. You’ll find a way to get the fuck out of my business. If he mentions it again, you tell him you don’t have anything to do with me anymore.” He makes a fist. “And you don’t, Bailey. Stop thinking this is some fairytale, because there’s nothing between us anymore.”

I used to think nothing would hurt more than unrequited love. I spent my adolescence loving Nic and knowing that he cared for me but not in the way I wanted. But this? Knowing we were so close to having a life together and now he’s not even willing to *try* to get it back? God, it’s so much fucking worse.

CHAPTER 8

BAILEY

Present day . . .

"The last time I did snakebites, I woke up in bed with Mason," I tell Emma. I lean forward on my barstool and add, "Married."

"All the more reason to continue the tradition," she says with a mischievous grin.

After dinner and going through her boudoir shots—which she absolutely adored, *thank you very much*—Emma convinced me we needed to celebrate properly. We drove over to one of her favorite bars in Destin. After we snagged two seats at the crowded bar, the first thing she did was to order a round of snakebites.

She bypasses the water I ordered and picks up both shot glasses, handing one to me. "It's tradition!"

I have no one to blame but myself. I'm the one who taught her this terrible tradition, after all.

"Come on," she says. "We need to celebrate!"

"Here's to your engagement!" I hoist my shot glass.

She clinks hers against mine and grins. "And to your *marriage*."

I grumble, then decide the reminder is as good a reason as any to get this alcohol in my system. I lick the salt from my wrist and throw back the shot, wincing like a schoolgirl when the heat hits my throat. I'm out of practice.

I reach for the lime fast and bite into it. My eyes water as the tart juice spills on my tongue. Emma pumps a fist in the air and cheers.

"I know you two," someone says from the other side of Emma.

I cough on my lime and wipe my mouth with the back of my hand. The guy is tall and built, with an easy smile and thick, dark hair that curls a little around the collar of his polo. I'm pretty sure he's one of the Gators' receivers, but I've never met him. "You might know her," I say. "But I'm pretty sure you don't know me."

"I do." He grins. "You don't know me, but I know you."

I roll my eyes. He's hot, but that's about as lame as a come-on line gets. "You don't say."

He points to Emma. "You're Keegan Keller's girl, the actress." He swings his hand around to point at me. "And you're Mason Dahl's wife."

Emma's head whips around so fast, I'm pretty sure she's going to need to see a chiropractor tomorrow. She looks to the guy and then back to me, shock in her eyes. And, yeah, I'm pretty shocked too, because *no one is supposed to know.*

Before I can decide what to say, I'm saved by a text coming through on my phone. I look down and see a message from Mia.

> ***Mia:*** *I thought we were best friends who told each other everything.*

My stomach lurches as I think of the secrets I've kept from her. For a dozen nauseating beats of my heart, it doesn't even cross my mind that she might be referring to my secret marriage to Mason.

Then I see the link at the bottom of the text. I click it, and the page it opens reads, "Mason Dahl, Gators receiver, secretly eloped in Vegas. You won't believe what was caught on camera."

My stomach climbs into my throat as I tap the *play* icon. The video looks like it was taken by someone's cell phone. It's slightly out of focus and not very steady, but when Mason and I walk down the aisle of the small Vegas chapel, you can tell it's us. I'm holding his hand and giggling, practically dragging him to the front.

Honestly, there was part of me that never really believed we got married. Like, maybe we bought rings and talked about it, but I couldn't imagine myself following through with it—no matter how drunk. How could I have made such an awful mistake, even completely trashed? But there I am, reciting vows that I can't quite make out in this recording, tears rolling down my face as I make my promises to Mason Dahl.

And if the world wasn't already in love with the Gators' wide receiver, they would be after watching this video and seeing him finish his vows by whispering in his bride's ear then kissing her so deeply that she was clinging to him when he pulled away.

I was clinging to him. That was *me*. I really am married to the one man I can't have. I want to spring into action, to *fix* this mess before it spirals into a disaster. But at the same time, I want to re-watch the video fifty times just to see the smile on Mason's face when I say, "I do."

I type out half a dozen partial responses to Mia, deleting each before I finish. The words I finally settle on are lame at best.

> **Me:** *I'm sorry. I promise I'll explain everything next time I see you.*

Then I open the text thread between me and Mason, fully aware that Emma and the hot dude are both watching me. Emma looks away for a beat before turning back to me, and when she does, the little bitch is *laughing*.

"This isn't funny."

She bites her lip. "It's a little funny."

"You're a bitch."

She nods. "Absolutely. Totally. And selfish, too. I want you to live here."

With shaking hands, I start typing, because this is going to affect Mason, too.

> **Me:** *Someone leaked our story to the press. There's*

even a video.

Mason: *Not someone. Me.*

Me: *WHAT? WHY WOULD YOU DO THAT? WTF, MASON?*

MASON

When I get home from my last meeting of the day, there's another collection notice in my mailbox for Bailey. Somewhere along the line, someone figured out we were married. The paper bills started arriving a few weeks ago, and then about a week ago, I started getting calls from people trying to track her down about overdue bills. I don't know every detail of her financial situation, but I've learned more in the last week than I've ever known before. Though Bailey may have many talents, managing money is clearly not one of them.

I toss it into the stack with the others and see my phone flashing at me from the counter. It's been blowing up with text messages and voicemails from friends and teammates since that video was released, never mind the deluge of texts from Bailey herself written in all caps and pulling on all sorts of colorful language.

I scroll through the notifications until I see a text from Keegan. I tap on it.

> ***Keegan:*** *Your wife and my fiancée are getting drunk at Gallagher's, and we're missing out. What do you say we divide and conquer?*

My wife. My lips curl into a smile despite myself. Sure, she's pissed at me and making me sweat my decision to release that wedding video to the press, and sure, my plans might royally backfire. But right now, all I can think about is getting Bailey out of Blackhawk Valley.

Maybe living here won't change anything. Maybe she's so dead-set on wasting her life in that town that no amount of time will convince her to leave for good, but I'm determined to give it a try.

When my phone rings and I see Mom's name on the screen, I close my eyes and take a long, slow breath before swiping to accept the call. I knew this was coming, since I didn't call to warn her before the video was released. I knew avoidance wasn't the most mature way to handle it, but I didn't want to hear her thoughts on my impulsive Vegas marriage.

"Hey, Mom."

"Hey, baby. I just saw the news." I can hear the tears in her voice, and I feel like an asshole. Mom is emotional when it comes to her kids, and even if I don't agree with the way she sees things, she does love us. "Your father wants you to know you *can* get an annulment. People get married in Vegas on a whim all the time and they have ways to fix it. It'd be like it never happened."

I walk to the back of the house and stare out the French doors to the ocean beyond. I count to ten before I let myself respond. I have to tread carefully here. "I don't want an annulment."

"Yes, well, you always did have a weakness for that girl, didn't you?"

Mom doesn't understand, and I have no interest in wasting my breath to explain. "Her name is *Bailey*, but you already know that."

"I just don't think you were considering your future, and—"

"I know what I'm doing, Mom."

"That girl was a *stripper*, Mason." She says the word as if it's an unclaimed pair of dirty underwear she's holding between two fingers to take to the trash. "You don't know what kind of diseases she's carrying, or—"

"Jesus. She's a woman, not a rodent."

"Please don't take the Lord's name in vain," she says calmly. "I'm just saying. We've been blessed with wealth, and there are certain types of people who like to take advantage of that."

"Do you see why I didn't tell you?" I ask softly.

"We're only looking out for your best interests, Mason. All your father and I have ever wanted is what's best for you. I'm afraid to ask, but . . ." She pauses for a beat, but I know her question before she asks it. "Was there at least a prenup?"

"That wasn't offered with the super-value wedding package, Mom."

"You're hilarious," she says.

"I don't want a prenup or need one." I squeeze the back of my neck, where the tension has returned with a vengeance.

"Well, now you have her. I'll be here when you need me, but I wish you'd listen before she hurts you more than she already has."

"Mom, I need you to back off on this."

She's silent for a few beats, and I hear the clinking of ice against a glass. I imagine her sitting under an umbrella by the pool, swirling her cucumber water in one hand, her phone in the other. "You need to remember that your decisions affect other people," she says. "I won't say anything more about it."

"Just trust me." Because one way or another, when this is all over, I'll prove Bailey is not who they think she is. When it's time for us to part ways, I know she won't take my money. "I know what I'm doing."

God, I hope I'm right about that. Mom might be worried about my bank account, but the only thing I'm worried about Bailey stealing is my heart.

Someone honks out front, and I go to the front porch. It's Keegan in his big SUV. The guys call it his *man-van,* since it was obviously purchased with his daughter, Jasmine, in mind.

"I have to go, Mom. We'll talk later."

"Love you," she says.

"I love you too. Try not to worry."

I end the call, and Keegan rolls down his window and sticks his head out. "Did you get my text?"

"I did. But I'm not sure Bailey will want me interrupting her girls' night."

"Come on! If you recall, the last time we went clubbing with our ladies, things got interesting."

I grunt. “You can say that again.” Then I sigh, because really, if Bailey is drinking in Destin, someone needs to keep an eye on her, and I’d just as soon it be me. “I’ll meet you there. I want my car.”

He grins. “Deal.”

CHAPTER 9

BAILEY

I felt bad about my shouty caps in my messages to Mason for about five minutes, but when it became painfully clear that he'd reverted to his habit of not texting back, I decided the man deserved way worse than shouty caps and ordered another round of snakebites.

"I take it this means you didn't know about the video?" the hot guy says. He hasn't lost interest, despite the fact that I'm married or that I've been obsessed with my phone since Mia texted me.

"That it existed, or that the whole world was going to see it?" I ask.

"Either?" He looks way too amused, his blue eyes crinkling in the corners, but I guess the situation might seem funny to anyone who's not me.

"Nope and nope," I say. The bartender slides the second round of shots in front of Emma and me, and I take this one with much less hesitation. Oh, look. I'm at a bar drinking irresponsibly, just like my sister thought I would be.

"I'm Hayden Owen," the hot guy says, offering his hand to Emma then me. "But the guys just call me Owen. I play wide receiver for the Gators."

"Nice to meet you, Owen," I say. "I'm Bailey."

"Mason's wife," he says, as if he's just *trying* to make me say it.

I grumble under my breath. What does Mason mean, *he* leaked our story? *Why?* Did I give him the impression that I'd made my decision? "So, I guess this means you saw the video?"

"Sure did." He stands and drags his stool around Emma so he's positioned between us. "It's so nice to meet the girl Dahl spent his rookie season moping over. He was one lovesick puppy."

Emma gives me a knowing look, but I snort. "I doubt he was moping, but if he was, I wasn't the reason."

"Hmm." Owen drums his fingers on his thigh. "You sure about that?"

"How do you know he was lovesick?"

"There are three types of rookies." He ticks them off on his fingers. "There's the type who's got Jesus in his heart and avoids the bars altogether. You know, the *not today, Satan* folks. Then there are the ones who revel in the groupies. Any time the guys are out, they're gonna go. And they're always going home with a different face."

"*That* sounds like Mason," I say, thinking of the guy I knew my freshman year—the guy he was before we started sleeping together. He did have a reputation, but I guess that all ended after me.

Owen grunts. "Yeah, right. Not since he's been a Gator, at least."

"So what category did Mason fit into?" Emma asks, leaning forward. She's loving this.

He grins. "He was the newly married, pussy-whipped boy. Those guys run home every night to their wives because they're scared of them or because they truly believe there's nothing better out there." He shrugs. "Doesn't really make a difference to me."

"He wasn't married his rookie season." I grab my water off the counter and drink. I'm not *quite* as irresponsible as my sister thinks. "We only got married a couple of months ago."

"Maybe you weren't officially together," Owen says. "But that guy? He never wanted to go out, and when we did, I couldn't even get him to look at the girls who were trying so hard for his attention. I thought, hey, maybe the brother's gay."

I laugh despite myself. "You thought *Mason* was gay?"

"In my experience, if a man isn't interested in a sexy woman trying to get him in her bed, there's a reason. I even sent a couple of my friends his way, thinking I was doing him a favor. Guys don't come out in the NFL like they do in other walks of life, so it was possible. But they all said no—Mason definitely didn't bat for their team. Now I'm meeting you, and it's all coming together."

I shouldn't like hearing this. I mean, it's probably not true, right? And if it is, I definitely shouldn't *want* it to be. But tell that to the giddy buzz in my belly. "You're full of ideas, aren't you, Owen?"

He grins and taps his head. "Yeah, I'm the brains of this operation." He looks me over. "You're easy on the eyes. I can see why he passed on all the pretty girls."

I feel someone watching me and turn to see Mason just inside the doors of the bar. He's talking to Keegan, but he's looking at me with intense and searching eyes that make my skin flush. Or is that the alcohol?

God, Mason looks edible tonight. His worn jeans are slung low on his hips, and his arms are likely to bust out of that shirt.

Owen follows my gaze and gives a low whistle. "I used to have something like that."

Reluctantly, I pull my gaze off Mason to look at Owen. "Like what?"

He gives a sad smile. "A connection so intense that other people could feel it when we were in the same room." He waves a hand between Mason and me. "What you two have is special. Don't throw it away."

"What happened to her?" Emma asks.

Owen looks surprised that she asked, then shakes his head. "She didn't have the courage to stay. And I didn't have the courage to go after her."

I want to ask what that means, because Owen intrigues me, and I'd rather sit here and listen to his stories than deal with the drama that's unfolding in my heretofore simple life. But Owen's contemplation of his beer tells me he's not interested in sharing any more, and Mason's on his way over anyway.

"You think I'm going to let you monopolize my wife all

night?" Mason asks. He stands behind me and settles his hands on my waist, dipping his head briefly to kiss my shoulder.

I turn to meet his eyes—*what is he doing?*—and he winks at me. Right. Because everyone knows we're married now, and so we have to play the part.

But I'm warm from the tequila, and my heart is all soft from Owen's description of Mason's rookie year, so being this close feels way too good to be safe. I slide off the stool and stand on the other side of it, facing the group.

Keegan joins us next, wrapping an arm around Emma's waist and whispering something in her ear that makes her blush.

"I need her to tell me your secrets," Owen says, looking at me as he talks to Mason.

Mason arches a brow. "My secrets?"

"Yeah. How does an ugly mug like you get a girl like her to marry you?"

Mason grunts. "Lots of alcohol and luck." His eyes skim over me with so much intensity that I blush. "A *lot* of luck."

"That was my guess. Now go away." Owen waves a hand. "I'm busy laying the groundwork with your woman so when she ditches you, I can take your place."

"You wouldn't have a clue what to do with her," Mason says, obviously unoffended by Owen's prediction.

"It's true," I say. "But to be fair, I have yet to meet a man who does." Really, I just want Owen to stop talking about me and Mason. I haven't even decided if I'm going to play along yet, so I haven't exactly taken time to iron out our cover story. Are we going to have one? He isn't really planning to tell people we *accidentally* got married, is he?

"I think she likes me, Dahl," Owen says. "Watch out."

I roll my eyes at Owen. "You do make me laugh."

"Did you show her the size of your penis?" Mason asks before looking at me. "That makes *all* the girls laugh."

I punch Mason in the shoulder. "Shut up and dance with me."

He drags his gaze over me and my stomach flips. He grins. "As you wish."

I was trying to get away from the conversation about my marriage, but the second we hit the dance floor and Mason pulls me into his arms, I realize my mistake. He's such a good dancer, and we've always moved effortlessly well together. He slides one hand to the small of my back and the other into my hair, and I want to press as close to him as possible. If dancing is my excuse to touch him, I hope we can stay here all night.

"If you move down here, I might have to spend my whole summer fighting off my teammates," he says.

"Owen was just being goofy."

He shakes his head. "Nah, he knows a good thing when he sees it."

I still my hips in the middle of a dance floor full of swaying bodies. Courtesy of the tequila and how damn good Mason looks in a pair of worn jeans and a fitted T-shirt, I completely forgot that I was angry with him. "You promised you'd keep our secret."

"You said you didn't want to take the focus off Mia before her wedding. The wedding is over." He tilts his head, studying me.

"Was there another reason for the secrecy?"

I tunnel my hands into my hair. There isn't any way I can answer that without some shitty consequences. "Do I have to live with you?"

He cocks a brow. "It'd be a little more convincing if you did, yeah."

"I have a job, you know. A life in Blackhawk Valley. Can't you just tell them it's a long-distance marriage?"

"You run a bar, Bailey. Pretty sure Keegan can find someone to cover for you."

He's right, and Emma even said as much at dinner, but from him and delivered like that, it burns. "Fuck you too."

"I'm not trying to be an asshole." He draws in a ragged breath. "It would mean a lot to me if you'd move in. Much more convincing if my wife isn't living six hundred miles away."

"Four months?"

"Give or take." He studies me. "Keep in mind, I'm gone at least ten hours a day most days, and I'll be out of town for games almost half of those weekends. What's the holdup? Afraid you'll fall for me?"

His tone is light and teasing, as if the idea is laughable, but is that really what he thinks? The lighting is shoddy in here, and while I can see his face, I can't see it well enough to make out the nuances of his expressions. But to be fair, even the brightness of the midday sun wouldn't give me what I'm looking for. Ever since the first time I told him I wasn't his girl, Mason's been too guarded to show his true emotions. "You haven't slept with me in almost three years because you want more. Maybe I'm afraid *you'll* fall for *me*."

Grinning, he spins me in his arms and pulls my back to his front. Instinctively, I start dancing, following his lead through the song. "Not a chance," he says into my ear. His breath is warm, and his mouth lingers by my neck. His hand slips under my shirt and his thumb grazes over my navel, sending a delicious shiver through me. "I'm immune to you now. Years of practice."

I'm too intoxicated by the rhythm of his hips and the stroke of his thumb along the waistband of my jeans to press the issue. I lean my head back into his chest, and we dance. His face is tucked into the crook of my neck, and I can feel the heat of his breath against my skin.

One song leads into the next before I realize we've been spotted. Mason might not think he's much of a celebrity, but around here, he's like royalty. I count at least three cell phones held in our direction, and there are probably more that I can't see through the crowd.

I spin in his arms and look up at him. His eyes are hazy, his lips parted. He was just as affected by our dance as I was. Satisfaction pools in my belly. "They're watching."

His eyes flick away from mine, and his chest expands with a deep breath as he scans the room and realization dawns.

"Think they've seen our wedding video?" I ask him.

"Probably," he says. He shakes his head. "But that's not why I was dancing with you. I just missed it."

My breath catches as I think of the night we officially met.

The party. The dancing. The hours after. "They're still looking," I say, when I pull back to meet his eyes. "What do you want them to see?"

His gaze drops to my mouth. "That's up to you, Bailey."

"This doesn't mean I'm moving in with you." I link my arms behind his neck. "I haven't decided yet."

"Understood."

I lift onto my toes because even with him bent down, I have to stretch to close the distance to his mouth. When my lips meet his, maybe the stars I see are from the flashes of the cell phone cameras around us, but more than likely it's just a sign of business as usual for me. This is the way I've always reacted to Mason.

He makes it good, slowly siding his tongue against my lips before opening over me and tilting my head back just so as he deepens the kiss. I know the crowd is watching, and I shouldn't let myself feel this too much. Whether or not I move in with him, this is the least I can do for Mason. Even if I don't come back after training camp, even if this is the last time we're in the same room before quietly dissolving our marriage, this kiss should help him convince everyone who needs convincing—for now, at least—that he is a happily married man.

When he breaks the kiss, he gasps in my ear. "Fuck, you taste good."

"That's tequila," I say, and his warm body rocks against mine as he chuckles. "And you promised a kiss didn't mean anything."

"I didn't promise I wouldn't *feel* anything. I'm a guy, Bailey, and the hottest girl in the room just kissed me. I'd be more worried if I didn't feel anything."

I bite back a smile. I've missed his flirtation. Before he gave up on me, I used to get it all the time. And then I hated that it was gone, missed his attention, and I'd tease him about his determination to stay out of my bed. In retrospect, that was a really shitty thing to do when I knew I couldn't have him. But I just wanted anything I could get. I didn't want to lose him completely. I still don't.

Is that why I'm actually considering four months as his wife? If I do this, there will be hell to pay.

CHAPTER 10

MASON

One PG-13 kiss, and she's frazzled. Her cheeks are flushed, her lips are swollen, and she's looking at me like I walk on water. I could take her to bed right now and happily keep her there for a week. It's been too damn long. But I won't. I know from experience that it wouldn't mean anything to her, and that inevitably pisses me off.

"I think I should get out of here before the fans and their cameras expect you to pin me against the wall or something," Bailey says.

I arch a brow. "That could be fun."

She smacks my chest. "Maybe another time." She pulls her phone from her pocket and opens up the app for Uber.

"What are you doing?"

"Getting a cab. I'm in no position to be driving anywhere."

"I'll take you wherever you want to go. I drove."

She turns, scanning the room. "Why didn't you get a ride with Keegan?"

I grunt. "He just got engaged. You really think he wanted to deal with taking me home before taking his fiancée to their bed?"

Her searching gaze stops when she spots them across the room, where Keegan has Emma pressed against the wall. She's gripping his shoulder as he whispers in her ear. I like seeing them happy.

"Good point," Bailey says. "Should we break it up to say goodbye, or just text and let them know we left?"

"Let them have their fun. You can drop Emma a text when we get in the car." In truth, I'm glad Emma and Keegan are so wrapped up in each other. Bailey's smiling and loose-limbed from the tequila, and I don't want to share her right now. Fuck, I never want to share her.

I offer her a hand, and she takes it and follows me out to the parking lot. The crescent moon is high in the clear night sky, and the air has cooled twenty degrees since I finished practice tonight. It's the magic of living by the sea. I wonder if Bailey would like that about living here.

"It's good to see them both so happy," she says, looking over her shoulder toward the bar entrance.

"It sure is." I unlock my car and open the door for her before going around to my side and climbing in.

"Did you know he was going to do it?" she asks.

I nod. "He was nervous about proposing. He worried it was too soon for her, but he didn't want to wait."

"She was ready." She grins then shakes her head. "Why do all our friends have to go through so much shit to find their bliss? Are they just stronger than everyone else? I think most people would have given up."

She turns her head and her gaze locks on the bar again, as if she can see through the walls to the couple in question. I take advantage of the moment and study her for a long beat. Something tugs in my chest—an ache for something I gave up on long ago. "If you're not willing to fight for it, it's not really your bliss, is it?"

She blinks and turns to meet my gaze. "I guess not." She looks around the car with wide eyes. "Holy hot car, Batman."

I grin. Before now, she hadn't seen my new Dodge Challenger, since I've never taken it to Blackhawk Valley. It's the only outrageous thing I bought for myself since signing with the Gators, and in the scheme of NFL players' outrageous purchases, it's pretty tame.

She skims her hand across the dash the way another woman might caress a pretty dress or a handbag. "Has Sebastian seen this?"

"I sent him a picture the day I brought her home, but he hasn't had a chance to drive her yet."

Her lips twitch. "Pretty sure he'd jizz in his jeans over this car."

"He can buy his own damn car now."

She sighs, and her face falls. "That's true. He could. I guess everybody from the old crew is doing pretty well."

"What about you, Bailey? Are you doing well?" We both know she's not—at least financially.

"I mean, I don't play in the NFL, but Keegan pays me all right, and I make a little spending money doing the photography thing."

Then why are you still living in the apartment in the bar? And why do you still wear the same tattered jean shorts you wore when we were back in the dorms?

Why is there a pile of bills for you at my house?

I don't want to pry. It's been a good night, and pushing her to open up only ever achieves the opposite. "Where are we going?"

"The Swan Motel," she says, and when she gives me the address, my brows shoot up.

If she were staying in Seaside, I wouldn't have to worry. Seaside is small and on the beach, and there really are no bad areas of town unless you have an aversion to tourists or assholes with too much money.

She's staying on the west side of Destin, about ten miles from the beach. The farther you get from the beach, the cheaper the hotels are, so I'm not surprised.

"You didn't have to get a motel, you know," I say as I merge onto 30A. "You could have stayed with me."

"Right. Because it makes total sense to plan a trip to ask for a divorce and then bunk with the guy I'm demanding it from."

"I can see your hesitation, but I still could have given you a room to sleep in. I have plenty of beds."

"What can I say?" she says. "I'm an independent woman."

I grunt. I'm not touching that one. But when I roll up to the motel, I decide to reopen the conversation of where she's staying. "This place is a shithole. Do they rent rooms by the hour?"

"Okay, *snob.*" She's so fucking cute when she gets pissed off. I miss that. I miss everything about her. "Not all of us can afford the Ritz."

I frown. "There's a world of options between the Ritz and this place, Bailey."

"Careful, Mason. Your privilege is showing."

There's a big banner taped to the wall out front, one corner hanging down, that reads *39.99 a night!* I dig my wallet out of my back pocket and pull out two twenties. "Here's money for your room."

"You're not paying for my room."

I slide my wallet back into my pocket and give her a hard look. "Sure I am."

"Mason, I'm not getting out of this car with your money."

"Damn right you're not. That's to pay you back for a room I won't let you use." I put my hand behind her seat and turn to look out my back window as I back the car out of the spot.

"Where are we going?" she asks as I pull toward the exit.

"I'm taking you to my house." When she puts her hand on my arm, I put my foot on the brake and sigh. "This place is worse than shady. Do they even wash the sheets between visits?"

Her jaw drops. "Oh my God, you are such a spoiled brat. It's ridiculous."

"Look me in the eye and tell me that room is somewhere you

want to spend your night."

She opens her mouth to speak, but when she meets my eyes, she closes it again. "It's pretty gross, but I don't need to be wasting money on a place to sleep right now. As I mentioned before, not all of us play for the NFL. I can't afford to be picky."

"You're my wife," I say, grateful for the excuse. I hate the idea of her sleeping here. "If people found out you were staying in a motel, they'd start asking questions. It's one thing when you're in Blackhawk Valley. You have a life there and presumably have loose ends to tie up. Until you make up your mind, let's not raise any questions about why you're not staying with me when you're down here."

"Okay." She folds her arms and leans back in her seat. "But only because my buzz is making me tired and I'm too lazy to move." She gives me a sleepy smile. "Can I at least go get my stuff, though?"

If she goes in her room, I'm not sure I trust her to come back. I wouldn't put it past her to lock the door to her room behind herself and refuse to come out. I turn off the engine and hold out a hand. "Give me your key. I'll go get it."

"Aren't you afraid I'm going to steal your fancy car?"

"You're my wife. If you leave with my car, I don't think it's stealing."

"Oooh!" She waggles her eyebrows. "So, what's yours is mine?"

If she knew me at all, she'd know it always has been. But this is Bailey, and even though she's rough and tough and independent, she's also an awful lot like a nervous stray who will run and hide if you get too close too fast. Tonight, I want to know she's safe in my house. "I'll be right back, okay?"

The room is as disgusting as I worried it would be. Maybe blood isn't splattered on the wall like I pictured, and the bedspread isn't visibly dirty, but the carpet is stained and there's an overwhelming odor of stale cigarettes despite the *No Smoking* placard on the door.

In the bathroom, wallpaper is curling off the wall. I gather all her things and go to the front desk to check her out before heading back to the car.

She's slumped over in the passenger seat, asleep with her mouth open and her hands tucked under her shirt as if she's cold.

My throat goes thick at the sight of her, at the thought of getting to take her home. I squeeze my eyes shut and try to cut off those thoughts before they lead me to a night in my bed with her. I know what this is, and I know what it isn't. We'll all be better off if I don't forget that.

CHAPTER 11

BAILEY

Four years ago . . .

Saturday nights are great money at the Pretty Kitty, but for once I'm glad for a night off. I'm hurting and stressed and want nothing more than to lose myself in a good, old-fashioned college house party. I can hear the music and smell the stale beer even before I come in the front door.

I'm still pissed at Nic for the way he wrote me off today. *"Stop thinking this is some fairytale, because there's nothing between us anymore."*

I'm still pissed at myself for telling him that Clarence came around. Maybe on some level I'm disgusted with myself for considering Clarence's offer. I contemplated a line I swore I'd never cross.

I need this party because I can't stop asking myself where I'd be tonight if Nic had wanted my help. I can't say I would have gone to Clarence easily, but it eats at me to know I wouldn't have rejected the idea outright. I would have considered it. And what does that say about me? Am I so close to whoring myself out?

"Bailey's here!" a girl shouts as I push my way through the crowd to the drink table. She's in my history class, but I can't remember her name. "Tequila?" she asks, and she takes a swig from a bottle before offering it to me.

I shake my head and point to the keg. "Beer's more my style." Actually, I think beer tastes like piss, but if I start chugging tequila from the bottle like that chick, God knows where I'll end up at the end of the night. I do my best to reserve hard liquor for smaller gatherings, where I know and trust everyone in attendance.

I find a red cup and stand in line to fill it. The chaos around me quiets the anxiety that's been gnawing at me since last night. This is exactly where I need to be.

My confession? The truth that I would never tell Nic? I *love* college. I was worried that I might not fit in with all these rich kids because, let's face it, aside from the students here on athletic scholarship, the only people who can afford BHU without getting into lifelong debt are those who come from some serious family money.

Personally, I fall into the lifelong debt category. I wanted a chance at a life outside of Blackhawk Valley and at a career that doesn't involve shaking my ass in front of strange men. I didn't want to become my mother.

Any apprehension I had about going to BHU has faded with the realization that I have as much right to be here as the next girl. It's not just the parties. I love the challenge of the classes and all the endless clubs and organizations. I even love living in the dorms—it beats Mom's trailer, where there's too much clutter and no AC.

Mia can't come out tonight. She got a babysitting gig, and she likes to take any opportunity she can to pick up extra cash. I'm not going to let that stop me. After seeing her brother today, I need to let my hair down and dance—just not topless on stage.

I'm halfway through my first beer and swaying my hips to the music when I feel someone watching. Turning, I spot a guy across the room looking at me with unabashed appreciation. He has intense green eyes, dark skin, and a smile that might have made my stomach flutter if I was a little less jaded. He looks vaguely familiar, so I'm guessing I've seen him around campus.

After meeting my gaze, he waits, as if he's sure I'm going to go to him. With those broad shoulders, thickly muscled arms, and big hands, it's a pretty safe bet that most girls would. But I'm not most girls and my heart still belongs to the biggest bad boy I know, so I just smile and return to my drink.

After a few minutes, he appears next to me. "You live with me."

I arch a brow. "Pretty sure I don't."

"Not *with*, near." Grinning, he takes one hand off his red Solo cup of beer and offers it to me. "I'm Mason from the quad down the hall from you."

"Hi, Mason from the quad down the hall. I'm Bailey."

"I know." His smile reaches his eyes in the most charming

way, and when his gaze slides over me, warmth swirls in my belly.

"How do you know?"

"I asked your roommate about you. I've been nursing a crush on you since the day I saw you move in."

That surprises me—not the crush, because *whatever*—but that a guy like him would admit to it. I'd expect him to play it cool and maybe be attracted to me but act ambivalent about whether I was interested in return. I like that he comes right out with it. It's refreshing, even if I don't have the time or emotional energy for cute boys with intense eyes and big hands. My life is way too complicated for *crushes* and *feelings*. "If you had such a crush, why didn't you introduce yourself before now?"

His lips quirk. "The day you moved in, you were wearing short white shorts that stole my capacity for speech."

"And after?" I'm surprised to hear the flirty cadence to my words. That's not like me. Maybe I should blame Nic and the way his words made me feel today. I deserve a fucking minute to flirt with a cute boy who makes me feel good. Hell, after Nic's speech, I deserve a whole damn month.

"You want to know the truth?" he asks.

"I always prefer the truth."

"I was hoping you'd notice me. You know, so I'd have a better chance when I finally introduced myself." He draws in a long breath. "But that wasn't working, and I'm not that patient, so . . . here I am."

My gaze snags on the guys walking in the front door, and my smile falls away. Clarence and the boys from last night. *Fuck.* Are they here for me?

A boy in a tailored shirt and tight jeans saunters over to Clarence and smacks something into his hand. *He's here for business.*

I hope it's too crowded in here for Clarence to see me. Maybe he doesn't care—that would be best—but I no sooner have the thought than his gaze sweeps across the room and lands on me. I react instinctively, looping my arms around Mason's neck and tilting my face up to his. "So are we going to dance or just stand here and make small talk?"

He blinks at me in surprise, but a beat later, a slow, sexy grin covers his face. "If the girl wants to dance, then I'll dance."

We ditch our cups and he settles his hands on my hips and holds me against him so the dance feels like something much more erotic. He's a good dancer. He knows how to move his body without resorting to that awkward side-to-side stepping most boys do.

I've almost forgotten about Clarence when he taps Mason on the shoulder.

Mason doesn't let me go, just arches a brow at the guy.

Clarence nods at me before looking at Mason. "Gonna need you to back off so me and my girl can go outside for a minute and talk."

Mason looks at me, and he must see the fear on my face. Or maybe he feels it in the way I grip his shoulders. "If she wanted to be outside talking to you, that's where she'd be. Why don't you get out of our way?"

Clarence's eyes narrow. "Do you think I'm afraid of a nigger?"

Mason stiffens, and he squeezes my hip and whispers, "Just a sec, okay?" before releasing me and turning to Clarence. I knew Mason was a big guy, but when he rolls his shoulders back to stare Clarence down, I swear he looks a foot taller and a foot broader than before. I don't miss the way he steps in front of me, as if he's creating a wall between me and this asshole.

"Everyone at this party knows why you're here, and I imagine the cop parked in the alley out back knows, too. Why don't you leave before somebody tips him off?"

Clarence shakes his head. "No pussy's worth this shit." He crooks a finger at his goons—never far behind—and leaves. Mason keeps his eyes on them until they're out the door.

I deflate in relief.

When Mason's attention returns to me, he watches me for a beat, and I wait for him to make some excuse to get away. I obviously come with trouble, and who wants to deal with that?

He touches my chin with two fingers. "I hope that was okay. It felt like you were afraid of him."

I shrug. "He makes me uncomfortable."

His green eyes search mine. "You okay?"

I nod. "Embarrassed that you had to deal with that, but otherwise okay." He probably doesn't even know I work at the Pretty Kitty and will run in the other direction when he finds out. I take a breath, preparing to rip off the Band-Aid. "I know him from work. The Pretty Kitty doesn't exactly have all the classiest clients."

"I heard you work there," he says, as if I just admitted I work the drive-thru at McDonald's. "I'm sorry you have to deal with assholes like that."

"They're a dime a dozen where I come from." I'm still waiting for him to realize that I'm not like him. Still waiting for a sign that he understands what I do and why guys like Clarence think they have some sort of ownership over me.

Instead, he looks around the party. "Can I take you to a late dinner or something? It's too loud in here."

Maybe he's a mind reader, because after seeing Clarence, I don't want to be here anymore, and I was already thinking up excuses to leave. I love college because it feels like a different world, miles away from my old life and the world that's got Nic in its claws, but tonight those worlds collided.

I smile at him and run my gaze over his toned biceps, broad shoulders, and narrow hips. "For some reason, I'm guessing you probably don't eat the same foods I do."

He shrugs. "I'd eat slugs if you'd keep looking at me like that."

And just like that, my vague affection for this clean-cut college boy turns into a full-on crush. "I'm not really in the mood for slugs, but I'm always game for tacos."

He takes my hand and laces our fingers together. "Tacos just became my favorite food."

CHAPTER 12

BAILEY

Present day . . .

I'm jarred awake when Mason scoops me up and lifts me out of the car. I wrap my arms around his neck and hold on tight before remembering myself.

"You can put me down," I murmur, but I'm tired, and his chest is warm against my cheek.

"Let me impress you with my ridiculous strength for a minute, okay?"

I try to laugh, but that takes too much effort, so it comes out more like a cough. "Okay." I'm so relaxed, and maybe I should credit the tequila, but I know the comfort of his presence is what has me so loose-limbed. I've always felt safe with Mason around.

I don't bother protesting anymore, or even opening my eyes as he carries me into the house. The moment reminds me so much of the night he found me in my apartment after Nic's funeral. He scooped me into his arms and carried me to the bed.

"Hold me. Don't leave," I whisper, just like I did that night, and I cling to him, just like I did then.

Sleep tugs me under again, and I'm half dreaming when he settles me into bed and tucks the covers over me.

Dream mixes with reality, past with present. In my mind, I hear Mason whisper, "I'm not going anywhere," but when I open my eyes, I'm alone in his big bedroom, the duvet pulled up to my chin, the ceiling fan clicking overhead.

I want him to come back and hold me like he did after Nic died. I want to be wrapped in his arms all night, but it's such a selfish wish that I don't dare tell him. Instead, I close my eyes and settle for the memories of Mason's soothing touch, his reassuring whispers.

I wasn't supposed to be overwhelmed with grief by the death of a man who didn't want me, and it was unreasonable to feel guilty about Nic's death when I wasn't driving the car that killed him. But grief doesn't care about *supposed to*, and guilt doesn't care about reason.

I'm not allowed to be Mason's wife. But the heart doesn't care about rules or promises that never should have been made.

I wake up alone and disoriented. At the foot of the bed, sunlight slants in through the sliding glass doors and seems to spotlight the ocean beyond.

The opposite side of the bed is fresh, unrumpled. Mason didn't sleep next to me last night. I put my hand on the pillow, trying to decide how I feel about that, trying to imagine what it would be like if I agreed to give him four months.

With the video released yesterday, it's unlikely his parents remain unaware of what we did in Vegas, but unlike Mason, I don't think that information is going to do anything to change how they feel about him marrying someone not of his social status.

I climb out of bed and wander down to the kitchen. On the island, I find a house key, my wedding band, and a note scribbled on the back of a takeout menu.

> *Bailey,*
>
> *I had an early meeting and didn't want to wake you. There's coffee in the pot and Pop-Tarts in the cabinet, since I know your aversion to foods that don't rot your teeth.*
>
> *I'll be home this afternoon. I hope you've considered doing me this favor and will think about what I could do for you in return.*
>
> *Here's your house key and the alarm code is 40236. Come and go as you please.*
>
> *Your adoring husband,*
>
> *M*

I rub the ring between my thumb and index finger and read

the note three times, because when I do, I hear his voice in my head, and that makes me feel all warm and fuzzy inside.

I slide the ring onto my finger, as if to test its feel, and find the Pop-Tarts in the cabinet. I shake my head at the unopened box. Mason doesn't eat crap like this, and I'm sure they were purchased for me. When did he do that? Last night after he tucked me into his bed, or this morning before he left for his meeting? Regardless, he went out of his way, and the simple gesture tugs at my heart.

I pull out my phone and text him.

> ***Me:*** *If the Pop-Tarts were a bribe to make me consider your offer, you're an evil genius.*

I send the message, and the doorbell rings. *Shit.* Can I ignore it? Pretend I'm not here?

Reluctantly, I leave my breakfast behind and go to the door. When I open it, a pair of familiar green eyes look back at me.

"Funny seeing you here, Bailey," Christian Dahl says. Then he pushes past me and into his son's house. I don't even protest—because one, seeing him again makes me want to puke, and two, he has more of a right to be here than I do.

Helplessly, I shut the door behind him and follow him into the kitchen.

"How are you?" Christian asks, spinning to face me. His sandy blond hair is shorter than it was when I first met him. I hope he matured when he cut off his man bun, but that's just wishful thinking. He's dressed to do business in a navy suit and tie, and I wonder if that's what this is to him—a business meeting, where I'm a pesky little detail he must contend with before he can close a deal.

"I'm fine," I say, my voice tight. "Mason's not here."

He wanders around the kitchen, examining my breakfast on the island, a picture of our friends from Arrow and Mia's wedding on the fridge. Between each destination, his shoes click on the tile floor. Everything is met with scrutiny. Nothing is good enough for his son, least of all me.

"I know he's not here." He returns that critical gaze to me and levels it at the ring on my left hand. "I came because I want you to look me in the eye when you tell me you're breaking your promise."

Four years ago . . .

I'm smiling. I'm smiling and I feel . . . *happy.*

Today, we found out that Nic's getting parole, and while I'm thrilled, I'm also nervous as hell, because I don't know what's going to happen if he gets out of prison and owes Clarence money. I wanted to find a way to resolve the situation before Nic was a free man, but aside from picking up more shifts at the Kitty, I'm drawing a blank as to what I can do.

Our relationship is complicated. Nic's worked so hard to push me away since he's been incarcerated that my friends would tell me to let him fix his own problems. But they don't know Nic the way I do. They don't understand that he pushes me away to protect me. They haven't seen his stubborn determination to get a leg up in this world, despite the consequences. They don't know that it's my fault he's in prison to begin with.

And yet, despite my worries about Nic's future, I can't get this stupid smile off my face, because I can't stop thinking about *Mason Dahl.* Which is weird and confusing and not at all what I expected. But Mason isn't what I expected. He's rough and sweet and so damn steady. I've never been with someone who treats me like he does, but I hope I can get used to it.

The Pretty Kitty is busy tonight. I'd normally be thrilled with the crowd—nothing says payday like a bunch of drunk guys with pockets still deep from their summer jobs—but tonight I'd rather be with Mason.

It's been a good night for tips, even if every time I walk on stage, I think of Mason holding me tighter, growling, "Don't go," into my ear. *"Find another job."*

"Are you embarrassed to be sleeping with a stripper?" I asked him tonight when I was getting ready for work.

"I'm not embarrassed," he said, sliding his hand down the front of my body. "I just don't want to share you." He slid his hands behind my back and cupped my ass. "I'm feeling a little possessive, Bailey."

"You're feeling something," I whispered, then I ended up being late for my unofficial shift because he picked me up and carried me to the bed. He explored me with those big hands and that demanding mouth until I forgot all about the Pretty Kitty and the money I very much need.

I don't want to do this job any more than he wants me to do it, but I have to. It's a necessary evil.

Vicky saunters up to me at the counter. She's in a short skirt that shows her hot-pink panties when she walks and a rhinestone-studded bra that I know from experience itches like a motherfucker. "Somebody's here looking for you," she says as she loads her tray with drinks.

I immediately tense. *Shit, shit, shit.* Clarence probably wants to give me one more chance to take him up on his offer before Nic's released. I was hoping seeing me with Mason might make him back off, but I guess it's not going to be that simple. As long as Nic owes him money, Clarence will believe he has a chance. "Where is he?"

She points a thumb over her shoulder and sighs. "Booth at the back. He asked for the bourbon."

"Did you tell him what it costs?"

She shrugs. "I don't think he cares. He looks and smells like money, you lucky bitch."

I grin like I know she expects me to, trying to hide my nerves. I don't want to tell her about Clarence. I don't want anyone knowing that Nic's still tied to him. Worst-case scenario, Clarence is asking for me. In that case, I'll deliver his drink and walk away, and if he tries to get more from me, Hammer will stop him. Best-case scenario, some rich man wants to pay for the pleasure of my company. Normally, that would be a good thing;

I'm just not in the mood to play the toy tonight. People think strippers make good money because of their hot bodies, but I've seen A-cup chicks with beer bellies take home more in one night of tips than I make all weekend. These men are here for attention, whether they know it or not, and good strippers make bank by giving it to them.

I pour the man's drink and flip my hair over my shoulder before heading through the crowd to the back booth. When I don't see Clarence anywhere, my shoulders sag in relief. I spot the bourbon drinker. Vicky was right. He looks like money. He has sandy blond hair pulled into a tie at the back of his neck, and he smirks when he sees me. It's not just the Rolex on his wrist or the crisp white dress shirt with the sleeves rolled to his elbows or the way he parts his hair. This man has an aura of wealth about him that's unique to men who've never wanted anything they couldn't buy.

We don't get a lot of guys in here with deep pockets, so if I'm smart, I'll take advantage of the opportunity to take some money off his hands.

"You asked for this?" I say, bending unnecessarily at the hips to deposit his drink in front of him. Straightening, I smile. "And for me?"

He has sharp green eyes, and he drags his gaze over me. I've been objectified enough times in this place to know what it feels like when a man is looking me over in a sexual way. This man is not. This man is sizing me up, cataloging my body like a piece of jewelry he might purchase to resell. "You're Bailey Green?"

I shift uncomfortably. I don't use my name in here. With a town this size, almost everybody knows it anyway, but I've never met this guy before and I don't like him calling me by name. "You can call me whatever you want."

"Why don't you have a seat, *Bailey.*" The emphasis he puts on my name makes me want to walk away, but the value of the watch on his wrist makes me stay.

"You're not the only guy in here who wants a drink." I try to keep my smile in place, but it's wavering. Does this guy have some connection to Clarence? I don't get that King Kong drug-dealer vibe from him, but what do I know? What else does some rich guy insistent on using my real name want from me?

He extends a hand. "I'm Christian Dahl, Mason's father."

The eyes. Shit. This might not be the *most* awkward meet-the-parents moment in history, but it's a contender for the podium. I try to keep my smile in place, but it's hard when I want to crawl under the nearest table and hide. Fuck the table—I'd rather crawl under a *rock* than be here right now. When the earth doesn't open to swallow me whole—damn the luck—I try to pretend this is totally normal. "It's nice to meet you, Christian."

Has Mason told his parents about me already? *Obviously, he did.*

"Now will you sit down?" he asks.

I suppose this could be worse. He could have gotten a lap dance or tried to talk to me while I was onstage. Yeah, it could be worse, but not much. I look over at Vicky, who's serving a round of beer to the booth beside us. She grins, no doubt making assumptions about me and the rich guy that are so wrong, I can't even . . . She waves me away, letting me know she'll take care of the floor while I talk to him.

The booths in here are semicircles big enough for men to lounge in comfortably and situated so they all have a view of the stage.

I sit opposite Christian, and panic seizes my chest. What if he's here to deliver terrible news? But he doesn't look like a man who's recovering from a tragedy. He looks like a cocky son of a bitch who thinks he has my number. "Is everything okay with Mason?"

"Not particularly," he says. He swirls his bourbon in his glass, takes a sip, and makes a face before pushing it away. I can't imagine Gary's cheap shit meets the standards of a man like this, and I'm oddly satisfied to see Christian drink cheap booze. Freaking rich people. "I understand you're involved with my son."

I'm not even sure how to respond to that. Mason and I haven't talked about what we are to each other. It's complicated, and we certainly aren't at the point where our parents need to be involved in the conversation. "We're friends," I say.

He smirks. "Right. Girls like you know how to get real friendly, don't you?"

That's the moment that I hate him. His "girls like you" comment? Fuck that noise.

I stand, and he smacks a hand on the table. "Sit."

"Fuck off," I say, not caring that this is Mason's dad. I wouldn't care if he was the president of the United States. He's already decided who I am, and he's wrong. "*Girls like me* can hold our own," I say, my voice a low growl that curls with anger. "*Girls like me* can put food on the table. Girls like *me* won't be bossed around by shallow rich men who confuse the size of their income with the size of their worth."

"That's a nice little speech," he says, cocking a brow. "But it doesn't change the fact that you were just on that stage letting men tuck money into your G-string. So why don't you save the self-righteous speeches and listen to what I came to say."

I hate myself a little for it, but I don't walk away. I fold my arms over my chest and stare at him. "You say what you need to, then I'm getting back to work."

"My son is going to be drafted. In just a couple of years, he'll be making more money than you've ever seen or dreamed of. But you already know that."

Now I do. Maybe I didn't when Mason approached me at the party, and maybe I didn't when I first got into bed with him. But since then, it's come up a few times, and I've gone to a couple of games to watch him play. Mason's talented, and I don't doubt he can make a career with football.

"And you probably know," his father continues, "that he comes from more money than you've ever seen or dreamed of."

That I *didn't* know. I could've guessed after the last five minutes, but before tonight I didn't have a clue.

He holds my gaze, but I'm not taking the bait. I refuse to justify my relationship with Mason. I refuse to defend myself and explain my intentions to this man—not that I have any. I just have a job that people judge me for and an asshole sitting in front of me who thinks what I do for a living says everything about my character.

"I get it," he says, dragging his gaze over my body again. "I totally get why a girl like you would latch on to a guy like Mason. He could change your whole life. 'Cause right now, I figure you have a few years of lying to yourself. You do this job and tell yourself you're just doing it to get through school, but soon, you take it outside the club because you can make even more cash that way. Then come the nights that you don't want to think about what you do anymore. Maybe your friend offers you powdered happiness—something that makes dancing seem fun again—then your checks start going up your nose or in your veins, then you're back in that trailer park nailing boards to cover the broken windows in the piece of shit you call home. Just like your mama did."

My eyes sting, and I clench my fists. If this man wasn't Mason's father, I'd probably swing at him. "You don't know anything about me." But anger simmers in my voice because he seems to know an awful lot.

"My son has a bright future. We've worked hard to make sure he has every opportunity. The last thing he needs is a girl like you bringing him down."

"I'm done with this conversation," I say.

"Are you? Because I haven't even gotten to the good part yet."

"The good part is where you leave."

"The good part is where I offer to write you a check, *Bailey*

Green. The good part is where you tell me how much it's going to cost me to make sure whatever is between you and my son never turns into anything more. I don't care if you want to fuck him. He's entitled to all the toys he wants, and right now, he seems to think he wants you. So sure, have your fun. But you'll never be anything more than the stripper he used to screw around with. Whether you take my money or not, I can promise you that."

"You obviously don't know your son very well," I say, but even keeping my voice low doesn't hide the way it's shaking.

"I know him better than a girl like you ever will. The way I see it, your choices are to take the check, pretend we never had this conversation, and make sure your little fling never becomes anything more. Or you don't take the check. Maybe you tell my son we had this conversation, and I won't deny it. But I will tell him you took the money, even if you didn't. And let me tell you something about my son: once I tell him you took my money, *that* will ensure you two never become anything more. Which will it be?"

CHAPTER 13

BAILEY

Present day . . .

"Are you making yourself comfortable in my son's house?"

"Right now, I couldn't be more *un*comfortable." I give him a tight smile. "Thanks for asking."

He rocks back on his heels and tucks his hands in his pockets. "Do you want to explain why we're in the same room together again? I'm *assuming* you have some sort of explanation."

"Um, because you drove over here and walked in the front door like you own the place?"

His eyes blaze. He never was a fan of my sarcasm. "Why are you in my son's life? In his house? Why are you married to him when you promised me—"

"I know what I promised." I swallow, hating the devil in front of me and the deal we made. "We're married because we were in

Vegas and I was drunk."

"Yeah, I saw the video. Along with the rest of the world."

I curl my hands into fists at my sides, and my nails bite into my palms. "It was a mistake, and we have every intention of dissolving the marriage."

"That was clever of you. Get drunk. Marry a rich man. No prenup and the perfect excuse to break your promise."

How could Mason have come from this man? Mason, who is so warm and giving, who believes the best of me even when I don't deserve it. "You always think everyone's after money, don't you?"

Christian arches a brow. "Weren't you?"

I don't answer. The last thing I ever wanted was for Christian Dahl to understand just how much I was giving up when I took his check and agreed to never have a relationship with Mason. I didn't want him to know how deeply I felt for his son. Now is no different. If he knew, he'd only find a way to use the information to hurt me more.

There was a point in my life when I didn't understand what it was like to want things that didn't cost money. There was a point when all the things I wanted could be bought—a better house, new clothes for school, a car to get to work when I turned sixteen, fancy makeup, the shoes all the girls were wearing. I wanted those things so much I ached with it. But until I made a deal with Christian Dahl, I had no idea what it was like to want something that can't be bought.

"What do you want, Bailey?" he asks. "How do I make this

go away?"

"I want a divorce," I answer honestly, because the little girl who believed in fairytales died a long time ago. I'm Tammy Green's daughter, and I know what happens when a girl like me tries to live in a world like Mason's. "We were planning to take care of it. But since you and your friends seem so set on playing matchmaker, Mason wants me to pretend to be his wife for a while." I cock my head. "Kind of ironic, isn't it? If you weren't so set on getting your son to marry the right kind of girl, he wouldn't be trying to draw out his marriage to me."

Christian's nostrils flare, and he folds his arms as he studies me. "You think this is hilarious, don't you?"

"I don't find anything amusing about a situation that makes me have to talk to you."

His eye twitches. "You said you're going to dissolve the marriage. *When*, exactly, do you plan on making that happen?"

"He wants me to move in until the end of the regular season."

A phone buzzes, and Christian pulls his cell from his pocket and frowns at it before looking back up at me. "You do what you have to do. Move your ass, be his wife, show him you're not who he thinks you are, and then get the divorce. Try to keep out of the press. We don't need any more attention on this embarrassing situation than you've already had." He looks me over, disgust curling his lip. "Maybe time with you under his roof is just what he needs to realize you're the trash I know you are."

The words take me back to when I was seven and got in a fight with a mean girl at school because she'd called my mom "trash."

I came home all teary-eyed and snotty with scraped-up palms from where I'd caught myself when she pushed me. Sarah had cleaned me up. *"Don't waste your energy trying to change people's opinions of her. We can't undo the choices she made."* The stern line of her mouth told me she blamed Mom and not the mean girl, and for the first time, my perspective of my world shifted as I realized that even my own sister couldn't forgive our mother for her choices.

"If the new year comes and you're still here, I'll make sure *everyone* knows your secrets. All of them. Do I make myself clear?"

My eyes burn with tears I refuse to let this man see. "Crystal."

MASON

> **Bailey:** *I'm not implying that all it takes to win me is a couple of toaster pastries, but you got the kind with SPRINKLES. So, I guess I'm moving in.*

I reread the text a dozen times to make sure I'm not imagining things. A grin stretches across my face. I can't help it. She's telling me exactly what I want to hear. Maybe she's only agreed to a few months, but she's giving me the chance to get her out of Blackhawk Valley for good. *The chance to have more time with her.*

I tamp down the second thought. Bailey's made it clear what she does and doesn't want from me. Expecting that to change now is asking for heartache.

"Have a picture of a naked woman on there or what?" Owen says, tossing me a towel.

"Not a naked woman, but a text from Bailey. She's going to move in."

Owen grunts. "Of course she is. She looks at you like you're a fucking mythical hero. There wasn't a doubt in my mind."

I shake my head and wipe my face and neck with the towel on the way to the locker room. "Nothing's ever that simple when it comes to Bailey."

I sit down on a bench in the locker room, ignoring Owen's laughter. I can't stop smiling, and reply with the only thing left to say.

> ***Me:*** *Of course I got the ones with sprinkles, and there's more where that came from.*

CHAPTER 14

BAILEY

My heart is racing as I knock on the door, but I tuck my hands in my pockets and promise myself that I have every right to be here, that I'm not doing anything wrong by showing up unannounced at my sister's house.

If she's seen the video of me and Mason in Vegas, she hasn't contacted me to ask about it. I don't think it's going to score me any points with my uptight big sis, so it's probably best if I tell her before she does. Preferably in person, so I can see on her face just how much ground I've lost in my tireless efforts to win her approval.

The door swings open, and I'm greeted by my sister's bright white smile. A smile that falls away as soon as she sees me. "Bailey. What are you doing here?"

"I was in the neighborhood." I try to keep my expression neutral. Defensiveness doesn't get me anywhere, and I don't think she'd be thrilled if I admitted I was afraid she might not call after Faith's dance class like she promised. "I thought I'd stop by and see you and Faith . . . if you're not busy."

"We talked about doing this tonight," Sarah says softly.

You would have found an excuse to put me off. "Sorry. It was a spur-of-the-moment decision."

She arches a single, perfectly plucked blond brow. "Imagine that. *You* doing something unplanned. I'm guessing that wedding video of yours is more of the same."

So she did see it. What is it about family that allows them to take your heart in their fist even when you can protect it from everyone else? I turn up my palms. "What can I say? I'm immature and impulsive."

"Aunt Bailey!" My sister winces as Faith rushes around her to race into my arms. "Mommy didn't tell me you were coming!"

"It was a surprise." I scoop her up and smooth her thick black hair as I lower my nose to breathe her in. When I meet my sister's eyes again, her face is resigned, as if she's disappointed. She likes to lead her life in a particular way, and that way involves controlling everything around her. Including people. She's not a bad person, just an obsessive, worried mother.

"You can't stay long." She opens the door to lead me inside. "Faith has dance in an hour, and we need to get ready."

I take it for the victory it is and carry Faith into the living room. I plop down on the couch and settle her onto my lap. "How old are you now?" I ask.

"I turn six in September!" she announces proudly.

"No way!" I gasp, as if this information takes me by surprise, as if every second of every day of her life hasn't been etched into my mind—each moment missed with her paid for with a chunk of my heart, lost forever. "You can't be more than three, maybe four."

"Six! I start kindergarten soon."

"Are you sure your birthday's coming?" I twist up my face. "I could have sworn you had a birthday *last year.*"

"I have a birthday *every* year!" She giggles. "Are you getting old, Aunt Bailey? Is that why you can't remember? Mommy says when she forgets things it's because she's getting old."

I lift my gaze to meet my sister's and, to her credit, she attempts a smile. Her mouth pulls down at the corners, though, and I see the concern there—worry that I might stay too long or ask too much, anxiety that my less-than-savory life choices might somehow ruin this perfect child.

What my sister doesn't understand is that she and I are two peas in a pod. We've both done whatever we deemed necessary to protect the people we love.

I shouldn't be surprised by the way she keeps her walls up. One summer in high school, when Nic had just gone to prison and I needed to get away from Blackhawk Valley for a while, Sarah took me in. That summer, she was everything a big sister should be—nurturing, protective, even adoring. But before and since, she's preferred to keep me at a distance both physically and emotionally. Mom had us ten years apart, and when Sarah moved away, desperate to find a new life in a place that didn't know her family, I was just a little girl.

"How long did you say you were in town?" she asks, and again it feels as if she's trying to throw up her defenses against me getting too close.

"I leave tomorrow, but when I come back next month, I'll stay for a while." I rub a lock of Faith's hair between my fingers. "I wanted to talk to you about that before I go."

I return my attention to Faith. My sister can direct her judgmental looks in my direction all she wants, but she's not the reason I'm here. I'm going to soak up every bit of this child I can. "How's dance?" I ask.

"Awesome!" Faith says, springing from my lap and demonstrating a pirouette. "I take gymnastics too!" She runs to the wall and kicks up in a handstand.

Sarah purses her lips. "Must be nice to be able to come and go as you please. I wouldn't think the people at your job would be okay with that."

I bite my tongue only because Faith's here, but if Sarah and I were alone, I'd snark that the flexible schedule is the upside of being a call girl. She knows I manage The End Zone, but I swear I'll never live down my choice to take off my clothes for money.

She turns to Faith, who is upside down again with her feet propped against the wall. "Give Aunt Bailey a hug and go get dressed for dance."

Obediently, she kicks down and rushes over to me, wrapping her arms around me. "Stay longer next time. You can sleep on the top bunk," she whispers, and my heart blossoms at being wanted, only to wilt seconds later as I admit to myself how unlikely it is that I'll ever be able to make good on that request.

I kiss her head. "I'll be back next month to give you a birthday present."

"Yay!" She scurries away and up the stairs, taking a piece of my heart with her.

When I turn back to Sarah, she's studying me. "Make sure your gift is appropriate for a six-year-old, okay?"

I cock my head and pretend to pout. "So Stripper Barbie is a no-go?"

Sarah rolls her eyes. "I don't let her have Barbies at all. She's six and doesn't need hypersexualized dolls manipulating her self-perception."

I stand. I wore out my welcome the second I walked in the door, and it's time for me to leave. "No Barbies. No problem." I might think she's being overprotective on this front, but it's not my place to say, so I keep my mouth shut. Like always.

"And don't buy anything too elaborate, please. I'm on a budget, and I don't want you making it look like I'm cheap."

I laugh. I can't help it. "And you think I'm rolling in money? I have creditors breathing down my neck and student loans that'll follow me to the grave."

"And yet a couple of months ago you were in Vegas. Maybe you need to reevaluate where you're spending your money." She turns her head to study the wall.

My best friend, Mia, paid for me to take that trip, but I don't explain. What's the point? It was humiliating enough to let Mia pay when I was supposed to be the independent woman, the girl who stripped to pay her way through school. I used paying for college as an excuse to take my clothes off and give lap dances to half the men in my hometown. My friends don't know I'm up to my ears in student loan debt, and I don't want them to.

"Not that any of your money issues are going to matter now that you're married to an NFL player," my sister mutters. "Well done, sis."

I flinch. If my own sister thinks I'm using this marriage to capitalize on Mason's wealth, why wouldn't the rest of the world?

"She looks happy." If I just keep the conversation on Faith, Sarah's judgment won't get to me so much.

Sarah nods. "I think she is. I worry so much about her not having a father, but I think it bothers me more than it bothers her." She takes a long, deep breath, but there's not enough air in the room to energize a woman who's been burning the candle from both ends for years and is running out of wax. "We make it work."

"You seem tired."

"I've been working a lot."

I've been thinking about being closer to Sarah and Faith since Mason first proposed I stay with him, so I take a deep breath and dive in. "So you saw my . . . wedding video?"

She rolls her eyes. "Me and the rest of the world. So proud of my drunk baby sister." She gives a sarcastic fist pump.

I ignore her jab, and the ache that springs in my chest. "I'm going back to Blackhawk Valley, but in a few weeks, I'll be moving down here. I could . . . maybe I could help out some. If you wanted to have a night out or something, I could—"

"Don't do this, Bailey. Whatever is going on between you and that football player, if you're not sure it's going to last, don't make promises about being here." She shakes her head and looks toward the stairs. "Faith might only see you a couple of times a year, but she's really attached. Don't tell her that you're moving to Florida if it's not going to be permanent. She already lost her father. I don't want to have to explain why Aunt Bailey's leaving, too."

I nod and swallow the tangle of emotions I've always felt toward my big sister. Maybe I should tell her the truth about my marriage, but it's so complicated, and I'm afraid the truth will only make her think worse of me and give her more reason to keep me from Faith while I'm down here. "What if we don't make any promises? I just want to see her more."

"And I want some rich NFL player to sweep *me* off my feet so I can quit my job and live on the beach." She flinches, then shakes her head. "I'm sorry. I'm just so tired tonight. Let me know when you're back in town, and we'll work something out."

"Thank you, Sarah."

"Fly safe," she says.

I head back to my car and spend the drive to Mason's whispering a prayer that I'm doing the right thing.

CHAPTER 15

MASON

Bailey is dancing in my kitchen. She's in her Wonder Woman pajamas with the bright red top and the skimpy star-spangled booty shorts. She sways her hips to a Chainsmokers song and mimes singing into a wooden spoon.

I just walked in the door and have a list I need to tackle before leaving for training camp on Sunday, but all I *want* to do is stand here and watch her toss her blond hair and be silly.

She spins, and freezes when she spots me. "How long have you been standing there?"

"Long enough." I grin, and hell, this is good. I like her here. I like her dancing in my kitchen in her ridiculous pajamas. I like that just in this moment, my house feels like home. "Nice moves."

She turns up her palms. "What can I say? Years as a"—she mimes air quotes—"'professional dancer.'"

"Did you ever use the wooden spoon on stage?"

She smacks it into her open palm. "Only on customers' birthdays." She wriggles her brows and steps closer. "Want to bend over for a demonstration?"

I laugh. "I'll pass." But then I catch the glint of the gold band on her ring finger and my laughter falls away. *She's wearing the ring.* I rub my thumb over my own gold wedding band. I pulled them both out this morning and held my breath as I put mine on my finger. I swallow the lump in my throat and decide it's better not to make a big deal out of her wearing it. But fuck. It *feels* like a big deal. I look at the timer counting down on the oven. "What's cooking?"

"A frozen pepperoni pizza. My personal specialty."

"What's got you in such a good mood?" Not that I'm complaining. I love seeing her smile.

She shrugs. "I had a good day." After a beat, she screws up her face and shakes her head. "I just came from seeing my sister and niece."

"Your sister is Sarah, right?" I vaguely remember Bailey talking about her once or twice. I've never met her. "What's she doing down here?"

She nods. "She lives a half-hour from here." She turns off the timer and grabs a potholder from the drawer. "She never comes home, so I visit a couple of times a year to see her and Faith."

She was down here twice last year? Thirty minutes from me and didn't bother to come see me? That burns. Last year was tough—rookie year always is, and even with Keegan at my side, I felt isolated. I missed Blackhawk Valley and seeing my friends every day. I missed having people I could share my triumphs with and people I could bitch to when things didn't go my way. I missed *Bailey* most of all. "How old is your niece?"

She freezes with the oven half open, and I wonder what it is about my question that makes her uncomfortable. "Faith will be six in September. I'm hoping I can spend a little more time with her when I come back to town."

"Is that why you agreed to stay?"

She pulls out the pizza and puts the pan on the stove. "It doesn't hurt."

There are those walls she holds so dear. She doesn't want to talk about her family. *Fine.* "I have to pack and then run a few errands. We're supposed to check in for training camp Sunday night."

She puts the potholder back in the drawer before turning to me. "No problem. I fly home in the morning, but I'll be back in August to play the part of *Mrs. Dahl.*"

I swallow, but it does nothing to fill the nervous emptiness in the pit of my gut. "Why don't you come sooner? You could get settled while I'm gone, enjoy the house and the beach."

She shakes her head. "No thanks. I'll just meet you here when you're back. I need to get things in order if I'm going to be away for four months."

"The house is here if you change your mind." I'm half afraid she will change her mind over the next three weeks—but about the marriage, not about coming down early. What if she has too much time to think and decides to stay in Blackhawk Valley with all the memories? I don't just want her to move in because it benefits me. I want to get her away from the creeps of Blackhawk Valley who see her as a stripper and nothing more. I want to save her from the past.

Nic Mendez is dead and buried, and I'm still trying to protect her from him.

MASON

Four years ago . . .

Arrow looks up from his biology textbook and watches me pace. When I stop, he arches a brow. "I've honestly never seen you this screwed up over a girl," he says.

"Why do you think this is about a girl?"

He grunts and shakes his head, putting his attention back on his textbook. "Forget I said anything."

It's been a shit day. My dad showed up in town unannounced, which is never a welcome surprise, and I was distracted and fumbled three times at practice. To top it all off, I heard that Bailey's drug-dealing ex is being released from prison on parole. Now, Bailey is late getting back from work, and I have a sick feeling in my gut that I've lost her.

I fucking hate the idea of her spending her nights letting other men look at her. I knew who she was and what she did when I approached her, and at the time, it didn't bother me. But then I realized she was more than a great pair of legs in a pair of tight white shorts. She was more than long blond hair and a pretty smile. I didn't expect her to make me laugh or *feel* things. I didn't expect to become so possessive. This is all new to me.

I sink into the chair. "Do you think she talks to Mia about me? Maybe I could ask Brogan . . ."

Arrow tenses then shrugs. "Sure. Ask Brogan what Mia says."

Laughter rings through the hallway, and I recognize the sound. It makes me smile without thinking, and something funny happens in my chest.

Arrow's gaze shifts to the door before coming back to me. "You don't have to play it cool, you know. Sometimes it's better to let them know how you really feel."

That's interesting advice coming from the guy who has it bad for his best friend's girl, but I don't say that. Instead, I hop off the couch and go down the hall to Bailey's room.

Our dorm is made up of quads—two double dorm rooms that share a living space and bathroom. Bailey's door is open. I step into her common area and get hit with the typical gut punch. When I first met her, the punch was pure lust. Now it's evolved into longing. I want *more.* She's talking to her roommate and has her shower caddy in her hand and a towel thrown over her shoulder. I've mentioned to her before that maybe a job that leaves you needing a hot shower isn't the best, but I don't think she appreciated it.

The laughter falls from Bailey's face when she sees me. But her roommate misses it and bites back a smile. "I'll get out of your way," she says before scurrying off to her room.

"Need any help in that shower?" I ask Bailey.

Her lips part, and her gaze drops down my body and back up. "I'm good. Just want to wash the scum of the earth off me before I fall into bed."

I step forward and tuck a lock of hair behind her ear. She closes her eyes and draws back a few inches. "You okay?"

"Why wouldn't I be?" Her tone is hard and defensive and feels an awful lot like being stiff-armed on the field.

"I don't know. When my girl flinches at my touch, I can't help but wonder." *Can't help but worry that you're thinking about someone else.*

She takes a step away and frowns. "Where'd you get the idea I was your girl?"

My abs tense as if she just landed a blow with her fist. This is about Nic Mendez. *Fuck.* I hate when my gut's right. "Aren't you? Do you belong to someone else?"

She shrugs. "I don't belong to anyone."

Okay then. "Well, have a good shower." I tuck my hands into my pockets and back toward the door, my pride demanding that I get away as fast as possible. "You know where to find me if you need me."

I head to my quad and force myself not to look back at her. Walking right by Arrow, who's staring at me curiously, I head into our shared room and slam the door behind me before stripping down to my boxers. I hit the lights and climb into bed.

Thirty minutes later, I'm still wide awake when I hear the

soft click of the door opening and closing. I see her, silhouetted from the streetlight from the window over my bed. She climbs in beside me without a word. Her hair's still wet, and she smells like the flowery pink lotion she puts on after every shower. I slide a hand over her back. She's in a tank and a pair of those fitted shorts that barely cover her ass and make me lose my mind.

I kiss her hard. She kisses me back—one hand behind my neck and the other roaming over my chest and across my stomach. My skin is on fire for her touch, my heart racing.

"You know you can do better than me, right?" she asks, breathless.

"What's better than you?"

"Maybe a girl who's looking for more than a good time?" She slides her hand into my boxers. Taking my dick into her palm, she wraps her fingers around me and strokes. "I can't be your girl, Mason."

Because you're in love with him?

I don't ask. Because she's here. Because she's in *my* bed, and whether she likes being called my girl or not, right now, she's mine. I grab her hand and pull it up over her head as I flip her over to her back and climb on top of her. I'm going to change her mind. I'm going to get this crazy idea out of her head that we can't be together or that she's not good enough for me. I'll do it by shutting up about the fact that she's a stripper. I'll do it by showing her just how fucking special she is. I'll do it by being the better man.

CHAPTER 16

BAILEY

Present day . . .

Mason: *Tell me if the dick pic asshole bothers you again.*

I get the text in the middle of my shift at The End Zone and bite my lip as I reread it. I've been back in Blackhawk Valley for two days, and even though we didn't spend more than a few hours together while I was in Seaside, I kind of miss Mason. No, I totally miss him, and this text proves exactly why.

I want to say I've never had a guy treat me like he does or care about me like he does, but that's not true. I dated around after Nic went to prison and pushed me away. A lot of guys were kind and protective at first, but once they got what they wanted from me, they stopped. Not Mason. Mason has always treated me like I matter.

***Me:** He won't. But even if he did, what could you do about it? I doubt leaving training camp to kick some loser's ass is worth the fine they'd hit you with.*

***Mason:** You underestimate how much I want to knock this guy out.*

I consider myself a strong, independent woman. Maybe that's why it means so much to me that he still tries. He never makes me feel weak in his attempts to stand up for me. He reminds me I'm not alone. I wouldn't have understood the difference four years ago, but now that I do, it's profound.

"You secretive bitch."

My head snaps up from my phone at the sound of the familiar voice. There's a beautiful woman wearing a Chicago Bears jersey standing in the middle of The End Zone. I want to jump out of my seat and hug her tighter than I ever have. After a year of living four hours from Mia, you'd think I'd be used to the time apart by now, but I'm not. She's my best friend, and I miss her so much. Since I haven't had the courage to call her since the news of my marriage broke, I was pretty sure I'd have to grovel to get her to forgive me. But here she is.

I may want to squeeze her, but I stay behind the bar and keep my distance, as if she's a wounded animal. I intend to proceed with caution.

"You're *married*," she says, hands on hips. "You got married over two months ago, and it didn't occur to you to *tell your best friend*?" She reaches across the bar and smacks me on the arm.

"Ow!" I rub the spot. "Violent much?"

"Sorry." She frowns. "I didn't mean to hit that hard." She lifts her chin. "But maybe you deserve it. *Married*?" Then she runs around the bar and squeezes me so tightly that I squeak. "I'm so happy for you."

"Don't be," I whisper. I look over her shoulder to make sure no one is eavesdropping. The End Zone might not be best place for us to have this conversation.

Releasing me, she backs up so she can see my face. "Why not? You married an awesome guy you've cared about for years. Why can't I be happy?"

I drop my gaze to the bar and grab a rag to rub at an imaginary spot. "It's temporary, Mee. We did it while we were drunk in Vegas, and we were trying to keep it quiet so we didn't detract from your wedding. We were going to take care of it, but now Mason needs a wife for a while." I shrug. "It's not permanent."

"But it *could be.*"

I shake my head. Bless her heart, the little optimist can't help herself. "No, it couldn't. Anyway, Mason is only trying to disentangle his career from a potential relationship with the team owner's daughter. He thinks our accidental marriage might put the matter to rest."

"Wow." Mia's shoulders sag. "That's disappointing."

I cock my head. "It would be disappointing if I could be his wife, but you and I both know I can't. So, it just is what it is."

Now she's the one to look around to make sure we have

relative privacy, but other than a couple of nearly senile professors chatting about Tolstoy in the corner, the place is dead. "Are you trying to tell me he still doesn't know about the deal you made with his father?"

In a moment of weakness a couple of years ago, I told Mia why I couldn't be with Mason. On the one hand, it felt amazing to finally have someone to confide in. On the other hand, she's been insistent ever since that I should confess the truth to him, and that's not an option. "You know I can't tell him. Even if I thought he could forgive me for taking that money—and I don't think he would—it wouldn't change how his family feels about me." I shake my head. Mia might know I took money from Christian Dahl, but she doesn't know why I'm afraid of him. How could she understand when she doesn't know I have other secrets? The only person who knows all my secrets is Mason's father, and that's because he had a vested interest in unearthing them. "I'll figure it out."

She squeezes my hand. "Don't shut me out just because you're ashamed of the choices you made. I'm your best friend. I get to know all your dirt. It's the rule."

My chest stings with guilt. "I'm moving down there after training camp and spending a few months pretending to be his adoring wife. After that, I'll come home and get back to running The End Zone like nothing ever changed."

She grimaces. "Arrow said they got an offer on the bar, and Keegan wants to take it."

My stomach knots. I might be coming back to a new boss. Or

no job at all. I can't say that I'm disappointed about not owning the business—I'm not passionate about The End Zone like I am about my photography—but the insecurity of a new owner is unsettling.

Mia studies me. "If you're still thinking about trying to buy this place, just tell them. They don't want to screw you over."

And make Keegan and Arrow stay tied to a business they don't really have the time for? Just for me? Keegan bought this place before he was signed, thinking he had no chance at a football career, and Arrow signed on as a silent partner to help with the money, not with any intention of running it himself. Now they both live elsewhere, and I suspect they've only held on to it this long for me. That doesn't seem fair. "I knew they were selling. It's not a big deal." I take a breath and change the subject. "How are you even in town? Aren't you busy with your new marriage and new house and new amazing life?"

She narrows her eyes at me. "You sound a little bitter."

"I might be." I sigh. "I'm glad you're deliriously happy, but I miss my Mia."

"Well, you have me tonight. We're here to visit our fathers before Arrow has to run off to the Bears' training camp." She makes a face. "I hate training camp. I swear, they find the most miserable location and run them hard during the hottest month of the year. Is Mason settled in okay?"

I've been home for two days, and other than our brief exchange just now and answering Mason's text when he asked if I made it home safely, we haven't talked. I wrinkle my nose and load a rack of pint glasses. "I'm going to need some practice at this wife thing. I haven't even asked."

She shakes her head. "Arrow said the only time he ever thought about walking away was during training camp last year. It's brutal." She pivots toward the entrance and waves at someone. "Hey, Ron! Long time, no see!"

When I follow her gaze and see that the Ron in question is the same one who sent me a picture of his junk, I drop the glass in my hand, and it shatters on the floor.

Mia jumps then puts her hand on my arm. "I'll go grab the broom." She rushes back to the kitchen before I can stop her, leaving me alone and face to face with Dick Pic Man.

"Leave my bar before I call the cops," I tell him.

His face flushes red, and his eyes dart away as he swallows. "I'm here to apologize, and then I'll leave."

I open my mouth to tell him to walk, not run, to the nearest exit, but then his words register, and I decide I deserve the apology he's offering. "Make it quick."

He wipes his sweaty forehead and shifts from one foot to the other. He stares at his feet while he talks. "I was drunk and pissed, and I never should have sent that. But I had no idea you were married. You should have told me."

What a loser. "Your apology lost all credibility with the *but*. You can leave now."

He lifts his gaze to mine for a moment before staring at his feet again. "You'll tell your husband I said sorry?"

Did Mason contact him somehow and tell him to apologize?

"Not if I have to look at your face in my bar again."

He lifts his chin, but his nostrils flare, and I can tell he's as pissed as he is embarrassed. "Understood."

"And if I ever hear of you sending a woman an unsolicited dick pic again, I'll fucking come after you myself." I prop my fists on my hips. "I mean it when I say I could take you."

He shakes his head. "You think you're this independent woman now, but marrying the rich guy doesn't make you any less bought and paid for."

What a motherfucker. "Excuse me?"

"What did you just say?" Mia asks behind me, her voice the screech of an angry mama bird. She steps forward and stands by my side.

Ron holds up his hands, palms out. "Forget I said anything. Congratulations on your *wedding*. I promise you won't see me again." He turns around and heads out the door.

"What the hell?" Mia asks.

"He was a regular at the Pretty Kitty," I say. "He saw me at the bank the other day, and when our reunion didn't go as he'd hoped, he sent me a dick pic and a nasty message."

"*Ron*? Seriously?" She sweeps up the shattered glass I'd all but forgotten about. "He always seemed so sweet. Didn't hang with the best crowd, mind you, but he was the quiet one."

I stare at the door even though Ron is long gone. "I think Mason may have contacted him and told him he had to apologize."

She sweeps the shards into a dustpan. "Bet that scared the shit out of him. I'm pretty sure Ron would mess himself if Mason was in the same room as him now."

Am I a hypocrite? I was just thinking how nice it was to have Mason on my side about this. But the idea of him contacting Ron without telling me makes me feel unsteady. I liked having the emotional support, but actually confronting Ron is completely different. "I don't know how I feel about it."

And what did he mean about me being bought and paid for?

The tinkling of glass shards into a paper bag pulls me from my thoughts, and I turn back to Mia. "How do you know Ron, anyway?"

"He was a buddy of Nic's. I never knew him very well, but before tonight he seemed all right, aside from following that guy Clarence around all the time."

My brain chooses that moment to lock a memory into place. I'd been remembering Ron in the context of the Pretty Kitty, when he'd come alone and sit by the stage for hours. I'd completely forgotten that he was one of Clarence's goons.

Does Ron think I slept with Clarence to pay off the money Nic owed him? Who else in this town thinks that?

MASON

Training camp means meetings, practices, weightlifting, film, more meetings, more practice, and at the end of the night, we're lucky to get an hour to relax in our rooms before falling into bed and passing out. This year, we're at a small private college about an hour from the Gators' facility in Destin, and I swear it's fifteen degrees hotter here than it is by the ocean.

My body feels bruised and beaten, and I want to text Bailey some more and sleep. But when I climb the stairs and go into the dorm room I've been assigned, there's a naked woman in my bed.

Given how few naked women have graced any bed of mine lately, I should probably be excited to see her. Objectively, she's hot. She's got that perfectly toned body, curves in all the right places—some God-given, some surgically enhanced. Her dark hair cascades down her shoulders, and her swollen lips are pursed in anticipation. But instead of being turned on by the sight of this woman in my bed, I'm thinking I should check the stove for a boiled pet rabbit.

Glenn Close's character in *Fatal Attraction* has nothing on Lindy McCombs.

"How'd you get in here, Lindy?" I ball my fists at my sides. After all the shit being thrown my way this week, I have no energy for Lindy's games. "Why are you naked? And what the fuck made you think you were welcome in my bed?"

She crooks her finger at me and smiles. "Why so many questions? Aren't there other things you should be doing with your mouth right now?"

That is just ballsy as fuck, and in this moment, the double standard pisses me off. If I showed up uninvited in a woman's bed in my birthday suit and started implying she should stop speaking and start using her mouth on me, I'm pretty sure I'd spend the rest of my life on the sexual offenders list.

But no. When a chick does it, it isn't crossing the line. It's sexual confidence, and I'm not supposed to be disturbed or feel like my privacy's been violated. I'm supposed to be turned on.

I'm not.

"Where are your clothes?" I look around the room, ready to grab them off the floor and toss them to her, but they're nowhere to be found.

"I thought you'd be happy to see me, so I didn't wear any."

I set my jaw. "You did not walk up here naked."

"Nope. I wore a trench coat." She runs a hand down between her breasts and over her stomach, stopping only when her fingertips are resting at the apex between her thighs. "I think my driver knew I was naked underneath. I think he liked it."

"Good. Why don't you let him give you a ride home?"

Her eyes blaze, and I know I'm being a dick, but given that she's naked in my fucking bed, I think it's fair to say the "gentle rejection" approach isn't working. Apparently, neither is the "I'm married, so back the fuck off" approach.

Lindy stares at me for a few long beats. Is she waiting for me to change my mind? *Dream on, lady.* Sighing heavily, she climbs out of my bed and stomps into the bathroom I share with the guy next door. She might have a few screws loose, but she's not stupid, and she knows this night isn't going to unfold the way she planned. When she emerges, she's wrapped in a long trench coat, and though I hate her being so close, I'm just relieved she's covered. "Why are you such a dick?"

I close my eyes and count to five before responding. "I'm *married.*" *And you're fucking crazy.*

"You're *still* punishing me for a decision I made when I was eighteen."

My jaw clenches at the reminder. "This isn't about that. I'm married. I've moved on. You need to move on too."

"But in April . . ." She saunters toward me and lifts her hand to my jaw. "That night *meant* something. I felt it. You felt it." She tries to smile, but it wavers. "You're telling everyone you and Bailey have been dating since college, but if you really loved her, you wouldn't have slept with me."

"You're mental," I mutter. I want to say more. Fuck, I want to *go off.* But at the end of the day, Lindy has more power over my future with the Gators than I care to think about.

"She was a *stripper*, Mason. A stripper who comes from nothing and has everything to gain by marrying you and then hanging you out to dry."

Damn my parents and their obsession with digging into all the people in my life. Damn them for telling Lindy everything. Four years ago, they found out I was dating Bailey and did enough research to conclude that she didn't meet the high standards they'd set for their son. Then they shared that information with Lindy as evidence that she and I should still be together. Not that any of that mattered then. Bailey took it on herself to make sure our relationship never turned into something serious.

But it fucking matters now if that information is going to make Lindy think that I don't take my marriage seriously or that she's welcome in my bed.

"She's not a stripper anymore," I mutter, reaching for the door to hold it open for Lindy.

"Just know I'm here for you when she gets what she wants and walks away. Until then I'll be your . . . what was it your dad always called Bailey?" She licks her lips. "Your *fuck buddy*?"

"Don't." The mental image of her and my dad laughing about my relationship with Bailey makes my stomach sour. Fuck both of them.

She smirks. "If you didn't want to be with me, you wouldn't have taken me home. It's okay to swallow your pride and admit you want me back."

"Don't kid yourself. We've slept together once in the last five years. I've *never* come back to you. And I won't."

Her eyes fill with tears, and she spins away. I wait until I hear the door to the stairwell slam before I allow myself to take a breath.

There are a few basic rules of personal conduct for NFL players who want long careers, and half start with the words "keep it in your pants."

Sleeping with Lindy in an attempt to get over Bailey was like taking arsenic to cure a head cold. Obviously, I'm an idiot.

CHAPTER 17

MASON

I wish I could have met Bailey in Blackhawk Valley to help her load up her stuff and keep her company on the drive back down here, but between her insistence that she didn't want my help and the fact that I'll be in deep shit if I miss practice or meetings this week, I had to let her handle it on her own.

I meet her in the driveway with what I hope is a casual smile. The truth is, I couldn't be more nervous about our arrangement. We've hardly talked since the last time we were together down here, and every time I sent her a text, I got the impression that she was irritated with me. It's one thing to move her in and get Lindy off my back. It's quite another to think I might make one of the most stubborn women I know give up her life in Blackhawk Valley.

Bailey climbs out of the car and stretches onto her tiptoes, her hands reaching high as if she's trying to grab handfuls of the perfectly blue evening sky. Her shirt creeps up, exposing her tan midriff and making me itch to move closer. To touch. To claim.

I walk to the trunk, and she cocks her head at me.

"I can get my own bags." She pops the trunk and reaches around me to pull out two suitcases. She sets them on the ground before shutting it again.

"Where's the rest?"

"This is it."

I look between her and her two modestly sized suitcases. My mom would require more luggage than this for a weekend away. "That's all you have? For four-plus months?"

"You have a washer and dryer, don't you?"

"I expected you to bring more." *I expected you to move in.* But in her mind, this is just a visit. And in my naïve fantasies, it's forever.

"I'm low maintenance, remember?"

I grunt. I'm not touching that. I grab the bags from the ground before she can and lead the way to the front door. I hear the soft pad of her tennis shoes on the tile behind me as I take the bags straight to the master bedroom.

"So, are you going to chain me to the bed while I serve my time, or am I free to roam the house?" Her words hit my gut hard, and I drop her suitcases and swing around, only to find her smiling.

"I didn't ask you to stay with me because I need a play-toy." Though I could get used to the idea of her tied to my headboard, her eyes watching me and hazy with pleasure as I work my way down her body. That isn't a bad idea at all. Except that it is. "It's really hard for you to believe someone might want you for something other than sex, isn't it?"

"Right," she whispers, looking around the room. "And you want me because you don't want your boss to set you up with his daughter. That's *so much better* than being wanted for sex."

"Maybe I have other reasons, too." I step forward and take her chin in my hand, forcing her to meet my eyes. I don't like the pain and betrayal I see in hers. "Don't you want to be here? Even a little?"

Her lips part as her gaze drops to my mouth. "I'm here to help."

It would be so easy to slide my hand from her chin into her hair, to lower my mouth and coax hers open. We could start day one in bed and stay there until my alarm buzzed for tomorrow morning's team meeting.

And if I did, I'd lose any chance of not falling apart when she left me in four months.

She steps back, seeming to shake off the moment. "I guess I should unpack."

I reach out to keep her from turning away, then drop my hand, stopping myself. "Bailey?" When she turns to me, I say, "Thank you for doing this. Thank you for staying here when you'd rather be home. It means a lot."

She gives a shaky smile. "What are friends for?"

I reach into my pocket and pull out the small black velvet jewelry box.

"What's that?" she asks, her eyes widening.

"Your ring."

She holds up a hand to show me that she's wearing the thin gold band I put on her finger in Vegas. "I have a ring."

"I thought you should wear something a little more convincing." I pull the princess-cut diamond solitaire from the box.

Her breath hitches as I slide it onto her finger. "Is that real?"

I laugh. "Better be."

"What the hell? Why would you waste your money? Are they going to let you return it?" Her voice is laced with panic.

"It's not a waste. I promise it'll hold its value just fine." I knew she wouldn't want anything too fussy, but she needed a ring as bold as her personality. I know I bought it with no intention to return or sell it, so I have no idea what will become of it. I'm not willing to look that far into the future yet.

"Jesus, Mason. What if I lose it or something?"

"It fits great. I don't think it's going to fall off."

She stares at it, her eyes wide, and I want a do-over. From the beginning. I would fight harder to win her heart from Nic before he died. I would tell her his secrets instead of trying to protect her from them. I would handle everything differently so we could get here the right way. Married because we wanted to be, not because we were drunk in Vegas. And both of us in love, not her with her heart in the grave with a dead man.

"Wow," she whispers. "Just . . . wow."

"There's a party Friday night. Kind of a welcome thing for

Lindy. I really don't want to go, but Bill will be pissed if I skip out." I watch her as she takes in this information. "Will you come with me . . . as my wife?"

She finally tears her eyes off her ring and looks up at me. "Of course. That's what I'm here for, right?" She fidgets with her ring. Normally, Bailey faces the world as if she's ready to attack, but right now she looks so vulnerable that all I want to do is pull her into my arms and protect her from the people who want her out of my life—the very people I'm asking her to face on my behalf.

"Are you okay?"

"I don't know how to do this." She grimaces as she meets my gaze. "I don't know what I'm supposed to do with myself."

"What do you mean?"

She shrugs. "I've worked my whole life. I can't just move into your fancy house and . . ." She shakes her head. "I don't even know. What do rich women do? Plan parties? It's not like you need me to decorate—not that I'd be any good at it if you did."

"Do whatever you want to, Bailey. Walk on the beach. Swim in the pool. Join a book club and make some friends. You work all the time. You deserve a break." She stares at me with a wrinkled nose and curled lip, as if I just suggested she spend her leisure time dining on rodents. "Think of it as an extended vacation."

"I think I'll find a job," she says. "Will you be embarrassed if your wife is working? Is that, like, a faux pas in your circle?"

What kind of circles does she think I travel in? Honestly, Keegan's one of the two guys down here I actually trust, and he's her best friend too. "I just want you to be happy. You could work the drive-thru at the Taco Bell across 30A if that's what makes you feel good, but don't do it because you need the money. I already told you I'd pay you for your time here. You're doing me a favor, and the least I can do is cover your bills."

She rubs her arms as if she's cold. "I don't want your money, and I wish you'd quit offering it." She chews on her lip and turns to look out the sliding glass doors that lead onto the second-floor balcony. "I want to help you, to be by your side and whatever else you need, but I also don't want people thinking I'm . . ."

"Thinking you're what?"

"Bought and paid for."

I flinch, suddenly seeing my offer to pay her as she seems to think others might. "The only thing anyone will know is that you're my wife."

BAILEY

Married life: day one couldn't be more awkward.

The only thing breaking the silence at dinner is the sound of our forks clacking against our plates as we eat our takeout. More accurately, as Mason eats and I push my food around. I have no appetite, and the heap of pad thai has cooled on my plate. Mason, on the other hand, seems completely normal. He finishes his inhuman quantities of food and politely sips his water as he waits for me to finish.

"Is it okay?" he asks. "I can order you something else, or—"

"It's fine," I blurt. "I'm not very hungry because I ate a lot of snacks on the drive. I'm sorry." I hop up from the table and take my plate and glass to the kitchen, feeling his eyes on me the whole way. I dig through the cabinets to find a storage container for my leftovers. He joins me in the kitchen and rinses his dishes. He loads them into the dishwasher and does the same with mine before I can get to them.

The tension between us is insane, and I'm embarrassed, because I know it's mostly one-sided. Mason seems at ease with our arrangement, whereas I feel as if I'm walking a tightrope. When his phone rings, I literally jump.

He puts a warm hand on the middle of my back. "Are you okay?"

"I'm fine."

He frowns but doesn't call my bullshit. "I have to take this. It's my agent. Make yourself at home, okay?" He puts his phone to his ear and walks into the office, closing the door behind him as he asks, "Any news?"

I wipe down the counters—not that they need it—and wander around the main floor. I don't know what to do with myself. I could pull out my laptop to edit some photos and reply to emails, but suddenly, the day's travel and stress seem to have caught up with me, and I don't have the energy for that.

I bite my lip as I stare at the door to Mason's office. I can't hear what he's saying, but the low rumble of his voice on the other side makes something stir in my chest. I've been walking around half panicked since the news of our marriage broke. Panicked he would find out the truth about my deal with his father. Panicked that there was no way out of this that didn't involve him hating me forever. But now it looks like that panic was all for nothing. This doesn't have to be complicated. I can live here and be the garlic to fend off the vampire would-be bride, and when she leaves, so will I. It's not that I have an amazing life waiting for me back home, but I sure as hell don't belong here.

I decide that the only cure for my mood is pajamas and a movie. I pull out the Wonder Woman sleep set Mia bought me, grab the throw off the back of the couch, and sink into the couch in the living room. I scan the offerings on cable before flipping over to Netflix and choosing *The Princess Bride.* When in doubt, go with the classic.

Princess Buttercup is still ordering around the farm boy when my eyes start to feel heavy. Maybe I'll turn in early tonight. As soon as Mason gets off the phone, I'll say goodnight and go to bed.

I force my eyes back open only to see the movie must have finished, because the TV has flipped over to the menu screen. The clock on the wall tells me it's after midnight. I'll take that as a blessing in disguise. As short as it was, marriage, day one, was awkward enough. Night one didn't need the additional weirdness of getting ready for bed together and trying to figure out how we're supposed to sleep. He didn't sleep with me last time I stayed here, but if we're presenting ourselves to the world as a happy couple, I can only assume we'll sleep together. Does one snuggle with one's temporary husband? Or are we supposed to fuck like old times while pretending we don't have emotions tangled up in it?

No, this is better. I turn off the television and return the blanket to the back of the couch before heading to the master bedroom. The bedside lamp casts shadows along the far wall and illuminates an empty bed.

"Mason?" I say softly, which is stupid. I know I'm in here alone. The bathroom door's open, and I click on the light and look around the gleaming white space as if he might have been hiding in there in the dark, but of course it's empty.

I head toward the stairs to check his office and spot a light coming from under the guest bedroom door at the end of the hall. The door is cracked, and I knock softly before nudging it open.

He clears his throat. "Come in."

When I open the door, my breath leaves me in a rush at the sight of him. He's sitting up in bed, leaning against the headboard. He's in nothing but a pair of boxers. His broad, dark chest is bare, and his long, muscular legs are stretched out in front of him. He puts his book down on the bed beside him as he looks at me.

"Is everything okay?" I ask.

He smiles softly. "Sure. Sorry I was on the phone so long. I was going to say goodnight, but you were sleeping, and I didn't want to wake you."

"So you're not going to bed yet?"

He skims his eyes over me, a vague smirk twisting his lips as he takes in my PJs. "I am in bed."

"We're sleeping in here?" I'm confused, but hell, I don't know, maybe this bed's more comfortable? Didn't he say the place came furnished?

"Bailey." He puts a hand up as I step toward the bed. "*I'm* sleeping in here. You can have the master."

My mouth works—lips opening and closing stupidly, like a fish out of water. I shake my head, trying to snap out of it. "I'm confused?" It sounds like a question, as if I don't even know how I feel, and I suppose that's appropriate.

"If we sleep together"—he drags his gaze down my body again—"we might actually *sleep* together. So you take the master, and I'll sleep in here. I have an early morning. I'll be gone most of the day, so I won't be in your hair."

"What am I supposed to do?" I sound like a whining kid complaining about being bored on summer vacation.

He cocks his head and studies me. "You mentioned wanting to get a job. What about doing your photography sessions down here?"

I look away. "I don't have any formal training. No one's going to want to hire me."

"Don't be so quick to write yourself off. You have a portfolio, right? When you have examples of what you can do, I don't think people care about formal training."

I shake my head. This area is so upper-crust, and there are hundreds of photographers who have way more talent than I ever will. His faith in me is sweet, but misplaced. "When I'm not job hunting, do you need me to *do* anything? Like run through the streets and make sure all the rich bitches know I'm your wife?"

He chuckles. "That shouldn't be necessary. I don't need you for anything until the party on Friday."

"Okay, listen, I have no idea how to be your wife." I prop my hands on my hips. "I don't know how to decorate a fancy house, or whether I'm supposed to tip the gardener, or even how I'm supposed to dress at this stupid party Friday night. But the one thing I know how to do, you're saying you have no interest in? Not gonna do it?" I don't know why I'm so angry. I'm being ridiculous. I wasn't even sure if I was going to sleep with him—tonight or *at all* during our stint as husband and wife—but suddenly his plan to make sure we don't sleep together is the most insulting thing he could have done. "Jesus, Mason, do you get off on not getting off?"

He closes his eyes and shakes his head as if he's not sure what to make of me. "What part of our arrangement made you think you needed to fuck me, Bailey?"

"I—I—I thought . . ." My cheeks heat, and I'm sure if I looked in the mirror right now I'd see a bright red flush covering them and creeping down my neck. "Wow. You sure know how to make me feel like a dirty slut."

"Shit." He climbs out of bed, and I'm struck by the sheer size of him. He's so tall and built, and his boxers hang low on his hips. He walks toward me and cups my face in his hands. "If I thought I could win you, if I thought at the end of this season you wouldn't happily pack your bags and head back to Blackhawk Valley, I'd take you in this bed and that bed and twice on the kitchen table. I'd fuck you in the shower, then from behind as you held on to the bathroom counter so you could watch yourself get off in the mirror." His Adam's apple bobs, and his gaze dips to my mouth. "So tell me, is there any chance for us?"

How many times will I have to refuse the thing I want most? "You know there isn't," I whisper, and it's like cutting my own heart in half.

He pastes on a smile as he drops his hands and steps back, but his jaw is hard. "Goodnight, Bailey."

I've hurt him, and I hate it. I want to patch the tense silence with excuses and false explanations, but I know how useless a Band-Aid is for heartache, and I'm suddenly far too tired to go through those old motions. "Okay. Goodnight."

"Sleep well." He looks me over one more time. The heat in his eyes is so intense, I feel it long after I've climbed into bed.

CHAPTER 18

BAILEY

According to Emma, the only things I need to blend in at this party are pearls, a little black dress, and a fake smile. She comes from a world full of rich folks, so I trust her advice on this. I look at myself in the mirror. Well, check, check, and check.

After a few days of job hunting by day and awkward marriage-of-conveniencing by night, I dedicated my entire morning to preparing for this party. I tried on every dress I brought with me, and once I decided they all made me look cheap, I went shopping. Only, the boutiques around here gave me such sticker shock that I called Emma in a panic. She talked me down and told me to drive to the outlet mall. An hour after I started digging through the sale racks, I found a dress that I deemed acceptable.

Unfortunately, Emma's out of town and won't be accompanying Keegan to the party tonight, which sucks, because

I'd prefer to have as many allies as possible.

I dig through my makeup bag for another hairpin, and when I look in the mirror again, I see Mason behind me. He must have gotten dressed while I was doing my hair. He's in gray suit pants and a white dress shirt, a tie in his hand, and he looks absolutely edible.

I turn to him and wait as he drags his gaze over me, from my low chignon to my dress to my red Mary Jane heels. Slowly, he brings his eyes back up to meet mine.

"So?" I ask. He's making me nervous. "Will this do?"

His tongue darts out to touch his bottom lip. "Fuck yes."

My stomach shimmies, and I feel warm all over. When he looks at me like that, it almost makes all those painful hours of shopping worthwhile.

He leans against the doorframe and tucks his hands into his pockets. "I asked around at practice today, and there's a lot of interest in your photography. *A lot.* I wouldn't be surprised if your phone starts ringing with calls from potential clients."

"Really?"

He nods. "Really. Kramer said his wife saw Emma's pictures and had already asked him to get your information."

I run up to him, throw my arms around his neck, and plant a kiss on his mouth. "You're the best!" I wave my arms overhead and wiggle my hips, doing as much of a happy dance as this dress will allow. "That's amazing. Thank you so much, Mason."

"Anytime." He settles a hand on my hip and studies me for a beat. "Will you be ready to go in about half an hour?"

"I just need to do my makeup and then I'm ready." I wait for him to say something else, but instead he nods, turns around, and leaves the room. "Glad we could get back to being awkward," I mutter. "What a relief."

MASON

I'm in over my head.

Bailey's been living with me for four days, and I'm already losing my mind wanting more.

I told myself I wanted to get her out of Blackhawk Valley, that I'd be happy if I could convince her to move down here, even if it wasn't to be with me. But how am I supposed to let her go in four months? Four *days*, and my favorite moments are when I'm at home with her. Four *seconds* with her lips on mine, and I want to throw all my stupid rules out the window.

I had to walk away or I would have pressed her against the wall and kissed her again. I would have slid my hand up her dress and whispered just how good she looks.

My phone rings, and I jog to it, grateful for a distraction. I keep a landline in my house for my security system and for my grandmother, who doesn't understand that I can't talk when she catches me at work or in a meeting. I answer it without checking the number on the caller ID.

"May I speak with Bailey Green, please?"

"She's not available right now. Can I help you?" I ask, then, too curious to risk a no, I add, "This is her husband."

"I was calling regarding Ms. Green's student loans. Could you tell me a good time to call?"

Student loans? "I think you have the wrong person. My wife doesn't have any student loans." She stripped to pay her way through school, and any time I tried to get her to quit, she'd remind me that she didn't want loans following her through her whole life.

"Okay, I'm looking for a Bailey Green from Blackhawk Valley, Indiana. If that's not your wife, I can make a note that she doesn't live at this number."

I swallow hard, but it doesn't do a damn thing to change the fact that something feels off in my gut. This has to be a scam. "If you gave her a loan, you know how to contact her. I'm hanging up now." I end the call. My grandmother got sucked into one of those phone scams once. Someone called her and said her son was stuck in Jamaica and had lost his wallet. Thank goodness some thoughtful person at the bank took the time to fact-check the story before wiring over the money, or she'd have lost thousands.

The call is still eating at me when Bailey comes down the stairs dressed for the party. Her little black dress is cut modestly below her knees but cradles her hips in a way that makes my hands itch to touch. She's wearing pearls and has her hair twisted into a knot that shows off her long neck and reminds me how much she likes to be kissed there. Once, I was intimately familiar with how I could suck just beneath her ear and her knees would buckle.

“I got a call on the landline,” I say.

She makes a face. “You have one of those?”

I attempt a laugh, but that *off* feeling is still making my stomach sour. “It was some company that said you had student loans through them. They said you’re behind on your payments.”

She walks past me, her heels clicking on the tile as she goes to the sink and gets herself a glass of water. “Damn. What they say is true—they really can track you down anywhere, can’t they?”

“I was worried it was a scam, so I ended the call.”

“It pretty much is a scam. The biggest legal ripoff millennials have to swallow every day. You should see my interest rates—just because I wanted a good education. Exorbitant, but I could go buy a new car at zero percent interest.” She drains her water, still avoiding my eyes.

The gnawing doubt in my gut grows teeth. I hate feeling as if I’ve been lied to, but it’s worse when it’s by someone I trust. “Why do you have student loans?”

She puts her glass in the sink before looking at me. “Not all of us were at BHU on a football scholarship. You don’t know how lucky you were.” She shakes her head. “I should have gone to community college. Nobody gives a shit that I have a degree from an expensive school, but I bought into the lie that if I got my education beside a bunch of privileged brats, I might get some of that privilege too. I was so wrong.”

“I was lucky,” I say. “I get that. But you said you were stripping so you didn’t have to take out student loans.”

"Unfortunately, as good as I was at shaking my ass, there weren't enough hours in a week to give the number of lap dances I'd need to pay that kind of tuition." She grabs a small red purse off the counter and thumbs through the contents. "Judge me if you must."

"Why did you make everyone believe you weren't taking loans?"

She spins on me. "It wasn't anyone's business but mine."

The lie eats at me. Maybe it doesn't matter. Maybe it shouldn't. But it's further evidence that Bailey's never given me the whole truth about anything. It's further evidence that she's never let me in and that I'll always know less about her than I think I do. Even so, I'd bet everything that this has something to do with Nic Mendez. Everything that's fucked up with Bailey goes back to him.

I stalk toward her until she backs against the counter. When she drops her purse, I stop myself and shake my head. I'm so sick of doing this dance where I ask questions and she evades. I am far too familiar with her moves. I don't want to care. "Keep your secrets. Hold them tight like you hold on to the fucking twisted notion that Nic Mendez was the only man on this earth good enough for your heart. I give up."

CHAPTER 19

BAILEY

He turns on his heel and storms up the stairs, leaving me alone and reeling.

I draw in one ragged breath after another, but my blood simmers with . . . something. Anger? Yes. *I am so fucking pissed.*

I cling to that and storm after him. I find him on the second-floor balcony pouring a glass of bourbon, as if this is just another night, as if he didn't just throw my painful past in my face.

"You know, once you were my friend," I say. "And maybe that's what I miss most about us. Maybe instead of judging me for my decisions, you could try being my *friend* again."

He puts his glass down on the table, his eyes locking on mine before he slowly stalks toward me.

I lift my chin, refusing to back down, because *dammit*, I shouldn't have to apologize for wanting Mason's friendship. Is that so terrible?

But my defiant stance doesn't faze him and he keeps coming, one step at a time, until he's finally up against that bubble he prefers to keep between us. He takes another step and he's inside it, but still not nearly as close as I want him. He takes another, and if I had the courage, I could reach out and touch him. Another step and he's so close that he has to bend his head down to maintain eye contact. So close that if I lift onto my toes, I could brush my lips against his.

I almost do, if only because fighting with him makes me feel as if there's something broken in me, and I want it to be over. I miss the soft stroke of his lips against mine. I miss the sound of his sweet murmurs as he unbuttoned my pants and slid my underwear off my hips. I miss the sex, but more than that, I miss the way he'd hold me after. He held me in a way no one else had ever bothered to. Not even Nic. Mason would pull me against him, my back to his chest, and he'd snuggle against me until I could feel the warmth of his breath against my bare shoulder.

I want all of that again, and what breaks my heart the most is if I'd known when I took that deal with his father—if I could have seen into the future and gotten a glimpse of exactly what I was giving up—I still would have done it. *I did what I had to do.*

Mason's eyes drop to my mouth. "I don't want to be your *friend*, Bailey."

"Yeah," I whisper. "You're making that really clear. All or nothing, am I right?"

His jaw hardens, and I wouldn't have thought it possible, but he moves even closer. My back's against the sliding glass door, and his body presses into mine. He shifts until his thigh is between my legs, and then he lifts a hand to my hair, sliding his thumb up my neck until he's cupping my jaw. I want to melt because I've missed this so damn much. I've missed *him* so damn much.

"I've never wanted to be your friend," he says, shaking his head. And it's a blow to the heart I'm not sure I'm strong enough to endure. When I told him we could be lovers but nothing more, we were friends…best friends. Then he moved down here and shut me out.

"I'm sorry my friendship was such a burden." Fuck, even my sarcasm sounds weak, but this whole conversation has me vulnerable.

"It wasn't a *burden.* It was a daily reminder of what I couldn't have. I thought that if I quit fucking you it wouldn't hurt so much that you refused to be mine." His thumb traces my bottom lip, and I tremble. "I thought if I could get the memory of your taste out of my head that maybe I'd be okay with being your *buddy.*" He sneers the word, his face twisting in disgust, but when the sneer falls away, it leaves raw need in its wake. "But I was wrong. I don't want to be your friend, because that means you're only giving me part of yourself, and I am the spoiled bastard you say I am. What was your word? Privileged?"

He dips his head down and turns his face to the side, sweeping the tip of his nose over the tip of mine. "I don't want your friendship unless it comes with your body. And I don't want your body unless it comes with your heart." He dips a little farther and brushes his lips so softly against mine that I almost wonder if I'm imagining it. Maybe he isn't touching me at all. Maybe the sensation is nothing more than air passing between our mouths.

He's chipping at the walls I keep erected around my heart. And what happens when they're gone? What happens when he sees me for who I really am?

"You say you want to be my friend," he says, "but friends don't lie to each other. They don't hide their pasts." His hand falls from my hair. I brace myself for his retreat, but he doesn't back away. Instead, he finds the hem of my dress and slides up my thigh, then between my legs until he reaches my cotton panties. "Is this it, then? Is this all you want from me?"

His knuckles skim across my center, and I should stop him. *Fuck.* I should stop him. I know what he's trying to do, what he's trying to say, and how I'll feel when this is over. But all I can think is how I feel right now. How it finally feels to have him this close—his heat, his touch.

All I can think is that if the rest of my life is going to be some sucky, lonely series of *if-onlys* and *what-ifs,* dragging from one day to the next, I just want this moment for as long as it can last. Maybe I'll wrap it up and hold on to it. Keep it for later when I can untuck it and examine the heat of his breath against my neck or the gentle graze of his fingertips along the lace edge of my panties.

He nips at my ear with his teeth, and I moan. His breath has gone shallow, and I can feel the tension building in him—that push and pull of wanting and knowing you shouldn't want. It's easy for me to recognize, because I've lived in that limbo for almost four years. Wanting him, knowing I can't have him.

"Fuck." Now his voice is shaking, too. "Tell me to walk away." Even as he says it, his fingers graze my inner thighs and tuck beneath the edge of my panties. "Tell me you don't want this, or I'm going to stand here and fuck you with my hand until I hear you scream, until I feel you fall apart."

I arch my back, shifting my hips into his touch, encouraging him with my body. He yanks my panties down in a single, swift tug and cups me. When he catches my clit between two fingers, I bite my lip.

"Nah, you don't get off that easy, Bailey. You have to tell me what you want. I'm sick of guessing. Tell me to walk away, or tell me to get you off." He closes his eyes. "Damn, I've missed the way you feel on my fingers."

I stay silent, and he backs away. It's not even a full step. The retreat was mere inches, yet it's still too far. He holds my gaze, but I don't have the courage to speak.

Reaching behind me, he opens the sliding glass door then steps around me to go inside.

I pull up my panties and chase after him. I'm wound up. My body is full and tight. I feel so vulnerable and needy, but this ache has nothing to do with sex and everything to do with *him*. "Mason." When he doesn't face me, I grab his wrist.

He spins, and his eyes scan my face, as they have so many times, looking for the secrets I can't tell him, looking for the truth that would break his heart.

"Touch me," I say. Because I'm weak. Because unlike him, I'll take something over nothing. I'm the starving stray cat who will gobble up the scraps of food when I know damn well it'll only remind me how empty I am, when I know damn well it'll only make me ache for more.

He steps forward, so fast and so close, one hand returning between my legs, the other at the back of my neck, tilting my face to his. He presses his mouth to mine. No more gentle brush of lips, no more faintly caressing fingertips. If every touch before was a question, this is a declaration.

His mouth is hot on mine, his kisses alternating between fast and slow, deep and shallow, as if he wants more and wants it now, as if he's greedy for it but is trying to slow himself down.

After years of telling myself I can't have this, that I can't have *him*, after years of him pushing me away every time we got close, the faintest touch of his hand could push me over the edge.

His fingers slip under my panties, and his groan tangles with mine when he slides a finger along my wet heat and then inside. "Jesus, Bailey." I gasp as he adds a second finger and drives into me, fucking me with his hand. "So good," he murmurs. "You feel so good."

He's claiming me, claiming my mouth as he slides his tongue inside and kisses me as he hasn't kissed me for years. Claiming my body as he teases my clit with his thumb. Claiming my neck as he trails his lips down lower and sucks on the sensitive skin across my collarbone.

He's branding me. *Mine. Mine. Mine.* And I wish it could

be true. I wish I could be his, not just for this moment, but for always.

MASON

I shouldn't be touching her. I shouldn't be tasting her lips or coaxing those sweet little moans from her mouth. I'd be a fucking liar if I said I wasn't hoping we'd get here, but I didn't want it to happen like this. Not with her lies still hanging in the air like burnt plastic, and her nowhere closer to opening up to me than she was four years ago.

I break the kiss and lean my forehead against hers, my hand still working between her legs, because I'm helpless. I want her too much, and after years of forcing myself to keep my distance, I've become powerless when she's too close.

"Tell me to stop," I whisper, and I know I sound like a broken record. I sound like some traumatized kid who needs to test his own limitations.

"I don't want you to." She slides her hand behind my neck and brings my lips down to hers. I don't know if it's her mouth or mine that's so unyielding, if it's her moan or mine that echoes off the walls. "Mason, take what I can give you. My body is yours."

My thoughts snap back together like a spring. I didn't think I could stop without her asking me to, but her reminder that this is where she draws the line is better than a cold shower and a kick to the balls.

I pull away and swallow hard. "We need to go or we'll be late."

CHAPTER 20

BAILEY

I'm in over my head.

I thought I could handle four months as Mason's wife, but four days in, and he's already too close to my secrets. It's like he's nosing around in the dark and has found them, but he doesn't know what he's looking at. And what's worse is that I just want to tell him everything. Every. Damn. Thing. Maybe I would if it were just about the promises I've made, but I'm so afraid of losing him. I don't think I have the courage to turn on the light.

After he took our little make-out session from sixty to zero in two seconds flat, we returned to our scheduled evening of awkward with a side of awkward. I smoothed out my dress and he got his keys, and here we are—pulling up to the party and ready to share our tension with the world.

I think I preferred the angry kisses and desperate finger banging to Mason's tense silence, but nobody asked me.

A man in a pressed black suit opens my door, and the valet takes Mason's keys. Yes, this is a party with a freaking valet.

I'll take, "How Do You Know You Have Too Much Money?" for a hundred, Alex!

I thought Mason's house was luxurious, but it's nothing like the house in front of me now. As much as I've been dreading a party for the woman Mason's parents approve of (i.e., my opposite), the upside of our fight is that, suddenly, I don't care about my dress or my hair and makeup. I'm far too focused on the frustration rolling off Mason.

This place makes me uncomfortable in my own skin. One look at this house—from its two-story windows to the dramatic, phallic fountain in the circle drive—and I want to run back to Blackhawk Valley and hide under the covers.

Laughter rings out from the back of the house, and normally that sound would put me at ease, but I know nothing will make me relax here. The luxury of this place is so goddamned intimidating to a girl who grew up in a trailer park and took off her clothes for money.

"You okay?" Mason asks. It's the first thing he's said to me since we left his place.

I squeeze his hand, knowing his warmth will give me strength, pull back my shoulders, and nod. I am who I am. My past is my past. And while I don't relish situations that make me question my worth, Mason was once my best friend. Being on his arm this summer is the least I can do if it's going to save his career.

We climb the steps and enter the house behind an older couple, and I realize the place is even more impressive on the inside. I've watched enough HGTV to know the value of marble floors and crystal chandeliers, even if they leave me wondering how anyone could actually *relax* in a house like this. The foyer opens into a wide-open entertainment area with a gleaming granite bar. The space boasts three separate seating areas with couches that look more ornamental than comfortable and a wall of accordion doors that open the inside space to the outside. Waiters wander through, handing out drinks and offering trays full of hors d'oeuvres.

Out back, people mingle around the pool. The men wear suits, and the women wear every variety of little black dress. Emma called it on the wardrobe.

"Mason," a man calls from across the room. He has gray hair, rosy cheeks, and a round stomach. He waves a hand, motioning for Mason to join him by the polished bar in the corner of the living room.

"Bill," Mason calls back, lifting his chin.

I grip Mason's arm. "That's the Gators' owner?"

He gives a subtle nod and pats my hand as he leads me through the room. "Relax," he whispers. I can feel the tension from our earlier conversation melting away. "Everyone's going to love you."

"He wants you to marry his daughter," I whisper. "I seriously doubt beating her to it makes me his favorite person."

Mason grins. "But it makes you mine."

I don't have time to respond before we're stepping up to the bar. Bill McCombs is shoving his hand in my direction.

"You must be Mason's wife," he says. I reluctantly release Mason's arm and give Bill my hand. "He's been keeping you a secret from everyone, you know." He skims his eyes over me in appraisal. "But now I see why. He just wanted to keep you for himself." His laugh is loud and forced. It makes me feel like everyone is staring at us.

"It's nice to meet you, Mr. McCombs," I say. He releases my hand, and I slide it under Mason's arm. I feel safer there. "Your house is lovely."

"Thank you, that's very kind. So how are you liking Seaside? It's beautiful, isn't it? My wife and I only recently moved here when we started the Gators franchise. Such a quaint place. Reminds you how much joy there is to be found in the simple things."

He just used the words *quaint* and *simple* to describe a town where there are homes this opulent. *Mind blown.* I smile politely. "I've always loved the area along 30A. My sister lives nearby, so I've been here before."

"Oh, is that so? Where's your sister located?"

My stomach twists the way it did when I was a kid and people would ask where I lived. I wasn't ashamed of living in the trailer park, but I hated the way people looked at me differently when they found out. I don't want this man to judge Sarah because of where she lives. There's nothing wrong with Sarah's town, but it's not part of this man's world. "She's over in Rock Hill."

He snaps his fingers and points at me. "Right." He looks at Mason. "That's the golf course community south of Rosemary Beach, right?"

"You're thinking of Rock Grove," Mason says. His gaze holds mine for a beat. "Rock Hill is about half an hour north of here."

"Oh, right, right," Bill says, but he obviously doesn't know the area or give two shits where it is, and I'm glad. With everything else I'm carrying tonight, I'm not interested in carrying the weight of his judgments. "So sorry your parents couldn't make it tonight," he says to Mason.

"They had a previous engagement," Mason says. "But they send their regrets and said they'll join you in the box for Sunday's game."

"Wonderful." Bill turns to me. "Will you be joining us in the box this weekend?"

Mason already gave me my tickets for Sunday's preseason game. "I'm sorry. I can't. I promised Emma, Keegan's fiancée, that we'd sit together."

He chuckles and shakes his head. "Well, probably better that way. A carefree thing like you wouldn't want to hang around a bunch of old people like us anyway." I'm not sure what that means or that I should read anything into it at all, but I don't get a chance to respond before he smacks Mason on the back—harder than necessary, if you ask me—and grabs his drink off the bar. "Lindy's out back. I know she's anxious to meet your bride."

MASON

"You look terrified," I say in Bailey's ear as we head out back.

"Sorry," she says. "Just nervous."

I'm more than a little grateful to have her on my arm tonight. It's not like I can't hold my own with Lindy, but she's upped her crazy game lately. Maybe if she sees me and Bailey together it'll finally sink in that it's over between us.

As we walk to the back, Bailey looks around the party with wide eyes. I try to imagine it from her perspective. I know she sees money and a place she doesn't belong, but I just see a bunch of assholes trying to one-up each other. Just because I grew up with money doesn't mean I value it more than I value people. The opposite is true. Growing up with money taught me that it causes more problems than it fixes.

Case in point: Lindy McCombs.

Lindy's red dress has a long slit up the front, and the sides float around her when she saunters over to us. Her eyes land on Bailey, and her jaw goes hard as she sweeps her gaze down her body and back up. "Is this the lucky girl?"

"Lindy, this is Bailey . . ." *Fuck.* Is she Bailey Green? Bailey Dahl? I guess to be Dahl, she'd have to file some paperwork to get her name legally changed, and that's obviously not happening. Better to not tackle the last name. "Bailey, this is Lindy, Bill's daughter and an old friend."

Lindy chuckles and tosses her hair over her shoulder. "Well, we were certainly more than *friends*, Mason." She looks at Bailey and says, "For years, we were *everything* to each other. But I guess that's all irrelevant now." She offers Bailey her hand. "It's nice to meet the woman who's held Mason's attention for so long."

"Nice to meet you," Bailey says. I slide my arm around her waist, and I feel how tense she is.

"Are you settling in okay?" Lindy asks. "I just moved here myself, but if there's anything I can do to help, don't hesitate to ask."

"I'm fine." She leans into me, and I don't even think she knows she's doing it. "I've spent most of the week job hunting."

Lindy looks to me. "She's still working? Is that necessary?"

Bailey shifts uncomfortably. "I want to. I like to stay busy."

"Girl, I can hook you up." Lindy waves to another woman standing nearby. "Jackie! Didn't you say that place by your husband's office is hiring? Mason's wife is looking for work."

The woman excuses herself from her group and joins our awkward little circle. "Sorry, who's looking for a job?"

Lindy points at Bailey. "This is Bailey, Mason's wife. She's looking for work, and I thought you told me the place by your husband's office was hiring."

"Seventh Heaven?" Jackie says with a laugh. She looks at Bailey and shakes her head. "You don't want to work there. It's a nasty strip club."

"But Bailey's a stripper," Lindy says. She puts her hand on Bailey's arm and cocks her head in mock thoughtfulness. "Or do girls like you prefer the word *dancer*?"

"Lindy," I growl. "Jesus Christ."

Every passing moment of this conversation, Bailey was inching closer to me, but now she steps away. "Excuse me," she says, her smile tight. "I'm going to find myself a drink."

She disappears into the house, and Lindy beams.

"Is she really a stripper?" Jackie asks, snapping her gum.

I turn on Lindy. "You're despicable. If only you were as ugly on the outside as you are on the inside, you might look in the mirror and understand why I don't want to be with you."

CHAPTER 21

MASON

"Are you planning on ever speaking to me again?" I ask.

Bailey's in the bathroom in her pajamas, her makeup washed off her face, her toothbrush in her hand.

It's the question I've been thinking all night. I have to give her credit. After Lindy's low blow, Bailey went through the motions of meeting everyone at the party. No one else mentioned her past or looked at her as if they might know, but I could tell it hung over her head with every person she greeted.

I was planning to stay most of the party, but I made excuses to get us out of there as fast as I could. Bailey didn't say a word the whole ride home, and now she's acting as if she's going to get into bed without acknowledging my existence.

I lean against the doorjamb and watch as she brushes her teeth. When she's done, she rinses out her mouth, wipes down the sink, and breezes right past me into the bedroom.

I feel helpless. I can't undo the embarrassment that Lindy caused. And I feel like a dick for even putting Bailey in that position to begin with. "If you're angry, I wish you'd at least say so."

"I'm angry." She doesn't look at me. She pulls back the covers, climbs into bed, clicks on the bedside lamp, and grabs her book. She grips it so tightly her knuckles go white.

I sit beside her on the edge of the bed. "Talk to me."

She closes her eyes. "I'm fine," she says, but her voice shakes, and I feel like the world's biggest asshole for asking her to do this, for taking her to the party, for putting her in this situation. "I just need a good night's sleep. When I wake in the morning, I'll have some perspective. This is temporary." She swallows. "It's not like I have to face those women for the rest of my life. Come January, I'm out of here, right? So, it shouldn't matter."

If things go my way, that's not how this will end, but she doesn't need to know that yet, and even if she did, this wouldn't be the smartest time to bring it up. "Don't minimize what happened." I touch her bare shoulder, and she flinches. "Holy shit, Bailey, just let it out."

"Fine." She tosses her book down, jumps out of bed, and folds her arms across her chest. "I'm angry and I'm hurt. You made me bleed and then threw me in the shark tank." She shakes her head. "I cannot believe you told her what I used to do. And you said you two slept together, not that you had a long-term relationship. I would have liked a little heads-up about that."

This is such a fucking shitstorm, and now Bailey's stuck in the middle of it. I should have seen it coming. If Lindy was ballsy enough to show up naked in my bed when she knew I was married, why wouldn't she do something to embarrass Bailey? I thought seeing my wife in person would make Lindy back off, but I underestimated her. "She was a high school girlfriend; that's why my parents are so obsessed with us getting back together."

"How did your *high school girlfriend* know I was a stripper?"

I meet her unsteady gaze. There are so many emotions swimming in her eyes, from anger to hurt to fear, and I hate that I'm partially responsible for them. "My parents told her years ago. They looked you up when we were dating, and they tell Lindy everything about my life. At the time, they were using the information in an attempt to convince her to break up with the loser she was dating and try to mend fences with me. I never would have imagined she'd bring it up tonight."

"Do you have any idea how that made me *feel*? I'm already so self-conscious with those people, and then to have her throw that out there like it was normal conversation." She presses her hand against her chest and squeezes her eyes shut. "I could handle people treating me like a whore at the Pretty Kitty, but there? In that dress?"

"You looked amazing. You were the most beautiful woman in the room."

Her eyes blaze. *Okay, obviously not the time to talk about her appearance.* "I looked like I was trying to be someone I'm not."

"Lindy is *awful*, and I'm sorry that she directed that nastiness at you, but don't let yourself think that everyone else there is like her." I stand and loosen my tie. "I'm sorry I put you in that position at all."

She bites her bottom lip, and her chin quivers. I step forward and skim my thumb over her mouth. "I hate seeing you this upset." I shake my head. "You're the strongest person I know. You do whatever you have to do to get by when the rest of us wouldn't have the courage. It's almost intimidating. Then sometimes I catch sight of these tender spots that make you so damn vulnerable that I . . ."

She finally lifts her eyes to meet mine. "That you *what*?"

That I know why you need me. That I know why I've never been able to make myself walk away. Suddenly, I'm fucking exhausted. My body is tired from training, and my mind is tired from this dance we've been doing since she moved in. My heart is tired of waiting. "I wish I'd met you before him. I wish you'd never had to become so tough."

"How is this about Nic?" Her voice cracks on his name.

"Isn't it? At the end of the day, he's always what's standing between us."

BAILEY

"How long are you visiting, Aunt Bailey?" Faith asks as she climbs into my lap.

"Faithy," Sarah says. "Come on, you're too big to be held."

I wrap my arms around Faith and squeeze. "Never!"

Faith giggles. "How long? How long?"

Sarah narrows her eyes, warning me without words to be careful what I promise.

"I don't know yet. But I'll be here for your birthday. Are you having a party?"

"Of course!" She squirms off my lap. Even though she loves to cuddle, she has too much energy in her to allow her to stay still for long. I reluctantly let her go. "We're going to Applebee's, and Brandon's going to come. Are you going to come too?"

"Faith, Aunt Bailey is busy. I doubt she can come, but she's here now."

I lock eyes with Sarah, and I know she sees my request there. *Please let me come. I promise I won't screw this up.* My sister gives a small, almost imperceptible shake of her head. I swallow hard. This is my penance for my choices, and I try to be patient, but sometimes I just want to scream at Sarah for being so unreasonable and self-righteous. Instead, I take a deep breath and think of Faith. "How about I bring your present by before I leave town?" I ask her.

"Presents!" she cheers, and tops it off with a cartwheel in the middle of the living room floor. "I hope it's a Barbie house!"

"Who's Brandon?" I ask.

"Mommy's special friend. He's really nice, and he works at the zoo with the dolphins. Isn't that the coolest?" I wait for more, but she holds her arms up in the air and says, "Watch me do a handstand!" She plants her hands on the floor and kicks upside down, and I know she's moved on.

"A new friend?" I ask my sister.

She wraps her arms around herself and shrugs, as if this isn't a monumental step for her. "He's nice."

Five years ago, on a stormy April afternoon, her husband told her he was "deeply unhappy," packed his things, and left his wife and their daughter for a new life across the country. Since then, Sarah hasn't been interested in dating, only in raising Faith and trying to keep their life together. She was a stay-at-home mom when Greg left, and she almost lost everything. She almost had to move back to Blackhawk Valley to the life she'd worked so hard to escape.

I nod. "I'd love to meet him someday."

"Sure. Maybe." She draws in a deep breath. "Are you going to the Gators game tomorrow?"

I shake my head. "They're in Kansas City tomorrow, so I'll miss it." It's been a week since Lindy's party and almost two since I moved in with Mason. As if things weren't tense enough between me and Mason before, the whole thing with Lindy made me feel even more insecure about our arrangement. He's gone all day, sometimes for more than twelve hours. Though we eat dinner together most nights, he's still sleeping in the guest room, and I catch myself wishing for more than I can have. Sarah doesn't need to know any of that, though. "I might travel for some of the regular season games, but I have a few clients who wanted to meet this weekend, so I thought it would be better if I passed on this one."

"How's the new life in your fancy house?"

"It's okay." I shrug and bite down on my bottom lip. There's jealousy on her face that I understand all too well. It's hard when the people around you seem to have all they need and you're struggling to get by. "I'm trying to get settled. Mason's told his teammates about me, and their wives' sessions are helping me to keep busy, but everything is different here."

"It's a good different," Sarah says, her eyes on Faith. "Back in Blackhawk Valley, girls like us will never be anyone but Tammy Green's daughters. Here, you can start fresh." She turns her gaze on me and gives me an encouraging smile. "I'll admit I was nervous about it, but I'm glad you moved here. Now you get a clean slate. You can start over like Mom never could."

Four years ago . . .

"To living on the right side of the law," Mia says, raising her glass of water and giving her brother a pointed look.

Everyone else raises their glasses, too. There are big smiles all around the table, except for Nic, whose smile is forced and whose gaze keeps darting to meet mine.

After the waitress clears our dinner plates, I excuse myself and go to the restroom. I heard the text come through from Mason right after our meals were served, but I didn't want to look at it in front of Nic. Now, I dig through my purse to pull out my phone.

> ***Mason:*** *Saw you walking down Fifth in your red dress, and now I can't focus on my homework. Come by tonight so I can get a closer look?*

I grip the sink and bow my head. I don't know what's worse—that I gave up Mason to save Nic, a man who doesn't want me, or that even though I know it was the right thing to do, I wish I hadn't had to do it.

I hold my hands under hot water and scrub them, but it doesn't help me feel any better. I want to leave here and go to Mason, but I don't want it to be just sex. I want to curl into his arms and tell him how relieved I am that Nic's out of prison, and how terrified I am that he's going to fuck up this second chance. I want to let him undress me and touch me, but I don't want to head to my own bed to sleep. I want to *make love* and let him hold me all night long. And I want to do all that without feeling like shit for loving them both.

"Always want what we can't have," I whisper to my reflection.

When I step out of the bathroom, someone grabs me from behind and pushes me into the wall. He's against my back, trapping me. I turn my head to the side to see who it is, but it isn't until his hands press against the wall on either side of my head that I know it's Nic. He takes one hand and drops it to my hip and places the other on my shoulder. "What'd you do?"

I planned on talking to Nic after dinner tonight, before he could talk to Clarence. Word travels fast. "I told you I'd take care of it."

"Where did you get the money, Bail? Where did you get that kind of money?"

"All that matters is the debt is paid."

He scoffs. "As if these guys are going to leave you alone now."

"Why wouldn't they?"

I feel his body tense behind me. "Now that you've given in to them, they'll find a way to get more. From me, from you—they don't care." He draws in a long, ragged breath, sweeps my hair to the side, and skims his mouth along the back of my neck.

Chills of anticipation rush through me. I've missed his touch for so long, and my body responds instinctively, but at the same time, guilt at the pleasure pierces my belly. What would Mason think about Nic kissing my neck? I shouldn't care. It doesn't matter. Mason and I can never have anything together. Not now. I shiver, and Nic groans.

"God, I've missed the way you smell, but now I'm going to be thinking about Clarence every time I'm close to you. I told you not to do it. It's tearing me up inside that you did it anyway."

The warmth in my belly goes cold. "I didn't."

"Don't lie to me." His fingers curl as he tightens his hold on me. I squeeze my eyes shut but tears leak out the corners. He loosens his hold. "Shit. I'm sorry." He dips his head to kiss where his fingers were digging into my arm, and I let him, but his hand isn't what hurt me. It's what he believes that hurts.

Tears sting my eyes as he slides his hand over the front of my dress. This is Nic. I've waited years to feel his hands on me again, but any thrill from his touch is overshadowed by the feeling that I'm betraying another man. "Clarence got a taste of you, and he's gonna want more. I can't even blame him. Look what I've done to you, and *I* want more."

"What did Clarence tell you?" I try to turn, but Nic's too close. He has me pinned against the wall so I can't see his face. Did Clarence tell Nic I fucked him? That I spread my legs to pay Nic's debt?

Nic's hand sweeps between my breasts before settling against my belly.

I wish I could see him. I can't see the expression on his face or the look in his eyes. All I have is the feel of his hard body pressed against mine.

I swallow. My stomach quivers like Jell-O. This is so like Nic—to hold me away from him while he drops bombs on my reality. He doesn't want me to see his face. He doesn't want to look in my eyes while he breaks my heart.

I hear his ragged inhale, his hard swallow. "Why'd you do something like that for an idiot like me?" He makes a fist and gently scrapes his knuckles over my navel. "You've already lost so much because of me. I told you I'd take care of this."

My heart aches. He said he'd take care of *me*, too. I was sixteen. He said he'd take care of me, and the next thing I knew, he was going to prison, and I was pregnant and alone.

CHAPTER 22

BAILEY

Present day . . .

"I told you he'd love them," I tell my client as I pedal away on Mason's elliptical trainer. "The camera loves you."

"Trust me," Naomi says. "I'm *not* photogenic when anyone else is behind the camera. You just have a gift."

"Thank you. I appreciate it. And thank you for telling your friend Heather about me."

"She's stoked about her session," she says. I can hear her kids playing in the background. Naomi was my tenth client since I moved down here, but my first that isn't a wife or girlfriend of a Gators player. When she called me on the suggestion of a friend of a friend, I had my first inkling that maybe I could keep busy through the end of the year. Now, only three weeks after I first moved in, word is spreading and only a fraction of my appointments are connected to the Gators. "I can't wait to see what you do."

"Don't hesitate to call if you want any additional prints." I step off the elliptical and wipe my forehead with the back of my hand. "Or anything else."

"Thank you so much! I'm sure we'll talk soon."

"Bye, Naomi. Tell your kids I said hi."

"I will. Have a great day!"

"You too." I end the call and grab my water bottle for a drink before hitting the floor for some ab work.

I don't make it public knowledge that I work out as much as I do, but the truth is, I put in at least six hours a week. I started hitting the gym in college. I eat like shit, and apparently, a diet of red wine and Pop-Tarts doesn't give you a great body. Since I had no interest in switching to kale and chicken breast, and my body was an important asset in my monthly income, I resorted to the treadmill.

As it turns out, that shit's addictive. So, the best thing about Mason's gorgeous house, other than it being right on the water, is the workout equipment he keeps in the spare bedroom. I don't think I could handle going to a gym and smiling at all the women there who are there trying to keep all their bits and pieces tight and firm for their rich husbands. It's nice to be able to get my workout in without leaving the house or having to hear anyone mention her thigh gap—because seriously, of all my concerns about my life, a thigh gap is nowhere on the list.

Though my body might look good because of my workouts, the process itself is gross, and I look disgusting when I emerge from Mason's exercise room on Monday morning. I'm dripping with sweat, and my face is beet red. The hair I piled into a knot on the top of my head is giving me that halo of frizz. That's what I look like when I see her—the chick with long legs and a beautifully rounded belly lying on the guest bed where Mason's been sleeping. Her dark hair is fanned out across the pillows. A steaming cup of tea is in her hand, her feet are crossed at the ankles, and her gaze is fixed on the TV at the foot of Mason's bed.

I don't know who this bitch is, but I do know she's officially spent more time in Mason's bed than I have, and I don't like that. I'm still gaping at her and trying to figure out what's happening when she turns and blinks at me.

"Who are you?" she asks.

I arch a brow. "I'm Mason's wife. Who are you?"

She hops out of bed so fast that tea splashes all over the comforter. "Oh shit. You're Bailey?"

Jesus. I'm trying really hard not to jump to any conclusions about the size and shape of her belly, but in my very well compartmentalized mind, there is currently a compartment that is sounding the alarm in panic.

"Yes. Who are you?" Whoever she is, she clearly has money, judging by the size of the rocks in her ears. Even though she's wearing casual clothes, I can tell by the way the cotton shirt hangs on her that it's not a cheap one.

"Who am *I*?" Her big green eyes stare lasers into me. "I'm the sister, Shell." She makes a face. "Well, the bastard sister, but the DNA test says my father has to pay, so that makes me the sister, and I flew all the way here to meet you and see my idiot brother."

"Oh." As luck would have it, that's the moment Mason comes in the door. When I hear him, I'm simultaneously mortified and relieved.

MASON

I look up from the stack of mail on the counter to see Bailey and my sister Shell coming down the stairs. Bailey's face is bright red, and although I think that might have something to do with the fact that she just worked out, her expression tells me there's more to it.

"You didn't tell your wife I was coming?" Shell asks.

Bailey turns to Shell. "I'll hold his arms if you want to take a swing at him."

"Hey now." I hold up my hands. "Let's not be hasty." Maybe she's thinking Shell can't do much damage with her little hands, but I know better. I spent one month of every summer growing up with her beating the crap out of me.

"You're a real asshole, you know that?" Bailey says. She points to my sister. "Look at her. And since I didn't know she was coming, imagine what I thought when I saw her."

I have to bite my lip to keep myself from laughing. "What makes me an asshole?" I just want to hear her say it.

Shell bites back a smile and holds up her hands. "I think I'll let you two fight this out without me." She winks at me before turning and jogging back up the stairs toward the guest bedroom.

"Do you know what I thought when I saw her in the bed where you've been sleeping? She's so pretty, and I had no idea she was coming, and . . ."

"And what?"

"And you aren't sleeping with me. What was I supposed to think?"

This time, I can't hold back my laughter. "Were you jealous of Shell?"

"No. I felt bad for her." She folds her arms. "Poor thing. Imagine being knocked up with your baby."

That punch lands right in my gut. I know she isn't trying to be cruel, but I wince before I can hide my response, and she sees it.

"Mason, I'm kidding." She steps closer and studies me. "Seriously. It was just a joke. I'm sure you'd make a great dad."

I don't want to have this conversation or pick at that emotional scab. I take another step forward and slide my arms around her bare waist. She's in a sports bra and short white shorts just like the ones she was wearing the first time I saw her. "Let's go back to the part where you were jealous."

"Only a little," she says. She lowers her voice. "It's weird living here, being your wife. I think I'm waiting for someone to find us out and expose our marriage as a sham."

I slide my hands up her back and pull her close, and she doesn't step away. Three weeks she's been here, and aside from the night of Lindy's party, I've kept my hands off her. She still hasn't explained why she has so much debt or given me any reason to believe she'd consider making her move permanent. Regardless, I'm losing my resolve to keep this a marriage in name only.

I skim my fingertips down over her damp skin to cup her ass—because when she's this close, I can't resist—and she doesn't protest. She turns her head and rests her face against my chest. We fit like this. So perfect. And for a minute, I don't really care about the rules I put in place for myself when she moved in.

"What have you told your sister?" she asks, cutting off my train of thought.

"What do you mean?"

"Does she know I'm only your fake wife?"

I pinch her butt, and she jumps but she doesn't pull away. "You feel pretty damn *real* to me." My voice has dropped lower, because it's hard to get words out with what I'm feeling—with her body so close, her skin slick with sweat.

I can hear her swallow as she pulls out of my arms. "If she stays here, isn't she going to wonder why we don't sleep in the same room?" She drags her bottom lip through her teeth. "You know, there's enough room in my bed for both of us."

"I'm well aware of that." I grin and decide to let her off the hook. "Shell won't sleep here. She prefers hotels with room service and private spas. She's only here for the night, then she's headed over to visit my parents. The poor thing."

"Oh. Okay then." Bailey averts her eyes, and it's so adorable.

I wonder if she's thinking what I am—that it would be nice to have an overnight guest so we'd have an excuse to share a bed. I wonder if she's realizing that we haven't had nearly enough time in public pretending to be husband and wife and if we don't have an excuse to touch soon, the tension between us is going to steal all the oxygen from this house.

Everything inside my chest is trying to escape to be closer to her. She looks hot in her workout clothes, and seeing her flushed like that reminds me of . . . other activities. "I should get in the shower," she says. "I'm meeting a client in a couple of hours."

Bailey's been working hard on growing her business down here, and her schedule's been full. She could have taken my money and spent these months living a life of leisure, but with clients lining up, she's busting ass to make contacts and find unique venues for her boudoir sessions. It's not just about the money. Her passion for her work shines through every time she gets a potential client on the phone.

"Do you want to have dinner with me tonight?" I ask.

She frowns. "I was planning on it. To meet your sister?"

"No. We'll be rid of her by five. Are you kidding me? All she does since she's been growing that kid is sleep. I mean go *out* to dinner. As in, let me take you to dinner and buy you a glass of wine. Then maybe kiss you goodnight."

Her eyes go wide as she stares at me, as if she's trying to decide if I'm punking her or serious. "What are you doing, Mason?"

I arch a brow. "I'm asking my wife out on a date." I saw her flash of jealousy when she thought Shell was my lover. She says she doesn't want to be with me, but she wouldn't be jealous if that were true. "Is that allowed?"

"I don't know," she says. "I thought we were doing this with your rules. *Is* it allowed?"

For three weeks, I've been coming home to her each night and telling myself I have to keep my distance. For three weeks, I've been going to bed alone while she sleeps in the bedroom down the hall—so close but not nearly close enough. I've been watching her blossom, watching her take chances for her business and get comfortable in my home. I've been keeping my distance and it's been hell. This is my last chance with her and I've been letting it slip out of my fingers. Why? Because I'm afraid it will hurt when she leaves? It hurts every time she walks away. I can't protect myself from that. "We'll go slow."

She twirls a lock of hair between her fingers nervously. *Fuck yes.* I want to make her nervous. I want to make her stomach dance with butterflies and her skin tingle. I want to make her *want* to stay with me. "Don't expect me to put out," she says with her bravest face.

"No expectations at all." I'm not sure if I stepped closer in the last sixty seconds or if that was gravity drawing us together, but here we are, closer than before and still not close enough. I want to kiss her now. I can practically feel her skin under my fingers and the soft give of her lips as mine sweep over hers.

This is my last chance with Bailey. I can't fuck it up.

My big sister likes to show up in my life randomly. Usually, she stays just long enough to give me a hard time about all my significant life choices and runs off again to do her thing.

When Bailey left to meet her client, I made a pot of decaf coffee for Shell and sat her down at the kitchen table to tell her the truth about my marriage. I might not want my parents to know, but I've never kept secrets from Shell.

I finish explaining how Bailey ended up my wife, living under my roof, and Shell doesn't look impressed.

"If you think you can stop Dad from trying to control your life, you're delusional."

"He can try all he wants." I fold my arms. "I don't need Dad's approval. I just need Bill to let go of the idea of me and Lindy together so he'll let me have a chance this season."

"You think he will?"

I shrug and look into my cup of cold coffee. "He's still giving me the cold shoulder, but until the regular season starts, it's hard to say how that will affect my career."

"So we should know more on Sunday," she says, nodding. "Good. I hope your plan works. All parts of it."

"What's that supposed to mean?"

"Can you seriously look me in the eye and tell me you talked Bailey—the girl you've been heartsick over for *four years*—into remaining your wife because you were worried about your *career*?" She arches a brow. "You didn't have any hopes of this becoming something more?"

"Not at first."

She grunts. "Bullshit. When you married her in Vegas, you

knew damn well that you wouldn't let her walk away without a fight."

I have to laugh because I know she's right. Every time I've thought I'd keep my distance, that I wouldn't expect this time with Bailey to turn into more, I've been lying to myself. "Maybe it will work out. Maybe this time she'll fall for me as hard as I've fallen for her," I say. I sip my coffee and wish it were something much stronger. "I have to try, Shell."

She puts her hand on the table next to mine. "The sister in me wants to hate her for not letting you into her life, but the woman in me sees the way she looks at you." She laughs and shakes her head. "I saw the way she looked at *me* when she thought I was your lover. This isn't about her not wanting you."

"Then what's it about?"

"I'm pretty sure Bailey's the only one who can answer that question, but my advice is that you stop focusing on making her fall for you and start focusing on being the safe place she needs."

"I am."

She tilts her head, sympathy softening her eyes. "Secrets are like bombs, Mase, and until you tell her yours, you're about as safe as a fallout shelter with no roof."

CHAPTER 23

BAILEY

Mason's holding my hand, and my belly is fuzzy with nerves.

I haven't been on an official *date* with Mason in nearly four years, and I'm nervous. He told me we were going to the Seaside Village to listen to live music and grab dinner from the food carts, so I wore a sundress and a pair of white sneakers. It's not the world's sexiest outfit, but you wouldn't know it by the way Mason looked at me when I joined him in the living room.

The village is bustling with the end-of-summer vacationers. When I first came down here, I wondered if Mason hated how busy it was, but he said it quiets down mid-September. That's right around the corner, and I'm looking forward to enjoying this beautiful space with fewer people.

"Wanna get some food?" Mason asks as we wander the grassy area, checking out the local artists.

"I'm starving. What's good here?"

He points to a trailer across the square. "They sell the best street tacos in town."

I grin. "We got tacos the first night we met."

He squeezes my hand. "I remember," he says softly. "Want to find us a table, and I'll go order?"

I nod and reluctantly release his hand. I'm a nervous eater, so I'm ravenous—or at least, it feels like I am. Picnic tables are scattered across the common area, and I find one tucked between two vendor carts and wave at Mason to show him where he can find me.

"It's my favorite photographer," someone says as I take a seat.

I look up and see Hayden Owen slide onto the bench opposite me. "Hey, Owen. What's up?"

"You know, just a typical Monday night off, trolling the beach for hotties."

I laugh. "Really? Any luck with that?"

He shakes his head. "Not a lick. You have any single friends?"

"Not really." I prop my elbows on the table and study him thoughtfully. "Too bad, though. You seem like you're not an asshole, which is my first requirement in setting up my friends."

"You've got my number. Absolutely not an asshole." He folds his arms and wraps a hand around each bicep. "Come on, there's gotta be someone."

I sigh. "Not really. There's a bad case of serious relationships running around our group, like it's contagious or something."

His lips twitch. "Not big on commitment yourself?"

My gaze drifts across the meadow to Mason, and I can't help but smile. "He married me while I was drunk in Vegas. What do *you* think?"

Owen laughs and shakes his head. "Fuck. Can't blame him. Boy did what he had to do, and now you're in his bed for good."

I'm not in his bed at all. But then, here we are, on a date. Maybe that'll change tonight. My skin tingles at the thought.

"I admire that." He lowers his voice. "Not that I'd tell *him*. Your husband's been trying to steal my place as our quarterback's favorite receiver, so you'll understand if I need to bust his chops and help him remember who the veteran is."

"Sure. I understand. Bust all you want."

"I hear your photography services are in high demand," Owen says. "You haven't even been here a month, and the guys are practically bribing Mason to get their wives in sooner than the others."

I laugh. "I have plenty of time for everyone."

"Do you have a business card?"

I shake my head. "No. It's not that kind of business—nothing that official. It's just something I do sometimes for a little extra cash."

"Well, give me your info, and I'll tell my friends about it."

"Owen, I don't do men."

He chuckles. "I meant my *female* friends."

I put two fingers to my lips, suspicious but not wanting to be a bitch.

"What?"

"*You* have female friends?"

His jaw drops, and he puts his hand on his chest in a picture of outrage. "I'm offended, Bailey. Why do you think I couldn't have female friends? I'm a really nice guy. You said so yourself—*not an asshole.*"

"I'm sure you are, but you just strike me as the kind of guy who doesn't know how to draw the line at friendship."

He wags a finger at me and tsks. "Quite the contrary. I insist on drawing the line there. And I have plenty of female friends."

I fold my arms. "Really?"

"Truly."

"Female friends you've never fucked?"

"Sure! I mean . . ." His eyes dart away before coming back to me. He extends a hand in my direction. "I mean, there's *you.* We're friends now, right?"

I can't help it. I laugh really hard. "That's what I suspected, but you can go ahead and give them my info if they're interested. I've gotta keep myself busy somehow." My gaze catches on Mason, who's heading our way with a tray of food and the biggest margarita I've ever seen.

Owen follows my gaze. "You should make that boy give you a real wedding. You know, with the fancy white dress and flowers and shit." He nods at me. "You deserve that."

"Ah, but there you go assuming I *want* the big wedding with a fancy dress and flowers and shit."

He arches a brow. "Don't all women?"

"No. Not all women."

"Huh." He looks sincerely baffled, and it's kind of adorable. "So, let me get this straight. You like football. You take naked pictures of pretty ladies."

"Clients are rarely naked."

"Okay, so sexy pictures. *Still.*"

"You trying to steal my date, Owen?" Mason asks as he sets the food on the table.

Owen looks at the food then back up to me. "You actually eat and enjoy *real* food, not that rabbit shit. And you don't like fussy things like fancy weddings."

I laugh. "That pretty much covers it."

"*And* you're hot—"

"Watch it," Mason growls.

Owen holds up both hands, palms out, as if defending himself against an oncoming blow. "Not being a sexist pig, just observing facts, and *objectively speaking*, your wife is not unpleasant to look at."

"Thanks, I think?" I pop a chip into my mouth, and Owen watches.

"I'm just gonna put it out there that if this whole marriage thing doesn't work out for you and Mason, you should look me up."

Mason takes the seat beside me. "Fuck off, Owen."

Owen just laughs, totally unashamed by being caught flirting with his teammate's wife.

Mason wraps his arm around my waist, pulling me against his side. "She's claimed."

I turn my head, twisting awkwardly to meet Mason's eyes. "*Claimed*? Like a cow at an auction?"

Owen chuckles. "I'm just saying you'd better treat her right. If you do, you don't have to worry about me, do you? And if you don't, well then, at least she knows she has options." He winks at me, flashing a dimple before looking at Mason. "That's the stuff of dreams you have in your arms right there."

Mason lowers his head and whispers in my ear, "Don't even think about it. I would fight him for you, and I'd win."

A shiver races through me, up my spine and down my arms, making my skin tingle and heightening my awareness of how it feels to have him close. I could get used to dating my husband. I like it a lot.

Owen gives a self-satisfied smile and stands. "I'll leave you two lovebirds alone. Have a nice night."

"We will," Mason says. "Now fuck off so I can enjoy my wife's company."

Owen walks away laughing.

Mason offers me the giant margarita. "I wasn't sure what you wanted, so I hope strawberry is okay."

Grinning, I take it from his hands and take a long drink. It's cold and sweet and makes my chest warm. "Perfect. Where's yours?"

He shakes his head. "I'm not drinking tonight. I'll have a drink of yours, but any more than that and I'll feel shitty at practice."

"You're really dedicated."

He shrugs and drops his gaze to my chest before lifting it back to my face. "There are plenty of other things for me to enjoy tonight."

My cheeks heat, and I scan the food in front of us as an excuse to look away. He got us chips and guac, salsa, queso, and at least a dozen different tacos. "Geez, Mase, hungry much?"

"You love tacos. I wanted to make sure we had enough."

I scan the smorgasbord of street food and shake my head. "I'm not sure how much of this is going to end up inside me."

"If I had a nickel for every time I heard that . . ."

I smack his chest. "Dirty."

He grabs my hand before I can pull it away and meets my eyes. "Thanks for coming out with me tonight."

"You're welcome. I'm having fun."

He brings my hand to his mouth and kisses my knuckles before releasing me.

My cheeks grow warmer, and I study the tacos again so he won't see how much his sweetness affects me. I want to ask him if he's finally planning to sleep in the same bed with me tonight and what this date *means.* Are we going to sleep together? Did I scramble to get a fresh wax for nothing?

Just breathe. I take another long pull of my margarita and search for a safe subject. "So, you remember our wedding?"

MASON

I have to be careful about the way I reply to that. I'm going to have to be careful about the way I handle all of this. "I remember flashes. Bits and pieces."

She takes a bit of the buffalo chicken taco and closes her eyes while she chews, only looking at me after she swallows. "No offense, but what the hell were we thinking?"

Note to self: don't watch her eat. You'll take her home before the night even gets started. "If I remember correctly, you were trying to get in my pants, and I told you we had to be married first."

She puts down her taco and turns to me. "You didn't."

I shrug. "It seemed reasonable at the time. I was drunk, and you were playing hard to get, like always. Can you blame me?"

"Yes." She nods vehemently and reaches for the margarita. "In fact, I'm blaming you right now. That was a terrible idea."

I want to ask her what makes it so terrible, but I know she'll feed me the same old shit about us coming from different worlds, and right now I just want to focus on tonight.

She turns back to her food and frowns. "So, *did* we sleep together?"

"Nah. You were too drunk, and the next morning when you were sober you were too fixated on the goddamned ring to give me a chance." It's been so long since I've been inside her, I wanted our next time together to mean something more to her than another slip-up, another mistake. She's not drunk now. She's wide-eyed and aware, and making me question all my very noble reasons for staying out of her bed.

She coughs. "I was too drunk to screw but not too drunk to marry? You're a shining example of hypocritical personal ethics."

I grab a taco—I think this is the BBQ pork—and shrug. "I have to be able to look at myself in the mirror in the morning."

"How's that working out for you?"

I grin. "You're on an actual date with me for the first time in four years, Bailey. If you ask me, it's working out great."

BAILEY

My stomach is full, my skin is warm from the margarita, and I can't get the smile off my face. We walk home hand in hand under the light of the moon to the sound of the rolling waves.

"Did you have a nice time?" Mason asks when we step onto the porch.

Nodding, I turn to him and put my hand on his chest. "You give good date, Mason Dahl."

He grins and cups my face in one big hand before slowly lowering his mouth to mine. The kiss is soft and sweet and far too brief. When he pulls away, I lean into him, resting my head against his chest.

"I hope we can do it again," he says, as if this is a normal date and he's about to drive away, not walk into the same house and sleep down the hall from me.

"I'd love to," I whisper, and he holds me and strokes my hair, in no more hurry to get inside than I am.

When my phone rings, I reluctantly pull away and dig it out of my purse. I'm surprised when I see Sarah's name on my caller ID. "Sarah?" I ask as I put the phone to my ear. "Is everything okay?"

"Yeah, of course. I . . ." Sarah clears her throat. "Listen, I was hasty when Faith asked you to come to dinner with us. I'm so used to it just being the three of us—her, Brandon, and me—and I said no before I really thought about it. Are you free?"

Mason opens the front door and waves me in. I step into the house and head to the kitchen to find my planner—not that it matters. I could have fifty clients scheduled Friday night, and I'd reschedule every one if it meant I got to go to Faith's birthday dinner. "Of course I am. Are you sure?"

"Yeah. She loves her Aunt B. I'm sorry if I get a little protective."

I write a note in my calendar—not that I think I'll forget—and Mason watches me curiously. "It's okay. Should I meet you at the restaurant?"

"No, no, just meet us over here if you can. Um . . ." She draws in a long breath, and I realize this isn't a simple case of her changing her mind. She wants something.

"What do you need, Sarah?"

"Brandon saw the news. I wasn't going to tell him about your husband, but that wedding video of yours has gone viral, and he. . ."

Seconds ago, I was warm from Mason's touch, but now my skin chills. I don't want anyone using Mason or trying to use me to get to him.

"Listen," my sister says, "I know it's awful for me to ask, but I was wondering if you could bring your husband with you to dinner. Brandon would just love to meet him, and I would too, of course. I mean, he's my baby sister's husband, so I should meet him, right?"

I could point out that she's manipulating me, or that I shouldn't have to play tit-for-tat to see Faith, but I don't. Faith's turning six, and I want to have dinner with her. If it's okay with Mason, it's worth it, right? "I'll ask Mason," I say, lifting my eyes to meet his. "But I'm leaving it up to him. If he can't come, does that mean I'm not welcome?"

She gasps. "Of course not. I know it's awful to ask you to bring your celebrity husband, but you should come either way."

I chew on the inside of my cheek. I don't believe I would have gotten this invitation if it weren't for Mason, but that doesn't mean I'm going to miss my chance. "I'm not trying to interfere with her life," I say, my voice low. "I've never done that."

"Can you blame me for being cautious? You can't deny that you're not the best role model. I know I'm uptight and need to relax . . ." I hear the clink of glasses and imagine her washing dishes. "I'm trying, okay? But it helps to see that you've got your life together, that maybe you've turned over a new leaf."

How is marrying a rich guy turning over a new leaf? I bite my tongue so the question can't escape. I don't want to fight. I want to see Faith blow out her candles and open her presents. I want to celebrate with her. "I'll see you Friday night, then. I'll ask Mason to come, but I'm not making any promises. He's really busy."

"Of course, we understand. I mean, he's an NFL player and all." She laughs nervously, and I feel nauseated. I feel bad for keeping the temporary nature of my marriage from my sister, but telling her the truth will only confirm all the reasons she already thinks I'm a bad influence on Faith. "I'll see you," she says.

"See you. Thanks, Sarah," I say before ending the call. I stare at my phone for a few deep breaths before lifting my gaze to meet Mason's.

"Is everything okay?"

I nod and set my phone and purse onto the counter. "Remember my niece I told you about?"

"Faith?" he says, and something tugs in my chest that he remembers. Of course he does.

"She turns six this weekend, and my sister wants us to come to her party. Any chance you'd be willing to go?"

He frowns and steps forward to pull me into his arms. "I'd love to." He tilts his head, studying me. "I'm a little surprised you're asking."

"I'm pretty sure you're the reason I was invited at all." I lean my head against his chest and close my eyes. My frustration with Sarah fizzles away when I'm in his arms. I feel so safe here. "Her boyfriend's a big fan, and he wants to meet you. Before he knew about our marriage, I wasn't invited to the party."

He pulls in a breath through his teeth. "That's awful. I'm sorry."

"My sister likes to keep me at an arm's length. She doesn't let anyone close."

He chuckles. "Are you telling me that's a genetic condition, then?"

I wrap my arms around his waist and squeeze. I don't want this night to end. I don't want us to remember that this is temporary or that I don't belong here. "I'm pretty sure she's ashamed of me. But I married an NFL player, so I guess I make the cut now."

"Why does she treat you like that? That's bullshit."

I pull back to meet his eyes. "I don't even care right now. I just know I haven't spent Faith's birthday with her since the . . ." I hesitate. "Since the day Sarah adopted her. I'm happy I get to be there this time."

"She means a lot to you, doesn't she?" He studies me, and for a second I think he might see the truth in my eyes. For a second, I wish he would. It doesn't matter how sure I am of my decision to let my sister raise my child; carrying the secret alone is exhausting.

"You have no idea."

He rubs my back. "I think it's time to say goodnight."

"Am I sleeping alone again?" I ask.

"That's why it's time to say goodnight. I'm trying really hard not to change my mind about that."

"Why?" I bite my lip. "There are a lot of things way more

worth your effort than staying out of my bed."

He chuckles. "We're taking it slow, remember?" He dips his head and skims his lips over mine. "And when I'm finally inside you again, I promise it'll be worth the wait."

A slow shiver shimmies through my whole body. I just might like *slow*.

CHAPTER 24

MASON

Another day of practices and meetings, watching film of our opponents and of ourselves in practice, analyzing weaknesses in them and in us, and then another meeting with the offensive coordinator after, and now it's been a thirteen-hour workday and I'm destroyed.

A few of the guys were going out for drinks and suggested I go with them. When I passed and told them I wanted to get home, there were grunts and nudges, chuckles, and the rookie wide-out said, "I'd want to get home if I had her waiting for me, too."

They think I'm going home to make love to my wife when the reality is that my evening plans only involve me and a dozen bags of frozen peas. I'm too exhausted to think about my complicated marriage. I just want to sit in front of the TV and watch some *SportsCenter* while icing my aches and pains and then maybe, just maybe, I'll get to kiss my wife goodnight.

When I walk in the door, Bailey's nowhere to be seen. I hear music out back, and I follow the sound to the patio. She has Ed Sheeran playing and she's swimming laps, her body flowing effortlessly through the water, her legs kicking back behind her as if she's some sort of mystical sea creature.

Is Shell right? Do I need to tell Bailey what I did? If I did, would she understand or would she leave before our time is up? Would she ever speak to me again?

When I think of letting her go forever, a thousand different memories pass through my mind. I think of the first night we met, when she kissed me and told me to take her back to my room. The nights after that when we couldn't get enough of each other, and filled every spare moment together naked. I think of the night she told me she wasn't my girl, and the way she pushed me away when Nic Mendez got parole, and insisted on calling our relationship *casual*. I think of how far from casual it felt to hold her in my arms as we watched them lower Nic into the ground. The way she shook as Mia tossed a handful of earth onto the coffin.

I think of the nights after. She'd come to me because she didn't want to sleep alone, and when she'd wake up from the nightmares—sweaty and panicked—I'd smooth back her hair and hold her tight and whisper in her ear until her breathing steadied and she believed that everything was okay.

Every time she pushes me away, I think of how she clung to me during those nights. How she needed me and how I could calm her in a way no one else could. I think all these things with a combination of love and frustration toward Bailey and a heavy dose of bitterness for the man who wasn't worthy of half of her love.

I'm sick of missing Bailey. I'm sick of walking around halfhearted. If my mistake of sleeping with Lindy and that night in Vegas can give me one last chance with the woman I've loved for four years, I'm taking it.

I don't know how long I stand there watching her swim through the water or how many laps I watch her complete, but the aches and pains I was so acutely aware of when I walked in the door are suddenly far from my mind. All I can think about is her.

When she stops, she puts her arms on the edge of the pool and gasps for breath, as if she wasn't going for a leisurely swim in the safe waters of a pool but was instead lost at sea and swimming frantically to shore.

"Do you creep on all your wives?" she asks without looking at me.

I peel off my shirt. "Only the special ones." I toe off my shoes and unbutton my jeans before pushing them from my hips, then I dive into the water in nothing but my boxer briefs. The water is warm from the hot summer sun, but it stormed this afternoon and the air is cool. I glide easily through the water to reach her, and she spins around to face me, treading water by the edge before I trap her against it with an arm on either side of her, stealing her space so she's forced to slip her arms around my neck to stay afloat.

"Did you have a good day?" she asks.

"Kind of shitty," I admit. "The coach is all about more live tackles in practice this year, so I feel like I've been beaten to a pulp, which is normal come October, but I hate feeling like this before the regular season has even started."

She licks her lips and studies my face. "I'm sorry."

"Don't be. It's better now."

I expect her to duck under my arm and swim away at any moment, but she surprises me by wrapping her legs around my waist. "Thank you for agreeing to go to my niece's party Friday."

"You're welcome. I'm happy to."

"Is this okay?" She locks her feet behind my back; the movement presses her hips against mine. Watching her swim through the water had me half hard, but the press of her heat against my cock finishes the job. "Or are you about to push me away again?"

"It's okay." Maybe it's not. Maybe this is a really bad idea. After all, sleeping with Bailey for a year after we first met never seemed to get me any closer to a chance at a real relationship with her. There's no reason to think it might now.

I slide a hand into her hair and lower my mouth to hers. She tastes like sweet red wine, and when my tongue sweeps across hers, she moans—a low and vulnerable hum I once mistook for lowering walls. I won't make that mistake again. I won't assume that just because she's giving me access to her body, more will follow. But I'm sick of resisting, and I'm terrified that when our time together is over, I might actually have to let her go.

I'm not even sure I'm capable. As many times as I've told myself I was walking away from Bailey, that I was finally moving on, I've never been able to do it.

She rocks her hips against mine, rubbing herself against my erection. I respond by pulling down a strap of her swimsuit and exposing one perfect breast to the night air.

I take it into my hand, lower my head, and skim my tongue across her nipple. She gasps and arches into me, and I draw her into my mouth. She cries out, the sound of her pleasure disappearing into the night sky.

Her legs are like a vise around me, tightening with each touch. She slides her hands into my hair and leads my mouth back to hers. Her kiss is the drug that makes me forget why this is a bad idea, and the rhythm of her hips moving against mine is the best kind of high. I hold her tightly and guide us to the shallow end, where I settle her on the steps and pull the other strap of her suit down so she's naked from the waist up.

I drop to my knees, spread her thighs, and kneel between them. I circle her navel with my tongue and slide a hand between her legs to rub her through her suit. Pulling back, I appreciate the way her bare breasts look in the moonlight, her eyes closed, her lips parted, her back arched in pleasure. With every stroke of my fingers, her legs spread farther and her hips lift off the step.

"You're so beautiful." I take her suit in both hands, guide it down both of her legs, and toss it away onto the pool deck. She's bare in front of me, and before I have a chance to take her in, she's grabbing my briefs in her fists. I help her, standing in the waist-deep water and stripping down to nothing before I'm even sure why. Then we're both nude, her hand between our bodies, her fist wrapped around me and stroking in a slow, steady rhythm that could make this end before it's even begun. I move her hand, pull her to me, and guide her back to deeper water. She wraps her legs around my waist again, only this time there's nothing between us. The heat of her presses against me, and then with a shift of her hips, the head of my cock rests at her entrance. She arches her neck, her face to the sky as she exhales two words. "I. Want."

Some part of my brain reminds me I'm not an idiot anymore. I don't fuck without condoms. That comes with consequences. But another part, a louder part, tells me that for Bailey, I would take the consequences, and with Bailey it wouldn't be *fucking*. I just want to be inside her.

"Are you sure?" I ask.

Her fingers curl into my shoulder blades. She shifts once, then twice, then I'm sliding into her, and it's so damn good. She squeezes around me, flesh to flesh. I bury my face in her neck and breathe.

"I've missed you." She rocks her body in time with mine.

I chuckle. "You've missed this."

She shakes her head. "No. I've missed *you*, Mason." I pull back enough to look at her face, and she meets my eyes. "I've missed *us*."

And in the long game of tug-of-war for my heart between me and Bailey, I happily lose it in this moment. I feel it pull away, feel her own me completely. "I've missed you too."

"Did you?" she asks, stilling. "You moved down here last year, and it was like I never existed. I thought you'd call more or visit or . . ."

"I was trying to move on, but it was hell trying to pretend I don't care."

Something crosses over her face, but before I can get a read on her, she shifts her hips and pleasure takes over and wipes it away.

The air is cool on my skin. The water warm. The patio lights cast shadows across her face and the stereo has shut off. It's just us in the warm Florida night, making love in the water to the ocean's rhythmic hum.

CHAPTER 25

BAILEY

"Bailey?" Mason calls when he walks in from the garage.

"I'm in the kitchen." I hoist myself on the island and cross my legs at the knee. Anticipation races up my spine as I hear his heavy steps coming toward me. I spent my day working but distracted by thoughts of Mason. What happened in the pool last night was sweet and intense, and I've spent all day giddy with nerves and anticipation for the moment he returns home from practice.

He comes around the corner, and my insides shimmy when I see him. When I first moved in, I thought he'd come home sweaty straight from practice, but it turns out that there's a lot more that goes into being a professional football player than running around on the field. It seems like he spends more than half of his "working" hours in meetings.

Tonight, he has on faded jeans and a green Gators polo that makes his eyes look an even deeper green than usual. He got a late start this morning and must have skipped his shave, because there's stubble on his jaw. My fingers itch to run over it.

He freezes when he spots me. "I'm pretty sure I would have blown off my last meeting if I realized what was waiting for me at home." He steps forward and grins. "There would have been hell to pay, but it would have been worth it."

His eyes go dark as he takes me in—from my red stiletto heels up to my blue-checked kitchen apron with nothing underneath. I did a photo shoot for a baker once, and some of the best pictures were of her in nothing but her apron.

I uncross my legs and swing my feet as I grip the edge of the counter. "Still trying to figure out this wife thing. Like I said, I'm not really sure what I'm doing. Does this seem about right?"

His chest rises and falls with a deep breath as he steps closer. He puts a big hand on each knee and slowly slides them up my thighs, guiding them apart so he can stand between them. "I'd say you nailed it."

I loop my arms behind his neck. "How was your day, *dear*?"

"Hard," he says, his hands inching higher on my thighs. "*Painfully* hard. What about yours?"

"It was long." My breath hitches when he sucks at the tender spot beneath my ear. "I feel like I've been waiting for you forever."

He slides a hand between my legs and groans against my neck. "That sounds awful. Let me make it up to you." Then he does.

Sex on the kitchen counter, followed by a shower, and ordering dinner in—because Mason's worn out and the only thing in the house I can cook is Pop-Tarts—and I'm feeling mighty content.

"I almost forgot." Mason hands me a business card. "This guy does my website. I talked to him yesterday, and he said he can make room in his schedule to get your site up and running."

I frown at the card for the graphic designer before looking at Mason. "My site for what?"

He opens the fridge and pokes around. Even though we just ate, he's hungry again. I don't envy his hours of training, but I'm a little jealous that he can eat so much—not that I'd choose the healthy foods he does. *Boring.* "For your photography business."

I shake my head. "I don't need a website."

"Sure you do. People will take you more seriously if you have a web presence. He said he'd get you set up on social media, too."

"I don't need people to take me seriously." I put the card on the counter. "Thanks for thinking of me, but I don't think this is necessary. I'm not launching an enterprise or something."

Mason closes the fridge and turns to me. "Bailey, you have natural talent, and you already have a line of football wives dying to get an appointment with you. Do you know what a great opportunity this is to launch a career? A *real* career? You've made it clear you don't want my money, so fine, don't take it. But you could start charging more for your sessions and stop living paycheck to paycheck."

"I don't take pictures for the money. I do it because it makes women feel good about themselves."

"And that's probably why you're so damn good at it." He studies me for a beat. "You're so afraid that everyone's going to look at you and see the trailer park girl who took off her clothes for money that you're afraid to try to be someone else."

"But that *is* who I am."

"That's who you were. That's where you're from. It's not who you are now, or you'd be getting ready to get on stage and not sitting here with me. They all want what you have to offer. I have guys trying to call in favors with me so their wives get bumped up the schedule." He presses a kiss to the top of my head. "If you'd believe in yourself just a little, you'd be amazed what life has to offer you. You'd be amazed who you could become."

Does he want me to be someone else? The last conversation I had with Nic, we fought about Mason. He said Mason was just another rich boy who manipulated women with his money. He accused me of selling myself to Mason. *"Just like you sold yourself to Clarence."* I told him he was an asshole. Told him he could go fuck himself because he would never be able to love someone like Mason could. Then he got the text from Mia asking for help, and an hour later, he was dead.

CHAPTER 26

BAILEY

"I'm not pregnant," Mia says, and it sounds like she's crying.

I push my phone closer to my ear and frown. I called to ask her a question and this was her greeting when she answered the phone. "Did you just say you're *not* pregnant? Like that's news? Were you *trying* to be pregnant?"

She sighs. "No, not yet, but my period was late and I started thinking maybe I was. After the initial panic, I decided I liked the idea. Then I told Arrow and the look on his face made me *love* the idea. But I'm not. I just started and I have cramps and I don't even know why I'm crying. Except that I'm not pregnant and I guess I was already feeling attached to the baby I'm not actually having."

"Oh, sweetie." I push aside the stack of prints I'd been working with when I called her and prop my elbows on the kitchen table. "You're still on the pill, right?"

She sniffs. "Yeah. I know. It's really effective. I was stupid to think I might be."

"I don't mean that." I bite my lip. I don't think I'll ever be okay with my best friend living across the country from me. "I mean, you can stop taking it now, right? If you both want a baby, you could try."

"I don't think we're ready yet. I just . . . I think I wanted the excuse to fast-forward to growing our family, you know? It doesn't change the fact that we're still young and it would be better to wait. It just made me really think about life and family and . . . I miss my brother."

To anyone else, the mention of Nic might seem unrelated, but I understand what Mia means. Her mother left before Nic died, and then when Nic died, it was just her and her father. Half her family was gone.

"I think I might want a lot of kids," she says softly, and the sound of tears has left her voice. "Not yet, but when we do start. Like four or five brats who will always have each other. I don't want them to be alone."

"You'll be a great mom." I look at the stack of pictures in front of me and let my fingers hover over the image of her brother leaning against a spray-painted brick wall. I'm sliced by a pang of guilt for never telling her about Faith. She thinks she's lost her brother forever, but part of Nic is still here.

Mia draws in a deep breath. "I'm sorry about my outburst. How are you?"

I rub the back of my neck, mentally debate telling her about the amazing sex Mason and I are having, and then decide against it. "I'm good. I'm going through some old pictures of Nic."

"Oh, Bailey," she says. "Honey, don't do that to yourself."

I shake my head as if she can see me. "It's not like that. I was just . . ." *Putting together a scrapbook to give to your niece when she's old enough to know who her biological parents are.* "Do you remember the name of that restaurant that paid Nic to spray-paint a graffiti-looking mural on their wall?"

"Abby's at Sunset," she says, a smile in her voice now. "He was talented, wasn't he? I'd forgotten about that."

"He always said he was useless with a pencil or paintbrush, but give him a can of spray paint and he'd give you the Sistine Chapel."

"He was such a punk," she says affectionately. "Oh, wait a sec, Bail."

I hear murmurs in the background then a muffled "I started," followed by more murmurs and a squeak from Mia.

"Hey, Bailey, can I call you back tomorrow? Arrow just got home."

I chuckle. "Absolutely. Tell your hubby I said hi."

"I will. Love you."

"Love you too," I whisper, and my chest aches as I end the call. I miss Mia. I miss open-mic nights at the Vortex and riding around in Nic's rusty pickup squeezed between her and her brother.

I flip through the pictures until I find one of the three of us that was taken shortly before Nic was arrested. Nic is giving a rare smile to the camera, I'm staring at him with total adoration, and Mia is watching me with worry etched into her features. She knew I was in love with him and never liked it. It wasn't that she was jealous or that she didn't want to share my attention. She knew her brother was trouble and was convinced being in love with him was going to screw up my life. To this day, she has no idea how right she was, but when I think of Faith, I wouldn't change a thing.

Ever since Nic died, I've been telling myself I was going to make Faith a scrapbook of the pictures I have of Nic. I know I can't give it to her yet, but every month that passes, my memories grow dimmer, and I want to put together something she can have when she's older and has questions about her parents.

I have the whole day off and no client meetings until tomorrow, so I decided it was the perfect time to get to work. Earlier, I gathered all my photos and emailed them to a local drugstore to get them developed, and now I have them spread out across Mason's kitchen table ready to be placed into the scrapbook.

Only it's a lot tougher than I anticipated. I wanted to put notes on each page, and I always imagined I'd have so much to say that it would be hard to have enough room. Now that I'm doing it, words are failing me. I want her to know we loved each other, despite our issues. But how do I describe young love, thrilling and overwhelming and too big to hold in growing hands?

I'm not sure why it's so hard to put this together. Is it because of what Mason said Wednesday night about who I was versus who I could become? Is it because sleeping in Mason's arms the last three nights reminded me of exactly what I sacrificed for Nic? Or is it just because Nic's memory has faded with time, and I've forgotten him enough that I don't know how to paint the picture for the little girl who will never be able to meet her biological father?

I'm so lost in my thoughts that I don't even know I'm not alone in the house until I hear him speak.

"This has gone on too long," Christian Dahl says.

I jump up from the table, backing away to put space between us. "What do you want?"

He pulls a pen and checkbook from his suitcoat. "I want you to name your price." He clicks his pen and arches a brow, and his facial expression reminds me so much of Mason that I have to remind myself he isn't a friend. This man doesn't care about me.

Mason would never try to buy me off.

"My price for what?" I ask, deciding I'm going to make him say it.

"How much to make this charade end?"

"I haven't even been here a month. I told you it would be through the end of the year." I hate explaining myself to him, but I hate talking about the end of my time with Mason as something inevitable even more.

"I don't want my son to get attached." He cocks his head to the side. "Come on. Surely a girl like you could use some money."

A girl like me. This man will always look at me and see the woman who shook her ass on stage for extra cash. He'll always see the girl who dared fall in love with a drug dealer. It's a wonder that Mason came from him. How could such a caring, unjudging, understanding man come from such an angry, bigoted one? Mason, who hated what I did but could understand it. Mason, who sees a human being when he looks at me and not a poor chick scraping by, desperate for cash.

"I don't want your money," I say. "I should never have taken it to begin with."

"But you did, and our actions speak louder than our words. I think Mason would agree."

I recognize the threat for what it is, but he doesn't fool me. He doesn't want Mason knowing about our arrangement any more than I do. "I had my reasons then, but I won't take your bribes now."

"I don't think you understand how much I'm prepared to pay you. You have some significant debt that I'm sure it would feel good to be free of."

I wrap my arms around my stomach. I always feel cold when this man is around. "Why do you hate me so much?"

"It's not personal, Miss Green. This isn't about you. This is about me protecting my son and my family's assets."

"Why don't you let him decide whether or not he needs to be protected? What are you so afraid of? That he might truly love a lower-class peasant like me? That he might decide he wants me to remain his wife?"

"We had an agreement." His voice is cold and hard. "Are you prepared to pay me back if you can't follow through on your end?"

I don't have that kind of money and probably never will, but in a flash, I realize I'm not powerless against Christian Dahl. He has as much to lose as I do, and he's just as scared of losing Mason as I am. "If that's what it takes, I'll figure out a way."

His nostrils flare. He doesn't know what to do with me. This is a man who truly believes he can buy anyone and anything. And I helped confirm that belief when I took his money.

"Right. I forgot. You have access to all kinds of money now that you're married to my son." He tucks his checkbook back into his pocket. "But you forget that I know about your child."

I turn up my palms. "Whoopdidoo," I say. "Ex-stripper from Nowhere, Indiana, let her sister adopt her daughter. Call the papers. Everyone's going to want this story!"

I hold my breath until I see that angry twitch of his jaw. If he called my bluff and told Sarah that he knew the truth—or worse, if he told Faith who her real mom is—Sarah would push me out of her life out of panic alone.

Christian laughs, and the sound is hard and cold. "I'm not worried. I know my son better than you do, and I know you'll be out of his life if he finds out the truth. I'll just save my money and let this take care of itself."

Those words are a storm cloud growing in the sky, and as excited as I am about Faith's party tonight, I know they'll follow me.

Christian combs his fingers through his hair. "Mason's mother and I are having an anniversary party at the end of the month. Find a way to get out of it. I don't want her to have to look at you on her special day."

I flinch. I've always considered myself tough, but Mason's father has a way of taking my heart in his claws and ripping it apart. "I'll see what I can do."

MASON

I pulled some strings to get out of my later afternoon meeting so I could go with Bailey to her niece's birthday party. I know she said I'm the only reason she was invited, but even so, I know what it means for her to let me in to this part of her life. I don't want to miss it.

When I drive into my neighborhood after practice, my father is heading out. I do a double take when I see his Escalade, and sure enough, when I look again, there he is. He has half his attention on the road and the other half on the phone in his hand, so he doesn't notice me.

What the fuck was he doing here? He knows I'm at practice all day long. He didn't call and say he was coming. If he knocked on my door and I wasn't there, why wouldn't he call or text to let me know he was in town looking for me?

It says something about the state of our relationship, that I don't honk to get his attention or call that phone in his hand to let him know I'm pulling in.

As I follow the road through the cul-de-sac to my driveway, dread tightens my chest. When I get inside, I find Bailey at the kitchen table, the makings of a scrapbook spread out before her.

"You're home earlier than I expected." She smiles at me but cuts her eyes nervously to the pictures in front of her. Was she planning to clean it up before I got home so I didn't have to be reminded where I stand? Or is she nervous because she was speaking with my father and doesn't want me to know?

I want to forget the worry in my gut and pull her into my arms.

There's nothing I can do about her feelings for Nic, but my questions about my dad are rooted in years-old baggage and probably a heavy dose of paranoia. Maybe he wasn't here at all. Maybe he was visiting one of my neighbors. "Was my dad just here?"

She straightens and gives me a plastic smile. "Yeah. He was."

So much for hoping. My eyes flick to the pictures spread out before her and stall. My kitchen table is covered with pictures of Bailey and Nic Mendez. Even when I have her living in my house, he finds his way in. Of all the times she could have done this, of all the places she could have assembled her precious memories of him, she had to do it here?

I shove my irritation from my mind and try to focus on the matter at hand. "What was my dad doing here?"

"I think he just . . ." She stacks pictures into piles. Are her hands shaking? "He wanted to meet me."

That might make sense if A) my dad wasn't a selfish asshole

who couldn't care less about the woman I'm married to since it doesn't benefit him, or B) if she hadn't already met him back at BHU when he came to town for a home game—more than once, if I remember correctly. "He's already met you, Bailey."

"Right." She taps a stack of pictures against the table, straightening them. "I mean he wanted to get to know me. We never had the chance to talk before."

Again, I'd like to believe that, but allow me to refer to point A. "He was here to talk?"

She grimaces.

"Bailey?"

"He doesn't want me coming to the anniversary party." She swallows and lifts her eyes to meet mine. "The truth is, he doesn't like me, and he thinks you and I are a passing fad."

"He's such a dick." I reach for my phone, and she puts her hand on my arm to stop me. "He had no right to come into my house and make you feel unwanted."

"But I am." She drags her bottom lip between her teeth. "We've talked about this before, Mason. You and I come from different worlds, and we can't blur the lines between them without consequences."

I mutter a curse. "What are you working on?" Even a scrapbook project about her love affair with a dead man is a better topic than my father and his continued efforts to control my life.

"It's a scrapbook of me and Nic." She grimaces. "I've meant to do it forever, and I've never had the chance." Her eyes skim over the open book and the two carefully laid-out pages before her.

There's a picture of them in front of a run-down trailer, Bailey on Nic's back, her arms around his neck. There's another of them lying on a blanket in the sunshine. Yet another shows Nic alone, holding his hand up in the universal symbol for "don't take my picture right now."

"You must really miss him," I say, and before she can answer, I turn on my heel and leave the room. I don't want to hear about how much she misses a piece of shit who would have stomped on her if he thought it would get him ahead, and I hate this sick feeling in my gut that tells me she's not telling me the whole truth about why my dad was here.

CHAPTER 27

BAILEY

The drive to my sister's house is laced with the same tense silence we suffered through on the way to Lindy's party. If that's a sign of the night to come, maybe I should have chosen to stay home.

Mason parks on the street in front of Sarah's mustard-yellow split-level and cuts the engine. I reach for the handle, but he grabs my hand before I can open the door. "I'm sorry I've been in a shitty mood all afternoon."

Today's been hard—his father's visit was a reminder that my time with Mason has to be temporary, and then he questioned me about it and I felt as if I'd been caught in a lie. "It's fine."

"It's not." He squeezes my hand. "I'm fucking jealous, Bailey. I walked in and saw you working on that scrapbook, and I just felt like Nic was back in our lives. I have you living in my house and sleeping in my bed, but you're still spending your days thinking about *him*."

I snap my head up, and he's studying me with those intense green eyes. Is that what he was upset about? The pictures? "Oh, shit, Mason. I'm sorry." I should have realized the reminder of Nic would upset him. "It's not like I'm fantasizing about Nic. I just have more free time living here than I've had in a long time, and I've been meaning to get that project done forever. But it can wait. If it upsets you, I can finish it after I move back home."

He closes his eyes and turns away. "It's not where you do it that upsets me. Only that you want to."

"They're just pictures. Memories." *And they're not for me.*

"I think you're wrong about me," he says, turning back to me.

"About what?"

"You think I'm spoiled. That I get everything I want." He shakes his head. "You're the only thing I've ever wanted enough to fight dirty for, and your heart still belongs to him."

My chest aches, because he doesn't understand, and I want him to. I reach across the console and place my hand on his shoulder. If he knew Faith was mine, he would understand why I was making the scrapbook. But I promised my sister that I wouldn't tell anyone, because she doesn't want it getting back to Faith before she's ready.

Why do we make prisons for ourselves with our promises?

Maybe his jealousy of Nic is a blessing. Maybe when I have to leave, he'll let himself believe I'm still pining for my first love. Maybe he'll never have to know how low I had to sink to do what I thought was right. Maybe he'll never have to hate me.

He looks at my hand on his shoulder, and silence grows between us like a heavy weight on my heart. He lifts his eyes to mine, and in one second, he's sitting there looking at me, and in the next, he's kissing me.

He sucks my bottom lip between his teeth and cups my face in his hands. He nips at my lips and strokes my jaw, then fists a hand in my hair and deepens the kiss until I want to crawl over the console and straddle him.

When he breaks the kiss, I'm breathless. I turn my face into his hand and press my lips against his open palm.

"Does your heart belong to him, Bailey?" He swallows. "Do I even stand a chance?"

I wish he'd only asked the first question. The second is so much more complicated. "Nic was my first love, but I didn't die with him."

Someone knocks on the window, and I look up to see a broad-chested guy. He points both index fingers at us and winks before turning and heading into the house.

"That must be Brandon," I say. I reach for my gift from the floor and open my door. The guy looked really amused about catching me and Mason together in the car, but I'm afraid my sister will be less amused. In her mind, our kiss will be "making out" in front of her house, a sign of my immaturity.

I grab the present, and Mason and I climb out. The car chirps when he hits the button. He plants a quick kiss on the top of my head, then takes my hand as we head to the house, where my sister is already waiting in the doorway, Brandon standing behind her and grinning at us like the huge fan of Mason that Sarah said he was.

"Nice shirt," Sarah says as she holds the door for us.

I look down at the T-shirt I threw on with my jeans this morning. It says, *I can't adult today.* I paste on a smile and pretend her judgment doesn't faze me. "Thanks."

"You must be the husband," she says, turning to Mason and offering a hand. "Bailey's told me a lot about you over the years, though it would have been nice if she'd told me about the wedding, too."

Mason grins and shakes her hand. "I would love to know exactly what she said about me."

"All good stuff," I say, and I realize Sarah isn't just blowing smoke to make this less awkward. I have told her quite a bit about Mason. He's been a fixture in my life for a long time now. I don't want to imagine a time when he's not.

"This is my boyfriend, Brandon," Sarah says.

The guy from out front grins at us. "Super stoked to meet you both. Sorry if I . . . interrupted something out there."

"You didn't," I lie, and Mason shoots me a look.

Faith runs out of the back room, and I hide her present behind my back. She wraps her arms around my legs. "Aunt B! Did you bring my present?"

"Was I supposed to bring you a present?"

She releases my legs and props her hands on her hips, narrowing her dark eyes at me. She looks so much like Mia when she does that, and it makes my heart tug with guilt over the secrets I've kept from my best friend. Mia's never met Faith. I've never given her the opportunity or reason to believe she might want to. Some secrets we have to bury deep.

"You're teasin' me," Faith says.

I grin and pull the wrapped box from behind my back.

"*Whatisit, whatisit, whatisit*? Can I open it, Mommy?"

My sister nods. "Yeah, baby. Go ahead."

"I'm not a baby anymore. I'm six years old, you know."

"I'm sorry. It's easy for me to forget."

"Because you're getting old," Faith says, matter-of-fact.

"Right. Because I'm getting old." Sarah laughs. She seems lighter today, more at ease with my presence than usual. I study her, hoping this is the beginning of a new trend.

Faith unwraps the gift with gusto, shredding the paper and letting it fall to the floor before opening the box and gasping. "New tap shoes!" She looks up at her mom and pulls them from the box. "Look, Mommy! Aunt B got me new tap shoes! I wanted these so much. Mine are old. They're hand-me-downs from Britney Haller, and she makes fun of me when she sees me wearing them, but Mommy said I shouldn't let that bother me because Britney's just trying to act cool, but I still wanted new ones that were mine and never anyone else's and you got them for me." She clutches them to her chest and dances in a little circle. "Yay!"

I watch my sister, waiting for some sign that this was a bad choice, that I've embarrassed her somehow, but she only gives a small smile as she meets my eyes and mouths, *Thank you.*

I exhale the breath I didn't realize I was holding. I feel lighter than I have all day.

"Best. Birthday. Ever," Faith says. She kicks off her sandals and slides into her new tap shoes.

MASON

That could be Mia's little girl.

The thought has buzzed through my head since the second I spotted Bailey's niece, and I feel like a racist jackass. Thinking that a little Latina girl looks like my closest Latina friend is just as bad as someone thinking I look like Reggie Miller because we're both black dudes with green eyes.

Seriously, I want to punch myself in the face for being one of those idiots who thinks all people of one ethnicity look alike. I've never been like that, but every time I look at Faith, I see Mia.

Bailey's on cloud nine after Faith's reaction to her gift, and her eyes follow the girl everywhere as she dances around the living room, showing off and talking at a hundred miles an hour. No, it's not that I think she looks similar to Mia. It's as if she could be Mia's daughter. If Mia and Arrow had a little girl, she would totally look like Faith.

Is it her eyes? Her smile? It's both, and it's more than that.

Brandon approaches me and offers a hand, pulling my creeper-like attention away from Faith. He's almost as tall as me and has the big barrel chest of a guy who likes his beer as much as his bench press. "I can't tell you how awesome it is to meet you. When I saw that video and realized you were Sarah's brother-in-law, I couldn't believe it. I watched you all last season. I'm a huge fan."

"I appreciate that." I look to Bailey, who's been coaxed into a dance with the birthday girl. "Thanks for inviting us. It means a lot to Bailey to be here."

"Of course. You two are welcome over here anytime!"

That's not the way I understand it. Saying as much will only add to the tension between sisters, so I only smile. "Thanks a lot. We'd love to have Faith come over sometime. Does she like to swim?"

"Oh, man, she's like a fish. Just try getting her out of the water! That would be fantastic. I'll definitely talk to Sarah and get something worked out."

"That would be awesome. Thanks."

He beams. "So how was training camp? Are you ready for regular season to kick off?"

I shift gears, prepared to talk football all night if it's going to help butter this guy up so Bailey can spend more time with her niece. He's a nice enough guy. He gushes a little, throwing out stats to impress me and mixing up some of my plays with some of Owen's from last season. It's no big deal, though. I know he means well, and he's obviously a fan of the team.

But through our whole conversation, I can't take my eyes off

Bailey and the way she looks at that little girl. Maybe someday when I'm an uncle I'll understand how it feels not to get the time I want with my niece or nephew. Even without that experience, I can imagine it would tear me apart if my sister kept her child from me. Family's important. As fucked up as mine is, I know that. And I get it. Sarah's conservative and doesn't like the choices Bailey's made, and Bailey . . . well, she's made some bad choices. Nic Mendez. Stripping. Hell, I'd even add staying in Blackhawk Valley to her list of bad choices, but that's probably just me wanting to pull her away from the ghost of her former lover. I swear he tried to bury her with him.

Faith appears in front of me and tugs on the hem of my shirt. "We're going to Applebee's for dinner."

Brandon grimaces. "Oh, is that okay with you and Bailey?"

Sarah wrings her hands. "Maybe we don't have to choose Applebee's, Faith. Bailey and Mason might want to go somewhere else."

"But it's your favorite, too," Faith whines at her mom. She looks at Bailey. "It's my birthday and Mom's Mommy-versary, because this is the day she adopted me. Please say we can go to Applebee's. Please, please?"

I'm pretty sure this offer is for my benefit, since I'm the guy in the room who pulls in the most money each year, so I'm quick with my response. "I love Applebee's."

Faith cheers. "Do you like the chicken fingers, too?"

"They're the best."

"Yes!" She pumps her fist in the air and pretty much steals my heart. Then, in a flash, I don't just see Mia in this little girl's smile.

I see Bailey.

CHAPTER 28

BAILEY

Tonight was amazing—from hearing Faith say "cheese" for pictures at dinner to watching her blow out the candles on her cake afterward. But none of it compares to this moment. We're all settled into the couches in Sarah's living room and Faith's snuggled on my lap, her eyes heavy and a half-smile curling her lips.

"Mommy, tell Aunt B about the day that I was born. The day you 'dopted me."

"The day I *adopted* you?" Sarah says.

"Yes. That day. Tell her about the day I was born."

Sarah and I exchange a look. "Aunt B doesn't need to hear that old story."

"I bet you could tell it," I say, looking down at Faith. "You've heard it enough times."

"I am a-dopted," Faith says with a very serious look on her

face. "And that means that I didn't grow in my mommy's belly. I grew in another lady's belly. The day I was born, she went to the hospital and my bi-logical mother put me in Mommy's arms and said . . ." She turns to Sarah. "What did she say?"

Sarah's face twists with emotion as she holds her daughter's gaze. "She said, 'I already love her so much, and I feel like I'm giving you a piece of my heart, but I know you'll be the mother she deserves. You can give her what I can't.'"

Faith nods. "Yes. And she told Mommy to take care of me and give me a family because she couldn't, and that's what Mommy did. And that's why I'm Mommy's daughter and not someone else's, and that's why my skin's a different color than Mommy's." She holds her arm next to mine. "Mommy says she's white, but I think she's more like a peach crayon like you, and I'm more like a light brown crayon because my bi-logical dad was Mexican American."

"That's right, baby," Sarah says.

I swallow, but the lump in my throat stays put. I have to give Sarah credit for this much. She's never tried to hide the adoption from Faith, and I like that they talk openly about skin color and ethnicity. Even if Faith doesn't know Nic's name, I like that she has an idea where she comes from.

Faith wiggles out of my arms to scoot over on the couch beside Mason. She turns and holds her arm against his. "But your skin is even darker than mine, so your mom *and* dad must be Mexican American."

Mason chuckles and studies their arms next to each other.

"That's a good guess," he says. "But actually, my dad is white like your mom, and my mom is African American—or sometimes we say *black*. That means her skin is dark like mine."

"Oh yeah," Faith says. "African American, like my friend Grace. She gets to put her hair in such cool braids. Does your mom have braids?"

Mason shakes his head. "Not anymore, but I think she did when she was a little girl."

She sighs dramatically. "Lucky duck."

"Your hair is very pretty," Mason says.

"Mommy says so, too."

"My friend Mia has hair like yours," he says. "She's Mexican American, too."

"Mia is a pretty name," Faith says, yawning. "I hope I can meet her someday."

"I bet she'd like that a lot," Mason says. He lifts his gaze from Faith to me. Maybe I'm just sick of being saddled with secrets, because I think he knows. I must be more exhausted from the weight of silence than I realized, because I *hope* he knows.

Mason's quiet on the drive home. It's a weird feeling, thinking he might know a secret I've never shared with anyone else. I was able to hide my pregnancy pretty easily. I never got very big, and by the time my belly really popped during those last couple of months, I was staying with Sarah, so nobody back home knew.

At least a hundred times since Faith's birth, I've thought of telling Mia. After Nic died, I wanted nothing more than to let her know that her brother was still here in a way. But I was too selfish. I was afraid Sarah wouldn't forgive me for breaking my promise and would let me see Faith even less than I do now. And even if I could get Sarah onboard, what if telling Mia after so many years of keeping that secret to myself just made her hate me? I was terrified she'd be hurt and I'd lose her.

But as strange as it is to have Mason know, at the same time, it feels right. On the drive home, he reaches over and takes my hand, squeezing it in his. The warmth and tenderness that rushes through me is so overwhelming, my throat goes thick with it.

When we get home, I follow him inside. He puts his keys in the dish by the door and kicks off his shoes before going to the kitchen and pulling a bottle of wine from the fridge.

Standing at the counter opposite me, he pours two glasses. He hands me one. "Do you want to talk about it?"

I open my mouth then close it, still holding the secret close just in case I'm wrong and he didn't figure it out. Mason just did me a bigger favor than he could ever imagine. Not only was he the key to getting Sarah to invite me to dinner, he somehow convinced them to bring Faith over for a visit next week. After giving me a gift like that, now is not the time to play coy. But after six years of silence, I don't know what to say. "I'm not sure I know how," I admit. "I've never talked about it before."

"Not even to Nic?"

Air leaves me in a rush, and the backs of my eyes prick with tears. There it is. He knows. I draw in a deep breath for courage. "Not long after I found out I was pregnant, he was convicted." I shrug, as if that moment hadn't crushed part of me forever. "I had his baby growing in my belly, and he was on his way to prison."

Mason reaches across the counter and grabs my hand. It's the gentle reassurance I need.

"I was just a kid with dreams of having a better life than my mom's, but there I was, following right in her footsteps. Then there was Sarah. She had her life together, you know what I mean? She's ten years older than me, and she and her husband, Greg, had been trying to have a baby for a couple of years with no luck. Because of our age difference, we've never been that close, but I thought to call her to confide my secret. It was like it was meant to be. We were on the same wavelength from the beginning. We both knew there was only one right choice. I was due at the end of the summer, so we made plans that I'd come stay with her until the baby was born, sign over my rights, and be back home in time for the start of my junior year of high school. It was the right thing to do for Faith, if not for me."

"What happened to the husband? Greg?" Mason asks.

I blow out a sharp breath. "Faith was a toddler when he decided this life wasn't for him. This baby they'd been praying for had all but landed in their laps, but it wasn't what he wanted or how he wanted it to happen." My gut twists. "He said he didn't feel the connection. That he'd wanted *his own* child, and Sarah had pushed the adoption on him, but I swear he'd been onboard until they brought her home."

Mason narrows his eyes. “What an asshole.”

“I have no way to prove it, but I think he couldn’t stand that she didn’t look like him. He’d complain to Sarah about how people would stare at them when they were out in public and he felt like they were trying to figure out why his child wasn’t white.” I shake my head, anger at my asshole brother-in-law as fresh as if it had been yesterday and not years ago. “Sarah told him that people stared because Faith was a beautiful baby, but he was so insecure, so worried people would think his wife had cheated on him.”

“People adopt babies who don’t look like them all the time,” Mason says. “This isn’t 1960.”

I smile at him, warmth blooming in my chest and pushing away that old anger. “I know, right?” I sigh. “He felt trapped. Family life wasn’t for him, he said. But he moved to California, and within a year he was remarried with a baby on the way.”

“I’d like to punch this guy.”

“You and me both. It ripped Sarah apart. It was hard for her, you know? He didn’t make a ton of money, but he had a decent job. She’d always stayed at home, first doing the homemaker thing while she tried to get pregnant, then as a stay-at-home mom to Faith. And then he left, and he didn’t just leave her and Faith. He left his job. For about a year, the only income Sarah had was from the odds-and-ends jobs she could do with Faith by her side. She almost lost the house, could barely afford groceries.”

He toys with my fingers and looks up at me through his thick lashes. “And then?” he asks, his voice a low rumble.

"It got better," I say, not sure what he's waiting for. "She made it through, and things got better."

"She made it through because you started stripping and sending her the money."

My heart tugs so hard that I instinctively squeeze his hand. He sees me so clearly that he guessed the truth. Years later, even Sarah, who took the money, can't forgive me for my choices, but Mason *understands*. "It seemed like the least I could do. That whole time was hell on Sarah. A year before she adopted Faith, she lost a foster baby. They had her from the day she left the hospital until she was nine months old. They really believed they'd get to adopt her, but the judge put her back with her mom. It wasn't rational, but I think Sarah was afraid she'd lose Faith, too."

"Do you want her back?"

"No!" I shake my head, and a tremor passes through my whole body, as if I need to shake off the secret thought he dared bring into the light. "I mean, yes. On a completely emotional, non-intellectual level, I'll always wish she could be mine. And if something were to happen to Sarah, I'd hope that I'd get to be the one to raise Faith. But Sarah's her mom, you know? I believed I was doing the best thing for her, and despite all the unexpected bumps in the road, I still believe I did. There was hardly enough room for me and Mom in our trailer. I can't imagine bringing a baby into that space. And then would I have finished high school? Would I have gone to college? Would I have been able to do anything other than strip to care for her? What kind of life is that?

Mom's gone every night, waiting for Daddy to get out of prison and praying he stays straight once he does? It's complicated. I can't pretend that I don't wish she was mine, because I've walked around with a piece of me missing since the day I handed her over in the hospital. She's wanted, but I loved her enough even from that first day to choose to walk around halfhearted. I love her enough that I'd make that choice again."

"I wish I'd had half your courage when I was younger." He shakes his head. "Half your selflessness."

"That's why I'm making the scrapbook," I say. "She'll never meet her father, so I want her to have these pictures. I want her to have something of him."

Mason puts his wine glass down and studies me. "You amaze me." Stepping around the island, he takes my glass out of my hand to put it on the counter. He pulls my body against his and lowers his mouth to mine, and I melt into him. We've kissed thousands of times before tonight, but now something's changed. He knows about Faith. I've been frozen in ice, and he's the sun, slowly setting me free.

His hands are gentle on me, sliding over my hair, slipping under my shirt, skimming across my belly. Every touch makes me want to get closer, to show him more. My love for Mason has kept me on the precipice for years, and I've always been afraid to jump. In this moment, I believe he'd catch me. He'd forgive me.

He unbuttons my jeans, but I stop him before he can push them from my hips. I can't let this just be about me. Not tonight. I fumble between our bodies until I find the button to his jeans.

It releases, followed by the slow slide of his zipper. I slide a hand inside his briefs, and we both groan. I drag my fist over him in long, tight strokes.

His hips jut forward as he thrusts himself against my hand. With a handful of my hair in his fist, he brings my mouth back to his. His kisses are harder now, deeper and more demanding. When we break it, our bodies rocking toward each other, I lock my gaze with his before I drop to my knees.

"Fuck, Bailey," he breathes.

I keep one hand wrapped around the base of his cock and settle the other on his hip as I open my mouth and slide it over him, taking him deep, using my tongue and my cheeks. He loosens his grip on my hair, and I moan as he gently guides me back and forth over the length of him. I can tell he's trying to slow me down, trying to make this last.

It's not long before he guides me to my feet, and I'm so desperate for him, I don't object. He leads me upstairs and into the bedroom. We watch each other while we strip, and when we climb into bed, he settles on top of me, his hands framing my face, his length positioned between my legs.

After tonight, I feel as if I'm naked for the first time, as if he's really seeing me and isn't running away.

"I can get a condom," he says. Other than our one time without in the pool, we've been using protection. "If you're worried about . . ."

"I'm on the pill, but if you'd rather . . ."

We stare at each other for several breaths before he grins. "I'd rather have nothing between us. I'm trying to be considerate."

"It's okay. I was on nothing but stupidity when I got pregnant with Faith." I lift my hips. "I like you like this."

His eyes close as he slides into me, and the sound of his satisfied exhale is as exhilarating as the way he fills me. "You feel amazing," he murmurs against my mouth.

We've had sex a hundred times, but tonight we find a new rhythm. Our movements are slower, our caresses more lingering. I'm liquid set free and slowly rolling out to meet the sea.

CHAPTER 29

BAILEY

I know we should sleep—he has to be up early for practice before the team leaves for New York for their first regular season game, and I have an appointment with a new client—but neither of us seems inclined. We made love and then showered together, and now we're in bed, lying on our sides and looking into each other's eyes.

"Tell me about Nic," Mason says.

At first I don't think I heard him right. Mason hated Nic, and tonight has been about us. "What?"

"Tell me about Nic Mendez. I've been a jerk about him, but I think I understand now why he was so important to you." He tucks my hair behind my ear and brushes my cheek with the rough pad of his thumb. "I want to know all of you, Bailey. Even the pieces that will never be mine."

Something in my chest aches at the idea of Mason believing

I picked Nic over him. I suppose in a way I did. But I was picking Nic's *life* over my happiness. Mason was so damn *good.* He could have anyone, and I was sure he'd eventually want someone better than me. "He wasn't all bad," I say. "He spent a lot of years trying to ignore me and doing his damnedest to convince me he wasn't interested. But I wore him down."

"Mmm." His chest rumbles with his groan. "To be pursued by Bailey Green. Poor guy. Sounds like a really rough life."

"I'd think you'd know something about it. I've spent an embarrassing amount of the last three years trying to get you to sleep with me again."

"Ah, yes, but I wanted more than your body." There's no bitterness in his words. Just truth. His hand cups my ass, and he tugs me closer so our hips are pressed against each other. "What else?"

"He was stubborn and reckless. But he could also be sweet and thoughtful."

"Thoughtful, like flowers and poetry?"

I laugh. "No. Nic definitely wasn't a poet. He didn't talk much at all, actually. I talked enough for both of us."

Mason's quiet now, skimming his knuckles back and forth over my arm as he listens. I've never gotten to talk about Nic like this, and it's both odd and touching that Mason is giving me the chance.

"He'd take me out. Neither of us had any money, so dates would be grabbing a pizza and a six-pack and going to the lake. Sometimes he'd drive me to the airport and we'd watch the planes take off in the dark. It was always a push-pull with him. Like he was the ocean and I was the shore. He'd come and then he'd pull away, and then he'd return only to pull away again, every time taking a little more of me with him."

"Do you think you two would be together now if he hadn't died?"

I shake my head. "I wasn't with him before he died. I still loved him, but he kept pushing me away."

"What would have happened if he hadn't been arrested? Would you have kept the baby?"

I roll to my back and stretch my arms above my head. "If he hadn't been caught, I imagine we would have tried to raise the baby ourselves. We hadn't gotten that far yet. He was arrested only a few days after I found out I was pregnant, and we were still trying to digest the information."

"I can't imagine what that must have been like for you." Mason settles the flat of his palm against my belly. "You were practically still a child and pregnant, and he wasn't there to help."

"Before he was arrested, I imagined he'd get us a little apartment, and he'd clean up his act. We'd be another young couple just scraping by, but it would be fine because at the end of the day, we'd get to come home to each other and maybe the baby would be the thing to finally make him go straight." I close my eyes, and it's as if the room disappears around me. I'm back in Nic's room watching him pace a hole into the carpet. He tried to be calm, but the idea of having a kid had terrified him.

MASON

Seconds stretch into minutes, and even though her body is next to me, her mind is somewhere else. The click of the ceiling fan overhead measures time while I wait, giving her the space the subject matter demands. I wonder if she's done talking tonight. Maybe I should let it go. Maybe I should tell her my own secret and just how well I understand what she's been through. She finally opens her eyes. "It's my fault he got caught."

"Bailey, no." I rub my thumb beneath her breasts. "Don't do that to yourself. He made his own decisions."

She swallows. "But it's true. I knew he was doing some minor deals for this guy in town—Clarence. Clarence had a way of keeping his boys under his thumb. Once you got in, it was almost impossible to get out. The day Nic got caught, I'd heard him talking to Clarence about an exchange. Nic wasn't going to be able to do it, because the other guy didn't like him. I called in a tip to the cops, thinking it was my chance to bring down Clarence so Nic could go straight."

"But Nic ended up being the one to do the exchange," I finish, because I can tell saying the words out loud is tearing her apart.

She nods. "If I hadn't made that call, they wouldn't have pulled him over. He wouldn't have been sent to prison, and we would have kept the baby."

"Nic made his own choices. He was arrested because he was

breaking the law." I press a kiss to her bare shoulder. "You don't need this guilt weighing you down."

"The worst part," she whispers, "isn't just that it was my fault he was arrested. The worst part is that, more than once, I've thought how grateful I am that he was put away."

I draw in breath. I didn't expect that. I thought she'd have done anything to keep Nic.

She rolls to face me again and curls her arms into her chest. "I hate that he had to go to prison and I still loved him, but we did the very best thing we could have done for Faith. I don't think I would have been brave enough to do it if he hadn't been in such trouble."

"You have more courage than anyone I know."

"Then why can't I find the courage to be with you?"

I pull her close and bury my face in her shoulder to hide my expression. I love that she's opened up to me, but I still don't know where I stand with her or if she still has secrets. Why else would she need courage?

I comb my fingers through her hair and pull back to look in her eyes. My secrets can wait. Tonight is about her. "He was your first love. I'm not asking you to forget him." *You can tell me the rest.*

"Nobody ever asks me about him. Even Mia. It still makes her sad to talk about him, and since she doesn't know about Faith, I'm always careful about what I say. So, thank you."

"You can tell me anything."

"People think I'm an open book because I don't mind talking

about the stupid shit people are quiet about. But I have secrets, too. Just like everybody else."

"I know."

"It's hard for me to share them."

"I know."

She flips over so her back is against my front. "I'm so tired of hiding my mistakes."

I wrap my arm around her and squeeze her tightly. Faith is her big secret, but there's more.

For now, I'll take what I've been given. I don't have a choice. She's not the only one with secrets. She said Nic was the ocean to her shore, taking more of her with him every time he'd pull away, and I understand that feeling all too well. I'm afraid if she leaves me again, I'll be an empty shell.

CHAPTER 30

MASON

Owen hands me a steaming mug of coffee and leans against the counter. "How'd the early meeting with coach go?"

"It was fine."

"*Fine.* Listen to you, communicating like a sullen woman."

Sunday was shit. The first regular season game of the year and they only put me in on special teams. I met with the Gators head coach this morning and asked point-blank why and got the runaround.

"Bill still giving you the cold shoulder about your new wife?"

I shrug. Bill McCombs needs to back off and let the people he hired run his team, but the Gators is a baby franchise, and he's been very hands-on—to the point where he never misses a team meeting and isn't afraid to tell his coaches how to do their jobs. Or when to bench a player who should be in the game. "Coach spent a lot of time this morning making sure I knew that the rookie is better than they expected."

"Fraser?" Owen shakes his head. "The boy can catch a ball, but he's gotta play catch-up between the ears if he wants a long career."

"I hate being on Bill's shit list." I squeeze the back of my neck. "How about we change the subject?"

"Sure. Let's talk about your wife instead." His face stretches into a shit-eating grin. "I am *always* up for talking about Bailey."

"You're lucky I need this caffeine in my bloodstream more than I want to throw this coffee in your face."

"I can't help it that you married the finest piece of ass I've ever set eyes on."

I glare at him. "Fuck you. She's so much more than a piece of ass."

He throws up his hands. "Exactly. Why the hell do you think I'm so jealous?"

I sigh. "You can't have her, so stop."

"You were pretty damn smart, marrying her like that. What's that old saying? If you love someone, let her go. If she returns to you, it was meant to be. If she doesn't . . . get her drunk and marry her in Vegas?"

My lips twist into a smile despite myself, then I go serious. "Can you blame me for trying?" I rub the back of my neck. "I don't want to lose her. I just have to make her fall for me before I run out of time. If she goes back to Blackhawk Valley, I don't know when I'll get another chance."

"How's Operation Fake Marriage going for you?"

I look out the window. From here, we can see down into the practice arena inside the Gators' complex, and there's my competition, putting in extra time and running plays with Dre. "Far better than I ever expected."

"Right," Owen says, "which totally explains why you say that like someone ran over your dog. Disappointed that it's not settling the playing field with Bill? It was a long shot, but it was worth it. And hey, if you get the girl in the end, Bill can fuck himself."

"That's a big *if*, Owen."

He hums. "The question is, at what point did this become less about your career and more about trying to win the girl?"

I take a long pull of my coffee. Didn't my sister essentially ask the same question? "It's always been about her. Even when I didn't want it to be." I turn back to him. "I have to try."

"You'd be crazy if you didn't."

"The man she loved died, and she's still not over him. She's starting to open up to me. Four fucking years, and she's finally telling me her secrets. But the days are going by too fast. She's been here almost a month already, and I think she's still planning to leave."

"You mean her old boyfriend? The one who was in prison?"

"He wasn't her boyfriend. He was just . . ." *More important to her than I ever could have realized.* "He was stringing her on. How insane is it that I'm the man in her bed every night and I still feel like I can't measure up to a dead man?"

He studies me for a beat. "You really think it's that simple?"

I know it's not that simple. Bailey's not the only one with secrets, and as much as I've told myself mine were justified, my sister's warning looms over me.

Four years ago . . .

I know I'm a first-level creeper for following Bailey's ex, but I had to. She's pulled away from me so completely since he's been released, and I know it's because of him. I just need to know she's safe, that he's turned over a new leaf. I fucking *hoped* that was what I'd find out. Instead, it took me a week to discover that the piece of shit is still doing the same crap that got him put behind bars to begin with.

I followed him to the Cavern tonight, but this time it's not because I want to see what he's up to. No. This time I'm following Nic because we need to talk.

I wait until he heads to the back door for a cigarette and I step in front of him, blocking his path.

He looks me over once before lifting his chin. "You're the guy my girl's been fucking? Mason, is it?"

It makes my stomach turn to hear him talk about her like that—saying *the guy my girl's been fucking* the way someone else might say *the guy my girl works with*. It's no wonder Bailey thinks so little of what she has to offer outside the bedroom. "Does she know you're still dealing?" It's the only question that matters, and I refuse to take the bait on anything else.

He stiffens, and his nostrils flare. He can handle that Bailey slept with me, but it riles him that I see him for what he is. "You think you know things? Rich boy, you don't know shit."

"She was over you. Then you got out of prison and started fucking with her mind again. You made her believe you're someone you're not." I shake my head. "If you can't stay clean, then you stay the hell away from her."

"Why would I do that? Because you said so?" His lips twist into a smile. "You think I'm going to back off just because you got a taste of her and want some more? Because lemme tell you, you're not the only guy who's had a good time with her. You're not special."

It's like he *wants* me to break his nose. "I'm not. But she is." I shake my head and back away. "Fuck this. You're not worth it. I'll just tell Bailey who you really are."

His face pales. "She won't believe you."

I shrug. "That's up to her."

He looks around, confirming we're still alone. "Say I'm willing to let her go so you can have your chance. What's in it for me? How much?"

CHAPTER 31

MASON

Present day . . .

"We were just putting together our RSVPs for the anniversary party," Mom says. It's her regular Saturday morning call where we catch up and she guilts me for not visiting more. "Were you planning on bringing Bailey?"

"Is there a reason I wouldn't bring my wife?" I hate that she's even asking, but more than that, I hate that there's part of me that doesn't want to bring Bailey. If she knew that, she'd think it was because I was ashamed of her, and that's not it.

I'm ashamed of the world I come from—the excess, the money. After seeing the reality that other people live in, after coming face to face with the conditions Bailey knew growing up, returning to my parents' world and all the luxuries they take for granted just makes me feel like an asshole.

I'm going to take Bailey to a party for which my parents shelled out thousands and thousands of dollars to entertain themselves and their friends for one night. I get it. They want to celebrate, and they have the means to indulge in this kind of extravagance. It's the only way they'd want to celebrate, and it's the kind of party their friends will expect.

But worse than all my shame about the extravagance is knowing how she'll be treated. My parents aren't good at hiding their feelings, and they don't approve of Bailey.

"Yes. Bailey and I will both be there, and if you could treat her like an equal, I might even stay all night."

"I was just asking." She sighs softly, but I can still hear the disappointment. "How's it going—your new life and marriage?"

I can tell I hurt her feelings, but fuck. When does it start to matter that she's hurt mine over and over again by judging the woman I love? "Things are fine . . . *good*," I say, correcting myself more forcefully than I should. But the truth is, even though Bailey opened up to me last weekend, I don't know if I'm any closer to getting her to give me a real chance. "It's been nice to have her here."

"Do you think it'll be different when the season's over and you don't spend so much time away from home?"

By *different* does Mom mean *worse*? Or am I just being defensive? *If Bailey's still here at all.* She will be, right? She's making friends here, and in only a month her business has grown into something she could make a long career out of. She opened up to me about her relationship with Nic and her sister . . . She's in my bed every night.

"It'll be great," I say.

"I hope so. It just seemed like it was all so sudden."

"I've been in love with her for four years. I don't think there's anything sudden about that." I make a fist and then release it. Things have been a lot better between me and my parents in the last couple of years, and having Bailey back in my life is making me defensive. "Mom, I need you to promise me something."

"What is it?"

"I know you do things because you have my best interests at heart, but I need you to promise me that you will not meddle in my marriage. I don't care how good your reasons are. If you have a concern, I need you to promise me you'll come to me with it and then trust me to make the right decision or to deal with the consequences if I don't."

"Is this about what happened in high school?" she asks. "Is it about the baby?"

I sink into a chair and rest my face in my hand. "Yes. Kind of."

"Is Bailey pregnant?"

"No, Mom. She's not. But maybe someday she will be." I close my eyes, because the thought slams me in the chest with hope. I want her to have my babies, but first, I have to confess my secrets and convince her to stay despite them. "Or maybe she won't. But regardless, this is my life."

"I'm sorry for what we did, baby. But look where you are now."

"It would have been nice if you'd believed in me enough to

think I could get here even with a child. I need you to let me live my life without you removing all the obstacles."

I can hear her sniffle and feel like a jackass for making my mom cry, but it needed to be said. "I promise," she whispers.

"Thank you. I needed to hear that."

"I'll talk to you soon. Love you."

"Love you too."

I grab a bottle of water from the fridge and walk to the back door. Outside, Bailey is lying by the pool. She told me she's a sun worshipper, but she looks like the goddess in her black bikini, her tanned legs stretched in front of her. As if she can feel me looking at her, she props herself up on her elbows, pulls off her sunglasses, and blows me a kiss. I grin at her. In moments like this, I believe everything is going to be okay, and I cling to that confidence before it can fade.

BAILEY

"Are you pregnant yet?" I ask Mia as I pour two cups of coffee from the pot in Mason's kitchen.

She smirks. "No. Are you?"

"Very funny."

The Bears play the Gators in their second regular season game at the Gators' stadium tomorrow, and this means I get to spend the weekend with my best friend, Mia, because her husband plays for the Bears.

I hand over her mug and add cream and sugar to my coffee. "Will you stay here tonight?" I ask.

Mia grins. "I was hoping you'd ask. Sleeping in hotel rooms alone while they travel totally blows. I wish they'd let him share a room with me."

I wiggle my eyebrows. "They know he wouldn't sleep if he shared a bed with you."

Her cheeks turn a pretty shade of pink. "This might be true. So how's it going? I want to know everything."

I bite my lip, but my mouth betrays me and smiles anyway. "It's been good. Everything, I mean. I've been able to work. I have four to six appointments a week already on the schedule through to the day I'm supposed to leave, and I can hardly keep up with the messages from other prospective clients. Who knew there was such an untapped market for boudoir photos?"

"That's great! And you were worried you wouldn't make any money while you were down here."

I swallow. "Yeah, money hasn't been an issue." *Any more than it always is,* I think, because I was barely staying afloat before. "I'm making more down here on my photography alone than I did in Blackhawk Valley running the bar and doing boudoir sessions. And I've gotten to spend time with my niece." Guilt rears its head at the mention of Faith, so I quickly change the subject. "Never mind that I get to look at the ocean every single day. I love it here."

"Are you thinking of making your move permanent?"

I twist my hair into a sloppy bun on top of my head and use the tie from my wrist to hold it in place. "Things had gotten pretty lonely for me in Blackhawk Valley. Everybody's gone. But I have part of the crew here. And there's a bigger market for my business, and my sister . . ." I shrug. "Yeah, I'm definitely considering the move."

She arches a brow and looks around the living room. "Like making *this* permanent? With Mason?"

"No." I shake my head. That's gotten more complicated since our night in the pool and Faith's birthday. It's gotten more complicated since I've gotten used to sleeping in his arms. "I still can't be with Mason. I can't change that I took that money or how his family feels about me. But maybe he and I could be friends?"

She folds her arms. "Friends?"

"Stop looking at me that way. I know better than to want more. This isn't just about the money, it's also about . . ." I blow out a breath. "Look at this place. I don't belong here."

"And yet being here has made you consider uprooting your life to move to Florida."

"Yes, Florida, but not Mason's house. Hell, not even Seaside, because no one can afford to *live* here."

She purses her lips and studies me. "Have you told Mason that you're thinking about making your move permanent?"

"I haven't. I have to figure out how to approach that. I don't want it to be weird for him to have his ex-wife live in town."

She shakes her head and walks forward to grab my hand. "Then don't be his *ex*."

"This is only for four months, Mia. That hasn't changed."

"But you're sleeping together," she says, because apparently, she knows me too well and can read my mind.

"We're . . ." I look away and my cheeks heat. "It just happened." Again, I try to bite back a smile, and she laughs.

"Okay, you don't have to give me details. I'm just making observations. We're talking about the future, so I think we need to keep in mind your evolving relationship with Mason."

"His dad visited the other day." I look outside but don't really see what's in front of me. I see the obstacles between me and Mason. "He pulled out a checkbook and asked for my number."

"Why?"

"He wants to make sure I walk away at the end of the season."

"You're not thinking of taking his money, are you?"

"No. God, no." I shake my head. "When I did it before, I had a reason. I didn't think I had a choice, but the fact that he's offering now shows just what he thinks of me. That's why I can't be with Mason. Even if I told him the truth, the past would never go away. My relationship with his parents would always be contentious." I turn toward her and away from the calming view.

"They made their bed," she says. "Let them lie in it."

"But what about me? Do I want to be the loathed daughter-in-law? Just the way Christian looks at me makes me feel like I need to enroll in a self-esteem course. How can I have a healthy marriage if he's so tied to it?" Just thinking about it, my heart races as if I've been running down the beach. "I can't undo what I did." I meet her eyes and think of Faith when I add, "Some decisions have long-term consequences, no matter how sorry you are or how willing you are to come clean."

"I want to believe Mason's dad is better than you've made him out to be."

I grunt. "He's worse."

"I refuse to give up hope. If Arrow and I can figure it out, I choose to believe you and Mason can, too."

I shake my head. "How on earth did I end up with an optimist for a best friend?"

"You just got lucky, I guess."

The bar is packed after the Gators beat the Bears. Mason didn't play much, and that makes two games in a row. Mia told me not to worry, but I could see the concern in her eyes when she watched them send the rookie out instead of Mason.

Mia convinced me to come here after the game, but she disappeared as soon as Arrow showed up. I scan the crowd for Mason, who got pulled away shortly after he and his teammates arrived half an hour ago. I can hang at the bar with the best of them, but tonight I'd rather be home with Mason, curled up on the couch and watching a movie.

"There are a bunch of guys from the Gators here tonight," the girl beside me says, scanning the crowd.

I force myself to smile and turn toward her. "There sure are."

"Have you seen Mason Dahl?"

I frown, my defenses going up. Does this woman know Mason? Is she some old girlfriend? Maybe a one-night stand? She looks like someone Mason should be with. Perfect skin, long hair, big boobs. *Rich.* "I'm sure he's here somewhere."

"I need to talk to his wife. I want her to do some pictures for me." She spins closer, shifting to a conspiratorial whisper before I have the chance to reply. "Did you know she does dirty pictures? The girls call them stripper pics because"—she inches closer and lowers her voice further—"she used to actually *work the pole*, you know what I mean?"

Who *wouldn't* know what she means? I blink at her, still processing the idea that the women down here call my boudoir portraits *stripper pics*. It was bad enough having Lindy know, but *everyone* knows? I have a packed schedule, and is this why? Because they want to dabble in being trashy for a minute? *Fucking fantastic.*

"Rumor is, that's how Mason met her, and their first night together was *paid for*. How raunchy is that? And he *married her*?"

"Rumor?" I ask, my voice cracking.

"Can you imagine a guy like that settling for a stripper when he could really have anyone he wanted?" She giggles and sways a little, and I realize for the first time that she's toasted. "Fuck, if he wanted me, I'd drop James in a New York minute and jump straight into his bed."

"That's says a lot about you," I mutter.

"Apparently, her pictures are really sexy and the boys appreciate them. *A lot.* Dre bought Julia diamond earrings after she gave him her set. This girl has the background for that kind of thing, you know? She knows what men think is hot. I think my husband would fucking *love* the idea of a stripper taking nude pics of me." She grins and rubs her hands together. "I can practically smell my kitchen remodel when I think about it."

The women are using my pictures to convince their husbands to give them diamond earrings and kitchen remodels?

My stomach turns, but I smile and extend my hand. "I think I'm the one you're looking for. My name's Bailey. I'm Mason's wife."

The laughter falls from her face, and to her credit, she looks truly horrified. "Oh my God. You must think I'm such a bitch. I'm so sorry. I'm kind of drunk."

"I noticed."

"Don't take the stripper pics thing the wrong way. Everybody *loves* your work. It's just that, I don't know, maybe we're all a little intimidated by your past. I'm so sorry. Please don't hate me."

I make myself take one breath and then the next. I don't hate her, but some days I really hate this world Mason's a part of. I hate the money and the greed and the superficial kindness. I miss my old life in Blackhawk Valley—the life I had in college, when all my friends were close. I miss the days when I didn't have to choose between loneliness and trying to blend into a world where I clearly don't belong.

"I needed money," I say, and it's so unlike me to defend myself that I immediately wish I could take the words back, but I've already started, so I continue. "I met Mason at a party, not at a strip club, but it's true I was a stripper. I've never tried to pretend I'm someone I'm not."

"Of course you wouldn't," she says, all cheer and friendliness. "You're *real.* Not like these fake bitches."

Does her easy willingness to put her friends in the category of *fake bitch* mean that I'm supposed to believe she belongs in a *different* category? I just stare.

"Can you forgive me and still take my pictures? James's birthday is coming up, and I just want to surprise him."

"With *stripper pics.*" Just saying the words hurts my heart. I'm proud of the work I do. It's not trashy at all. Climbing a pole and shaking my ass may have been cheap, but not the pictures I take.

Mason sidles up to me. "Oh, I see you've met Jimmy's wife. Hadley, isn't it?"

Hadley cuts her eyes to Mason and back to me. She looks like a kid who just got caught skipping school.

"Yeah," I say, not taking my gaze off Hadley. "She already knew all about me."

He grins and lowers his mouth to my ear so Hadley can't hear him. "I told you word would spread. You've totally got this. Run with it. Make it something big."

Tears burn the back of my eyes. I spent years stripping for money and never feeling ashamed of it. It was the best choice for me at the time, and I'd rather exploit my body on my terms than someone else's. But in this world and in this context, I feel shame, and *that* pisses me off. Why should I have to feel ashamed just because they're laughing behind my back? Why should I have to explain myself when it was my choice to make?

"How much longer do you want to stay?" I ask Mason, trying to keep my blue mood from my face and voice.

He turns me toward him and wraps his other arm around me, holding my front to his. "You wanna get out of here sooner rather than later?"

I nod, too worried that tears might come out with my words.

"I'll take you home and keep you in bed for a while," he murmurs into my ear. He cups my face in one big hand and rubs his thumb along my jaw line. "I could definitely get onboard with that plan."

CHAPTER 32

MASON

"Are you sure you're okay?" I toss my keys into the dish and place my hands on Bailey's shoulders. She was quiet the whole ride home.

"I'm fine."

What is it about that word that's so completely unconvincing? "That's been your response to everything I've asked you since we left. The game was fine, you had a fine time at the bar, you're fine, meeting people was *fine*. I might not be a woman or a genius at reading them, but I am quite familiar with the concept of *fine* meaning anything but."

Her eyes blaze. "That's the most sexist thing I've ever heard you say."

I drop my hands. She's in the mood to fight. Well, *fine*. I think I'd rather her fight and scream at me than clam up like she has. "Okay. Then I'm a sexist asshole, but it's true. You're not fine."

"No. I'm not. But who cares? I made an appearance at the bar and acted like your wife. Mission accomplished. Who cares that I'm a joke? Except you. Maybe you care. Hell, I'm kind of embarrassed on your behalf."

What the fuck is going on here? Weren't we good yesterday, and now we're back to this? I take a breath and pray for patience. "What exactly are you embarrassed about?"

"They don't understand why you'd marry a stripper. Isn't that kind of trashy?" She leans forward and lowers her voice to a whisper. "Rumor has it, the first night we slept together, you paid for it."

I squeeze my eyes shut, and my blood turns cold. "Who said that?"

"They all said that. The *girls*. The players' wives and girlfriends. Hadley told me that they call my business *stripper pics,* and they think I'm good at it because after years of being a stripper, I know what turns men on."

Oh, shit. I don't know Hadley very well, and I've never liked her much. This certainly doesn't help her case. I have a lot of trouble believing that all of the guys' wives and girlfriends would think of Bailey that way. The thing with football is that even though we make good money once we're here, most of these guys didn't come from wealthy families. Many players were first-generation college students, guys whose parents never would have been able to afford to put them in peewee ball if they hadn't been able to play on scholarship.

I know Bailey is insecure about her past and her social status when it comes to being around people she deems higher class than her, but her childhood isn't that far removed from the one a lot of these guys experienced. And their wives come from all different walks of life, too, so if they're calling her business stripper pics, it's most likely because they're uncomfortable with the idea of posing for sexy photos, not because they're mocking her past.

"I'll talk to James about Hadley."

"You're telling her husband on her?"

"Yeah, I am. I won't have anyone talking about my wife that way. I knew she was immature and catty, but that's over the line."

"You can't talk to every one of your teammates about me. One, that's absurd, and two, that's even more embarrassing than having them talk shit behind my back."

"I don't need to talk to all of them," I say, treading carefully. "Hadley's just one person, and I think she's made it clear that she's not a very good one."

"She talked about it like there's this whole rumor mill that gossips about me that way." She shoves her hands in her hair and stares up at the ceiling as she tugs on it.

I have a sister. I know girls can be mean and two-faced, but I feel helpless. I don't want anything scaring Bailey away, but on an even more basic level, I can't stand seeing her this hurt.

"And you know what I hate the most? I hate that I fucking *care*. Before I came here, if you'd told me that a bunch of your NFL player friends' wives called my business *stripper pics*, if you'd told me that they all believed I was a whore, I wouldn't have cared. But now I do. Now it feels like this giant insult. I've lived here, and some of those women *know* me, and still that's all they see when they look at me."

"Maybe Hadley, maybe a couple of others too, but not everyone. The guys love you. You are *more* than your past."

"You know that's all Lindy sees." She pauses for a beat and meets my eyes. "You know that's all your parents see."

I step forward, pull her hands from her hair, and place them at her sides before cupping her face. "Can we talk for a minute about what *I* see?" I study her—her big eyes, her perfect bow-shaped lips. "Because I see the most beautiful woman I've ever met. I see a woman who has sacrificed more for the people she loves than anyone else I know would." I drag my eyes over her body and back up to her face. "I see someone who's so precious to me, I hate letting her go when I wake in the morning. Someone who's so good right here." I place my hand to the middle of her chest, between her breasts. "Someone who has such a good heart that I know I'm the luckiest sonofabitch anywhere because she gave me a chance. I see a woman I don't want to lose. A woman I'd fight for and give anything for, even if that means telling bitches like Hadley where they can shove it or buying you the house next door to your sister in Rock Hill so you don't have to deal with the bullshit of girls like Hadley when I'm not around."

"Mason—"

"Anything, Bailey. I see a woman I'd do *anything* to keep in my life. Even things I shouldn't." I swallow back my guilt. "I see a woman who's so unaware of her worth that even as I stand here and say it out loud, I know she doesn't believe she can take what I'm offering."

Tears slide from her eyes and down her cheeks, where they wet my thumbs. "I hate them," she says. "I hate them all so much."

I'm not even sure who she means—women like Hadley and Lindy? Everybody in this town? The people from her past? But I just whisper, "I know," and pull her into my chest, saying a silent, desperate prayer.

Please stay with me. Please let me prove this can work.

BAILEY

"Why do you always know exactly what to say?" I ask. That little speech about what he sees when he looks at me might as well have been stolen from my dreams.

Mason rubs my back. "I just say what I mean."

He's so warm, and it feels so good to be in his arms. I feel like I'm safe. Like I'm forgiven. Like I'm enough.

When I reach up to touch his face—to make sure this is real and that he is too—my hands are shaking. "I've done things, Mason. If you knew all my secrets, you might not want me forever."

"You don't have to worry about that. I've wanted you from the beginning, and I've never stopped. The question is whether or not you want me."

I bite my lip. "Of course I do."

His exhale is heavy, and he pulls me fast against his chest. "Thank God. I'm so fucking in love with you. I don't want to pretend I'm okay with doing this life without you."

"I love you too," I whisper, closing my eyes, searching for my bravery. I always thought people who fiercely pursued their dreams were fearless. There's nothing more terrifying than accepting the life you want. There is no test of your own self-love and acceptance as great as trying to live your dreams. Do I deserve this? Am I good enough to keep it? What if I'm not?

He pulls back and his lips part. "Say that again."

"I love you?"

He swallows. "I'm going to need to talk to the coaches about taking the next week off."

"Why's that?"

"The girl I've loved for four years finally loves me in return. If I had my way, I'd keep her in bed for a week straight."

Joy surges in my chest, but I play it cool and put my finger to my mouth. "Wouldn't we get bored?" Mason scoops me into his arms, and I squeak. "What are you doing?"

"I'm taking my wife to bed," he says. His voice is so low and husky it's like fingertips grazing between my legs.

I loop my arms behind his neck and grin, because scary is also good. So damn good.

When we get to the bedroom, he lowers me to my feet and turns me around so he can unzip my dress. As it falls into a puddle around my feet, I hear his intake of breath, feel the heat of his eyes taking me in. I step out of the dress and turn to face him. "Do you like?" I ask. I'm wearing a new black lace panty set I bought when Mia and I went shopping yesterday. It was a splurge, but seeing his face now makes it totally worth it.

His nostrils flare and his eyes dilate. "Fuck yes." He unbuttons his shirt in record time, pulling it off and tugging his undershirt over his head. "You're perfect. Everything about you is perfect."

I stand, and he comes toward me, shirtless and strong and beautiful. His hands settle on my hips, his thumbs skimming over my navel and then along the lace below. He lowers his mouth to mine as he explores my body as if he's never seen it before. His kiss is long and slow, and his hands follow suit.

"I wouldn't change a thing about you or about your past," he says. "Because you're here now and that's all that matters."

"I have a child, too."

The words jerk me from my peaceful, post-coital half-sleep state, and I'm sure I didn't hear him right. We're in bed, naked limbs tangled together, one of his hands in my hair, the other flat against my back as he looks into my eyes.

"You do? A child?"

His jaw hardens just a bit before he lets out a long breath. "Yeah. I don't know his name or where he is, or anything about him other than the day he was born."

I never imagined Mason would have secrets like mine. Isn't

that the perk of having money? You don't have to have secrets. "What happened?"

"I wish I could say I was as noble as you were." He grimaces. "I think it's amazing what you did. You carried a baby and let her best interests lead your decisions. I wasn't that mature."

"I was terrified, Mason. Not a martyr."

He tucks my hair behind my ear. "You were amazing."

"Tell me what happened with your child."

"I was in high school and in love. I was an idiot. I didn't *care* for sex with condoms. She was on the pill so I figured it didn't matter, but apparently, if you're not great about taking your pill regularly, it matters quite a bit.

"It was my senior year. I had a full ride to BHU and it really looked like I could do something with football. And then she got pregnant." He releases me and rolls to his back, stretching his arms above his head and looking at the ceiling. "I was so scared. But it was my baby, you know? Like, sure, it was scary, but there was joy there, too. How can you not be happy about a child? But my parents had other plans for me, and they were beyond disappointed."

My stomach knots, because I can already predict where this is going, and I don't like it. "Oh, no."

"I had a full ride, but I knew I wouldn't be able to have a job. If she came with me, how were we going to take care of the baby while I was busy with school and football and everything else?"

I place a hand on his chest just so he won't feel alone. Because I never knew this about Mason, and I can tell that sharing this story is a big deal. He grabs my hand and squeezes before bringing it to his mouth and kissing my knuckles.

"So I told my parents that the way I saw it, we had a choice. They could either help us out so she could come with me, and I could move forward with my football career. Or if they didn't want anything to do with it, I could decline the scholarship, stay with her, get a job, and be a father to my child. To me, there was no option that didn't involve being a father."

"That's amazing. You were brave. I can't imagine being with someone who'd be willing to give up so much for me."

He turns his head and meets my eyes, his gaze intense before he turns away. "My parents didn't see it that way. They saw options I wouldn't have considered. And while I shut down that conversation before they even got it started, she listened to what they had to say, and when they pulled out their checkbook, she took what they had to offer." He swallows hard. "She didn't believe in abortion, so she ruled that out, but adoption . . . well, she was scared too. She wasn't ready to be a mom, and I can't blame her for that. I *don't* blame her for that. But it's that she made the decision with them and not with me. It's that they took a decision that should have been part mine out of my hands. I always felt like my parents meddled too much in my life, but I never realized how far they were willing to go to control me."

I cling to his hand and squeeze my eyes shut. God, if I'd known, would I have taken the money? Christian knew exactly what he was doing when he made that offer. He warned me that

Mason would never forgive me if he believed I'd taken the money, but I had no way of realizing how deep those feelings went. "Your father really didn't want you to be with her, did he?"

He huffs. "Quite the opposite. He was banking on us ending up together—but only after I'd finished college and been drafted, only after she'd finished her marketing degree." He makes a throaty sound that's pretty close to a growl. "It wasn't enough to plan out my life. He wanted me to follow his plan, on *his* timetable. My opinions, my feelings, all irrelevant."

"That's insane. I'm so sorry, Mason."

"If my parents ever try to get to you, just tell me, okay? My father doesn't understand that the world is not his to control."

I squeeze my eyes shut, wishing his understanding of his father's true nature would work to my benefit but knowing that the opposite is true. "So that was the end between you and the girl?"

He draws me against his chest and kisses the top of my head. "She could have talked to me. She could have told me she was scared or that she didn't want a baby. But she just disappeared instead. Left me and gave our child away without even warning me."

Could you ever forgive her? I think, but I'm too afraid to ask the question, too afraid what the answer might mean for *us*.

"It's better this way. My son has loving parents who wanted him, and I'm not stuck in some loveless marriage with Lindy."

Lindy was the one who had his baby. Lindy took his father's money, and now he hates her more than I'd realized he was capable of hating anyone. What happens when I tell him I took Christian's money too? I'm glad he has me clutched so tightly to his chest. Maybe he won't notice I'm shaking.

CHAPTER 33

MASON

"We should start using condoms again," Bailey says. I frown at my phone as I climb the stairs to my hotel room. One, I wouldn't relish going back to having a barrier between us when we make love, and two, this isn't the conversation I expected to have when I called to say goodnight.

It's been six days since she said those magic words to me—*I love you*—and I told her about Lindy taking money from my parents. I'm in San Diego with the team, and I should probably be dreading tomorrow and another game on the bench. Instead, I can't stop thinking about my wife waiting for me at home.

"Why are you thinking about condoms?" I ask.

Bailey sighs. "I was just thinking about your story and how Lindy got pregnant when you were in high school. I'm good about taking my pill every day, but I don't want you to think I'd be offended if you wanted to double up."

"I'd only be worried if I weren't prepared for an accidental pregnancy. But it's your body, Bailey. If you want to use condoms then we will."

"No, it's not about that. I just thought it might be a tricky subject for you, given your past."

I round the corner and jog up the last flight of stairs. I can't believe we're having this conversation on the phone, but she brought it up. "I don't want extra protection, because I don't mind the idea of you carrying my baby." She's silent a beat too long. "Do you hate that idea?"

"I don't think we're ready for that yet, but . . ." She draws in a long breath. "Now I wish I hadn't brought this up on the phone, because I want to kiss you."

I grin. "Yeah?"

"Yeah."

"Tell me what you're wearing." I keep my voice low as I push out of the stairwell and walk through the hotel hallways to my room.

Bailey laughs. "You did *not* just ask that."

"Fuck yeah I did. And in a minute, I'm going to throw the lock to my room and make this a FaceTime call so I can see for myself."

Everyone prefers home games to away games. Not only are you playing on your own turf and have a stadium full of cheering fans on your side, you get to sleep in your own bed the night before the game. I hated leaving Bailey this morning. Knowing I wouldn't be home until late Sunday night was harder still.

I slide my key into the slot over the door handle, and the light flashes green before I push in. "I'm waiting."

"If you must know, I'm in a pair of your flannel pants and a Gators T-shirt, and they both fit me way better than I anticipated, so instead of being all content as I snuggle into my husband's clothes, I'm playing around on my tablet and looking at easy weight-loss plans."

"I hope you're kidding." I drop my key on the minibar, pull my wallet out of my back pocket, and undo my belt.

"About the outfit or the diet?"

"The diet," I say, unbuttoning my shirt. "I kind of like thinking of you sitting around my house in my clothes. I bet you look adorable." I turn around and almost jump out of my skin when I realize I'm not in the room alone.

Lindy puts her finger to her lips, signaling that I should be quiet. At least she's wearing clothes this time. I guess I'll count my blessings.

"So adorable," Bailey says. She groans. "Tell me when you're ready to switch to FaceTime. I want to see you."

I scowl at Lindy and point to the door. She shakes her head. "I'm gonna need a rain check. Lindy's here."

"Lindy?" Her voice wavers on the name.

"Yeah. Unfortunately." I give Lindy a pointed look. "I just need to get rid of her and then I can call you back."

"I don't like that she's there."

"That makes two of us."

Bailey laughs. "I wish you were home. I've gotten spoiled the last few weeks, and now my body doesn't like to sleep without you."

"I feel the same," I say softly. "I'll call you later, okay?"

"Okay. I love you."

"Say it again," I say, because I don't give a fuck that Lindy's waiting for me. That will never get old.

She laughs. "I. Love. You."

"I love you, too. Miss you already." I end the call and toss my phone on the bed before giving Lindy my full attention. "This again?"

"How's your *wife*?" She shakes her head. "So fucking clever, marrying you in Vegas. Kind of wish I'd thought of it myself."

"Yeah, except I wouldn't have married you because I can't stand you."

"Right. Because you are madly in love with Miss Stripper Pics and her magical hooha."

I rub the back of my neck. I should have known that *stripper pics* thing started with Lindy. "Stop with that shit. Seriously, I had no idea you were so immature. How did I ever think I was happy with you?"

"Because you *were*." Lindy's expression softens, and she lowers her voice. "We could get that back. That's why I needed to talk to you about your wife."

"In my room? At night?"

"I didn't think you'd want me doing that in front of the guys."

"You don't need to talk to me about shit. Though if you'd talk to your dad and let him know you've moved on and he can quit fucking with my career, that would be fantastic."

She shakes her head. "You're the most naïve man I've ever met. You really think this is going to end happily?"

"I don't need to hear your opinion about my marriage or your thoughts about my wife."

"Are you so sure she's better than me? Do you think I was weak to be influenced by your parents but she's immune?"

I don't like to talk about the past, but here she is, shoving it in my face. "I think some people have more integrity than you'd ever understand."

"Really?" She shakes her head. "You're so smart, but you can be so dense."

"What are you talking about?"

"Mason, I'm a woman. I see the way she looks at you. That girl is in love with you."

"I know. Lindy, I'm in love with her too."

"Yeah, but the difference is, she's going to walk away. She's going to leave you."

My gut clenches like she just put her fist in it. "You tell yourself whatever you want."

She tilts her head to the side, and for a moment, her face shows real sympathy. "She's been in love with you for years but she wouldn't let herself be with you. Don't you wonder *why*?"

"It's complicated."

"Is it? I think it was complicated for *me*. Your parents talked to me about *your* future, *your* life, *your* hopes and dreams, and *our* baby. *That* was complicated."

"How complicated was it when you used their money to buy yourself that Porsche? I bet you looked terribly conflicted driving around with the top down." I shake my head. "You didn't even need the money. But if you didn't have to play by your daddy's rules and go to the college he chose to get the car you wanted so badly, then you won, right?"

"I'm *not* the villain. Your parents made me believe that you would resent me if I had that child."

I lean against the wall, as far from her as I can get. "You've explained yourself to me before. I'm not interested in hearing it again." I point to the door. "That's the way out."

"Stop sticking your head in the sand," she says, standing. "In Bailey's case, it's just about money. You can't get any more basic than that."

Her words send a chill through me. It's not what she's saying—I wouldn't put it past her to lie—it's the certainty in her eyes. "What do you know?"

"You know your parents aren't above bribery, and you know how they felt about her. How they *feel* about her." She turns up her palms and shrugs her shoulders to her ears. "I don't know anything, Mason. I'm just a girl who sees the red flags when they're there. I'm just someone who can feel it in her gut. This girl isn't any better than I am. She's worse." She shakes her head. "I did what I did because I loved you. I did it for *us*. For *our future*. But if I'm right about her, she won't be able to say the same. In her case, it wouldn't have been complicated. Greed is simple and selfish."

"I want you to leave."

"You can bury your head in the sand all you want, but it's not going to change the truth."

"I said leave."

She sighs heavily. "I'm just trying to warn you. You may hate me, but I still care about you."

I hold my breath until she's out the door, and when it shuts behind her, I immediately grab my phone, but I stop before calling Bailey.

I shake my head. No, Lindy's trying to make me question Bailey because she's jealous. She can't be right when I just had a conversation with Bailey about a potential pregnancy.

But I can't stop thinking about her words. If Bailey was willing to strip to send money to her sister, is it so far-fetched to think she'd have taken any money my parents offered? As I reach for my phone to call my mom, I hate myself, but the seed of doubt's been planted.

"Mason," Mom says. "Is everything okay?"

"Yes, everything's fine." We already had our regular Saturday morning conversation, so I'm sure this call takes her by surprise—a sign that I'm not doing great in the son department. "I need to ask you something."

"Of course, what is it?"

I'm ashamed of how long I hesitate, ashamed that it takes me so long to get the question out of my mouth. I don't want it to be true, but I need to know. "Mom, when I was at BHU, did you offer Bailey money?"

She gasps. "What?"

"Did you give her money to stay away from me? Or pay her in exchange for a promise to never have a relationship with me?"

"Did she tell you that?" Mom doesn't get angry often, but I hear it in her voice now, simmering quietly. "Mason, that's not true. I didn't like the girl because she was a stripper, but—"

"*She* didn't say it. I'm asking."

"No. Mason, absolutely not. I lost a year of my relationship with my son after making that mistake once. I wouldn't do it again."

I draw in a long breath, and it feels like my lungs are filling for the first time since Lindy put that piece of poison in my brain. "You understand why I had to ask."

She's silent for a beat. "I do, but I wonder why you asked me and not Bailey. With a question like that, shouldn't you have been able to ask your wife?"

BAILEY

"Next time Mia's in town, I'd like to bring her over to meet Faith."

My sister stiffens and purses her lips. "What?"

I draw in a deep breath. I didn't expect this would go great, so I'm prepared. The fact that I feel like I can even bring it up says a lot about how far we've come in the time I've been here. Yesterday, Sarah and Brandon brought Faith over to watch the game and swim. The Gators lost by fourteen, which was brutal, but more frustrating than the loss was that Mason barely got to play. They put him on special teams to receive the kickoff a few times, but he saw more play time in his first game last year than he did in this one.

When he got home, he took me straight to bed, kissing and touching me with a desperation I didn't quite understand. After, he told me about Lindy's visit and that she's still determined to win him back. When I asked him if that was what he wanted, he kissed me again, harder and more desperately than the first time around. *"You're all I want,"* he whispered as we made love again.

Today, I'm spending the afternoon with Sarah and Faith, and it's been awesome. First, because *she* invited *me* over, and second because she hasn't been rushing me out the door.

Now Faith is out back playing on the playset, and Sarah and I are cleaning up the kitchen.

"I know you're not ready to tell Faith about me yet," I say, treading carefully. "I wouldn't expect you to tell her that Mia is her aunt. But Mia lost her brother, Sarah. And I think it would do her heart a lot of good to know about Faith. If she met her, she'd see that Nic's still here in a way." I see the worry on her face, and I reach out and squeeze her wrist. "No one is going to take her away from you. Faith is your daughter. I was sure when I made that decision that it was the right one, and I stand by it. I just want Faith to meet Aunt Bailey's best friend, okay?"

Tears spill out the corners of her eyes. "Okay. I guess that'd be fine." Then she surprises me by stepping forward and wrapping me into a hug. "Bailey, I'm so afraid I'm not good enough to be her mommy. If I weren't, maybe I wouldn't be so scared."

"You're a fantastic mother." I turn her toward the windows so she can look at Faith playing on the swing set beyond. "Just look at her."

She wipes away tears and turns to watch Faith pump her legs on the swing. "I'm so afraid I'll never be the mother you are."

I frown at her. "What's that supposed to mean?"

"I'm ashamed of what you did for me. I'm ashamed that I let you, ashamed that I needed you to, and ashamed that I never would have had the courage to do it myself." She draws in a breath and looks down at her hands. "If I'd been able to figure out how to cope after Greg left, you would have never had to take that disgusting job. I just kept thinking, how much more is she going to sacrifice for us? And I was left torn between wanting to let you have a relationship with Faith and wanting to push you away so you wouldn't feel responsible for taking care of us."

"Sarah, I made my own choices. I know how you feel about them, but at the time it was a choice I was comfortable with making. I wouldn't do the same thing now, because I have a different relationship with my body today than I did then." I look away, realizing this says a lot about what Mason's done for me. He's changed a lot about the way I see myself. I was always pretty clinical when it came to thinking of my body, but now taking off my clothes for strangers *would* feel like an invasion of my privacy.

"I hate that you felt like you had to." Her face crumples. "And I hate that I was so afraid of someone taking her away from me that I let you. You were always so brave, like a mother should be."

I pull her into my arms and stroke her hair. "Giving her to you and giving you help when you needed it are my proudest accomplishments, but *you* are her mommy."

We hug each other for a long time, and years of animosity seem to melt away, replaced by a new understanding.

CHAPTER 34

MASON

Does your wife know you paid off Nic Mendez to stay away from her? What's it worth to you that she never does?

Those two questions make up the entirety of the message from a guy named Ron Abrams, whose Facebook profile lists him as working at Blackhawk Valley Financial Bank. I probably never would have seen it if the guy who manages my social media accounts hadn't flagged it and sent me an email. *This is a couple of weeks old, and it's probably bullshit, but I thought you should see it just in case. Let me know if you want me to reply. Otherwise, I'll delete it and block him, just like we handle all the other crazies.*

Ron Abrams is the asshole who sent Bailey the dick pic. He was full of apologies when I called his place of work and talked to the branch manager about him lifting people's phone numbers from their accounts. He's sure as fuck not going to see a dime from me, but that doesn't mean this isn't something I need to deal with.

I close the email application on my phone and put my head in my hands as I mentally rehearse the conversation where I tell Bailey I paid the man she loved—the father of her child—so he'd stay away from her. If I'd never done that, I probably wouldn't have given a second thought to Lindy's claim that Bailey took money from my dad, but my own guilt made me question her, and I feel shitty as hell about it.

Bailey stomps into the living room, tears the remote from my hand, and turns off the TV.

I lift a brow. "Maybe I was watching that." *I wasn't.*

She waves a folded paper in my face. I can't tell, because she's moving it too quickly, but I think it might be a bill. "I just got off the phone with the company that holds my student loans, and do you know what they said?"

"That they were paid in full?"

"Yes!" She smacks my shoulder with the bill. "They said they'd been paid in full by *my husband*. Do you want to explain, please?"

"It seems pretty self-explanatory." I take a breath and push out of the chair, because she's pissed, and I want to give her my full attention when she's raving. Her hair's wild around her face and she just looks . . . hot. "I paid them in full."

"Why? Why would you do that?" Tears spring into her eyes.

If I thought this was fun a minute ago, my brain shifts gears so hard that I'm surprised there isn't smoke. "Whoa, what's wrong? I did it because I *could*. Because I wanted to."

"You didn't have the *right*." She holds the paper in front of my face. Sure enough, it's an old bill. "That's a lot of money."

"Not to me it isn't." Okay, so it is. She was carrying some pretty heavy debt, but I knew how much it weighed on her. It was worth it to take that away.

"Fuck you, Mason. You shouldn't have done it. I don't want to owe you money." The tears don't fall down her face. No, she's too stubborn for that, but her hands are shaking.

"You don't owe me anything. It was a gift, Bailey. I don't expect you to pay me back." Stepping forward, I take the bill from her hand and toss it onto one of the chairs. "You're my wife."

"I'm your *fake* wife."

It's a fucking punch to the gut I should have seen coming. "Right. Because you have one foot out the door, no matter how I feel about you. No matter how *you* feel about *me*." I shake my head. "Is it all guys, or is it just me, Bail? Is it that no one but Nic is worth staying for, or is it just that I fall short?"

"Why are you doing this?"

"Because I'm sick of living without you."

She shakes her head, her jaw hard. "You wouldn't think that if you knew about the things I've done or the mistakes I've made."

"Then tell me. Tell me and let me prove I can love you through anything." I tuck her hair behind her ear and brush my knuckles over her cheek. "Just give me a chance," I whisper, and even though it's the first time I've said it out loud, I feel like my heart's been whispering those words for four years. "Give *us* a chance."

"A chance?" She shakes her head. "Don't you see what I've been doing here? I don't just want to give you a chance—I want to give you *everything*." Her bottom lip quivers. "But I want to *give* it to you. I don't want you buying it."

I don't know if it's her words or the look on her face that slams me in the chest, but I gather her to me and hold tight. "I'm sorry. Jesus, I never want you to feel like I was trying to buy you. I wanted you to be free of the burden of that debt, but I should have asked you."

"Do you really think we can do this?" she asks, her words muffled. I release her, and she steps back to look at me. "We come from different worlds, and I want to believe it doesn't matter, but I keep seeing all these reminders that it does."

I take her hands. "Do me a favor and close your eyes."

She frowns. "Why? So you can magically make my debt reappear?"

I laugh. "No, not that. Will you?"

She nods and closes her eyes. I don't say anything else for a breath, because I just want to look at her—her residual blush from raging at me, her soft eyelashes on her cheeks, the way her blond hair looks even lighter across her tanned shoulders. She squeezes my hands. "Okay, now what?"

"Now I want you to imagine your life in ten years." I swallow. I'm nervous, but at the same time I believe it when she says she loves me. "Your life as you'd paint it in a picture. Think about where you're living. You're working—what is your work? You wake up in the morning—who's next to you?"

She opens her eyes, and her chest rises as she inhales. "You know who's next to me."

I cup her face in my hands and dip to kiss her. "Does the rest really matter?"

BAILEY

"Do you have a dress you could wear to a party this weekend?" Mason asks.

"Sure. I have lots of dresses. What's the plan?"

It's been a hectic week for him. They had an away game in San Diego last Sunday, and tomorrow they'll host a Thursday night home game. I know he's frustrated at practices and feels as if he's fighting a losing battle for time on the field, but he's also been quieter than usual when he gets home at night. Or maybe I'm the one who's quieter. Since I found out about him paying off my student loans last night, I've been walking around with my stomach in knots about how to approach telling him the truth. It wasn't until I said the words out loud that I realized I do want to give our relationship a real chance—but I can't do that without telling him about the money I took from his father.

Mason shifts awkwardly and avoids my gaze. "It's my parents' anniversary party. They've been married for thirty years."

Everything inside me stills. "Your father asked me not to come."

"I've talked to my mother. She knows you'll be there. It's fine."

"Maybe fine with *you*, but what about me?"

He draws in a breath and looks out the window. "I'm not any happier about going than you are."

"I don't get a choice, then?"

When he turns back to me, his eyes search my face. "My father's an asshole, and he made you feel like shit by asking you not to come, and I apologize for that. For him. But I won't let him dictate my life or who is in it. He did that before, remember?"

My heart squeezes, and for a beat I forget about Lindy and think the "before" he's talking about is with me.

He takes my hands in both of his and squeezes. "You don't have to go. But we're together. And if he made you feel so unwelcome that you won't attend, then I'm not going either."

That would break his mother's heart, and obviously he wants to be there or he wouldn't be asking me to do this. I shake my head. "I don't want to make a scene."

"My parents and I don't have a good relationship, and I've been dreading their party."

"Are you dreading it because you don't want to see them, or are you dreading it because you don't want them to see you with me?"

He flinches, and I wonder if I hit on the truth. "I want you with me. The rest is unimportant."

"Mason, your parents don't like me."

He tenses, and even though it would be ridiculous, I wait for him to deny it. To defend his parents or to tell me that no one could hate me. But he nods and says, "I know. They had different plans for me."

"Ouch." It shouldn't hurt, because I knew that, but it does. I don't want him to accept it. I want him to defend me to them. "Lindy was their plan for you."

"Not *better* plans, Bailey. Just different plans."

"How are we supposed to make this work?" I ask, more of myself than of him. I want to tell him the truth. I even wrote him a letter that I planned to hand over if I couldn't make myself talk. But if I tell him now, this party he's already dreading is going to be that much worse for him.

"There's nothing to make work," he says. "We go, we talk to some people, dance, drink champagne, and then sleep it off in a resort downtown."

That's not how it'll go if I tell him now. "If we get to the party and they're unhappy that I'm there, I can leave."

"No. If they want me there, then you're going to be there, too. They're going to have to get used to that." He brings my hands to his mouth, kissing my knuckles. "You're not just a girl I drunkenly married in Vegas. You're my forever."

I bite my lip. "How am I supposed to deny you anything when you come up with lines like that?"

He grins. "I speak the truth."

CHAPTER 35

BAILEY

The game was amazing. After the rookie wide-out dropped the ball a third time in the fourth quarter, the coach finally put Mason in, and he helped the quarterback lead a drive down the field that ended in a thirty-yard touchdown pass and a Gators victory.

When I get home, I'm still buzzing with happy energy, but it all fizzles away when I see Mason's mother sitting on a stool at the kitchen island. She's all long limbs and grace, her back ramrod straight and her legs crossed at the knee. There's not a single extra ounce of fat on her, and yet she doesn't look hardened or sick. She's beautiful.

"Hello?" I offer hesitantly. "Mason's not here. He should be home soon though."

"I know." She gives a small smile. "I'm here to speak with you, Bailey."

Oh, shit. All this time I've thought of Mason's parents in general as the bad guys, but the truth is it was easier to stand up to his father. This woman is classy and elegant, and from everything I've read, she's wicked smart, too. She intimidates the shit out of me.

"You're quite beautiful," she says, looking me over. It doesn't really feel like a compliment as much as an observation. "There's quite a bit of chatter about your pictures, too. You have an eye for female beauty and a natural talent for capturing it on camera. I can appreciate that, of course."

I swallow hard, not wanting to speak until I know where this is going.

"But I suppose all that really matters," she says, seemingly unfazed by my lack of response, "is that my son's in love with you."

Even though I hear Mason say it every day now, my stomach flip-flops, and I feel as if I'm falling when I hear his mother say those words. I know he does, but I don't just want him to love me. I want him to love me and for that love to be strong enough to withstand the weight of my mistakes. "He's not a kid anymore." My voice shakes a little.

"I'm aware of that. But I need a favor from you."

"Please don't ask me to stay away from him." I shake my head. "That was a deal I never should have taken."

She frowns. "It was one my husband never should have offered."

"I'll pay you back." My skin feels tight at the promise. I already want to pay Mason back for my student loans, and I owe the bank back home for the new roof on Mom's trailer. It just feels like my life is this race to catch up, and I'll always be in someone's debt. But this is a promise I need to keep. "I never should have taken the money, and I need to pay it back."

"That's not what I'm here to ask, Bailey. I don't want your money. Not a cent."

"What do you want?"

"I want my son." Her smile is brittle. "I want him to stay in my life, and if he finds out what my husband did, he'll push us away. I don't know if he could forgive us a second time."

"Because of the baby," I whisper, and when I see the shock pass over her face, I realize she didn't expect me to know.

"Yes. Our interference with Lindy's baby almost made us lose him forever."

I swallow hard. "Maybe you don't deserve his forgiveness. Maybe neither of us do."

"Maybe we don't." She uncrosses her legs and stands. "But I'm here to tell you that if you and Mason want to be together, I'll stand behind you. In return, all I ask is that you keep our secret." She hands me a small business card with her phone number on it. "Call me for anything. I can't lose my son."

I shake my head, and the truth hits me with so much intensity that I want to be free of my secrets immediately. "If we keep this secret, we've already lost him."

"I need to tell Mason."

"Um, one second, okay?" Mia whispers. I hear the swishing of sheets. "It's just Bailey," she says to someone on her end. It's most likely Arrow, and he's most likely in bed because it's—I look at the clock—*after two a.m.*

"I'm sorry, Mee. I didn't realize how late it was." I've been stewing about this for hours since Mason's mom left. Mason's asleep, and I tried sleeping too, but that was useless. I tried reading but couldn't concentrate. I didn't realize how late it had gotten. "You can go back to bed."

"Absolutely not," she says, yawning. "What are best friends for if not for middle-of-the-night, real-life crisis freak-outs?"

I'm pacing Mason's living room, and even though I need privacy for this conversation, I'm glad he's home. This house is too big and too empty when he's gone traveling with the team. If I stay, that's something I'm going to have to get used to. *If he even wants me to stay after he learns the truth . . .* "His mom visited me. Apparently, she didn't know Christian paid me off, and she's terrified that when Mason finds out, he's going to shut them out of his life forever. She sat here and begged me not to tell him." I shake my head, but no matter how hard I try I can't forget the look in her eyes.

"The truth comes out," Mia says. "You can't outsmart it or

outrun it. And you'll never have the relationship with Mason that you want—that you *deserve*—if you keep trying to hide it."

"I know," I say. "That's exactly it. I saw how panicked she was, could see that the possibility of losing him for good haunts her. And I don't want that to be me. I want Mason, and I need to tell him I took that money. It's our only chance."

"I agree." I hear a kettle whistling and imagine Mia pouring herself a cup of tea.

"I'm ashamed."

"I know you are, sweetie. But you had reasons for doing what you did. Good, noble reasons."

"I could have been honest sooner." Panic claws at my chest. "If I'd told him years ago—"

"But you didn't. And if you wait another year or another five years, you'll still be kicking yourself for not telling him sooner."

"I'm in love with him."

Mia laughs. "Why don't you tell me something I didn't figure out years ago?"

"God, you're such a bitch."

"You love me," she says.

"I do. Thank you, Mia."

"It's going to be okay, Bailey. Just be patient when you tell him. This stuff takes time to process, but I know he'll forgive you."

I swallow hard. When Mia finds out about her niece, will forgiveness comes as easily as she believes it will for Mason? "I hope you're right."

I end the call and type Mason's mom's number in my messaging app. My stomach knots as I type out the words.

> ***Me:*** *I won't ruin your party. But after it's over, I'm telling him the truth.*

CHAPTER 36

MASON

"Are you ready for your parents' swanky party?" Owen asks. We're the last people to leave the complex most nights, but tonight we're both heading out early so we can drive to St. Augustine for my parents' anniversary party. I'd like to point out my many late nights to the coach, but I know he sees who's putting in the work and who can perform when it's game time. At this point, all I can do is hope he'll find the courage to put me on the field when Bill has given explicit instructions that he wants the rookie to have more game time.

"There is no *ready* when it comes to facing my father," I say. "But I am ready to spend the night in a ritzy hotel with my wife."

"Hotel sex," Owen says, nodding. "I hear ya."

"Fuck off." I rub my temples, where a throbbing headache has been lingering all day. "There's an asshole back in Blackhawk Valley trying to blackmail me, and I need to tell Bailey about it."

"Blackmail you about what?"

"Nic Mendez," I mutter. His name leaves a bad taste in my mouth, but maybe that's guilt.

He cocks his head. "The dead boyfriend?"

I dig my thumbs into my temples. "Bailey and I both have secrets. I feel like they all come back to him."

Owen folds his arms. "What did you do, brother?"

I shake my head. "I just didn't want him dragging her down with him. If he loved her—if he *really* loved her—it wouldn't have been so easy to keep him away."

His forehead wrinkles. "Did you pay her boyfriend to break up with her?"

"I just wanted him to stay away. He was going to ruin her life, and I loved her too much to see that happen."

"And you paid him off?"

I let out a breath. Why does he have to be so fucking direct? "Yeah."

"That's really shitty."

"He took the money. Fuck, I was offering my silence in exchange for him to stay away from Bailey. He's even the one who suggested I pay him. But yeah, it was pretty shitty. If it was as justifiable as I told myself at the time, I imagine I would have told her by now."

"And now someone's threatening to tell her if you don't pay up." He nods, piecing it together. "What are you going to do?"

"I have to tell her. When you have four years of pushing and pulling between you, you can't move forward until you're standing together on solid ground, and the only way there is through the truth."

"Great, so do it tonight on your drive to St. Augustine."

I rub the back of my neck, where I have knots on top of knots. "This party is going to be hard enough on her. My asshole father straight up told her he didn't want her there." I shake my head. "I'll tell her after." I meet Owen's steady gaze. "You think she'll understand, don't you?"

"I can't answer that. You're going to have to find out the hard way."

BAILEY

Mason's breath catches when he sees me.

To me, there's nothing that makes me feel sexier than being wanted for who I am—my mind as much as my body. I guess that comes from my time as a stripper. Body parts become less sacred when you show them to just anyone. But I'm not so enlightened that I don't get a little thrill when I come down the stairs and get that kind of reaction. He doesn't say anything at first. He just looks at me, slowly taking his eyes from my face to the swell of my breasts, to my hips, and all the way to my legs to my completely impractical shoes.

When he does smile, his grin is so wide, he's like a little boy at Christmas, but then it goes away in a flash, and his brow wrinkles with his frown.

"What are you frowning about?"

He shakes his head. "I just can't believe you're mine." His tongue darts out to wet his lips as he gives me that slow, intense once-over again. He shakes his head. "I'm just afraid this has all been a dream, and I'm going to wake up."

I'd be running to him right now, but that line turned my brain to mush, and for a beat, I don't even remember how to make my feet move. But as soon as I can, I cross to him, slide my hands behind his neck, and bring his mouth down to mine. "I don't want to wake up," I whisper.

"Me neither," he says. He cups my face and kisses me—long and slow and full, a kiss that is a claiming and a discovery all at once. This isn't just a meeting of mouths and tongues. It's our hearts, open and joining, finding a rhythm together in a way we've never allowed them to before. "I love you," he whispers.

I melt more. Something dangerous is happening to me. My insides are all gooey, liquid and vulnerable, as if he's in there and could destroy me with a single word. I'm not sure that this is something I should like, but I do, because it's Mason, and I know he won't destroy me. He'll hold my hand. He'll lift me up. "I love you too," I say against his mouth.

He keeps my face in his hands as he steps back and studies me. "Say it again, Bailey."

I smile. "I love you too. Haven't you heard me say it enough by now?"

He shakes his head. "Never." The intensity in his eyes used to scare me. It made me want to hide from him, made me so sure he'd see my ugly secrets. But now it's everything I want. My secret looms between us like a storm cloud I want to ignore.

He pulls my hand away and nips at my bottom lip. "You're such a brat."

I place the flat of my palm against his chest and push him back. "We'll go to the party like we're supposed to, and then we'll go back to our room and see how long you can keep me in bed without me getting bored."

"Challenge accepted."

I force a smile, but I'm scared. I've made up my mind to tell him the truth after the party, and he might not want to spend a second alone with me when that happens, let alone all night in bed. By the time we're settled into his car, my mind has latched on to our destination, and jittery, fuzzy nerves distract me so much that I'm sure I'm terrible company. The truth sits on my tongue, thick and paralyzing, like setting cement.

The drive passes too quickly, and the next thing I know, we're pulling up to his parents' party. I don't want to face them.

When the car pulls up to the party, a man in a tuxedo and bowtie opens my door and helps me out.

Mason gives his keys to the valet and comes around after me to take my arm. As we climb the steps to the art museum where they're having the celebration, Mason seems as tense as I am.

"Are you sure you want me here?" I ask.

He squeezes my arm. "Absolutely." He meets my gaze. "I'm here because I'm expected to be, and I want you here with me because—" He smiles and looks me over. "Because looking at you in that dress is going to be the best part of my night."

If his smile reached his eyes, or if I didn't have an ugly history with Christian Dahl, maybe that line would put me at ease.

I watch all the fancy people in their fancy dresses milling around the room. Trepidation builds in my stomach.

Now that I'm so close to giving Mason the truth, I want to get it over with. The idea of waiting another second is making me miserable. It was always so important to me that I never lied to him. I held back some truth, but never lied. Tonight, in this context, my secrets feel like lies.

I'm in a daze as we walk through the party. Everyone greets Mason with hugs and big smiles, and me with kind curiosity and welcoming handshakes. There's a string quartet playing, and waiters circulate with hors d'oeuvres.

I see his parents across the room and immediately recognize Lindy speaking to an older couple by the dance floor. *Lindy, the mother of his child.* It changes the way I see her; it changes the way I think of them together. Now, as much as I hate it, I see myself in her. I see how desperately I grappled for any affection from Nic after his sentencing. I see that frantic need for approval. I see her loneliness.

Her gaze lands on us, and she excuses herself and comes our way.

"Mason," she says when she reaches us. She grasps his forearms and kisses the air beside each cheek before turning to me and doing the same, and I'm struck by how fake she is—how fake this whole world is. I want to leave. "So nice of you two to make it."

If Mason picks up on her jab at our arriving late, he doesn't indicate it. If he thinks it's presumptuous of her to greet us like it's her party, he doesn't say.

"Your parents are going to be glad to see you regardless," she says. Then, with a pointed look toward me, she adds, "I'm almost surprised you came. You're the courageous little thing, aren't you?"

What does that mean? Does she know about the money? I mentally redact all my sympathetic thoughts. I was hurt when Nic pushed me away, but I wasn't a bitch. I paste on a smile, lift my chin, and say, "From what I hear, you wouldn't know courage if it bit you in the ass."

She flinches and pulls back her shoulders. Another couple calls her name. "Excuse me," she says with a tight smile before walking away.

"Sorry about that," Mason says. "She can be awful."

"Why do you let her?"

He's distracted, and I can't shake this sick feeling that he wishes we hadn't come. Or is he wishing I hadn't come?

I'm being paranoid, and I try to talk myself out of it, but the hair pricks at the back of my neck the way it does when I find myself several stories up and unexpectedly getting a view of the ground below.

Someone puts a glass of champagne in my hand, and I drink it too quickly. I'm introduced to countless people, and with each name and face, Mason goes stiffer by my side. There's more champagne, more faces and names, more forced laughter.

My cheeks hurt from smiling, and my head spins.

I turn to Mason between introductions. "Excuse me, I need to find the ladies' room for a minute."

He squeezes my hand and points to a hallway on the opposite side of the gallery. "Right that way."

Christian spots me on my way to the restroom. We haven't even greeted the guests of honor yet. Was that coincidence or intentional on Mason's part? "Hello, Bailey," he says, his voice as slick as oil. "You look lovely tonight. Is that the dress you picked out to bury my relationship with my son?"

I give him a polite smile and walk right past him, but then I force myself to stop and turn around. I take a breath and look him in the eye. "I don't know what he's going to say or how he's going to take it, but I do know that I'm not willing to keep this secret anymore."

"Yes," he says, smiling. "That's what you keep saying, and yet here we are. I told my wife she didn't need to worry."

"I'm sorry," I whisper. "I wanted you to have tonight. I wanted *her* to have tonight, but tomorrow . . ."

He chuckles. "Tomorrow, you'll be moving out."

My chest squeezes. Is he so sure Mason will want to be rid of me? I search the room for Lindy and find her glaring at me while a man talks to her. Yes, maybe he will, but like Mia said, if I just give him time and space . . . "You don't know that."

"What I know is how much you hate me," he says, scanning

the room. "I see it in your eyes."

Am I supposed to deny it? He's my father-in-law, true, but it takes more than legalities to change a relationship.

"And when you find out just how much my son is like his father, you'll be out of my hair." He grins and drinks a full glass of champagne in one pull. "I don't know why I didn't see it sooner."

"Why you didn't see what?"

"The way to get rid of you." He pulls something from his back pocket and hands it to me. It's a white envelope. There's no writing on it, but it's sealed. "You don't need to look at it now. Unless you want to leave, which I would consider an anniversary gift."

I stare at the envelope in his hands while my heart races faster and faster in my chest. "Are you trying to trick me into taking money?"

He laughs. "No, your chance to profit has passed."

People are starting to stare, so I snatch it out of his hands. "Whatever is in here, I'm showing to Mason."

He raises his brows. "My son hates me either way, but at least this way I can ensure Bill will give him a good career and stop benching him. Knowing your filthy hands will never end up with my money is an added bonus." He waves to someone behind me. "Mike! Good of you to come!"

I rush to the bathroom and lock myself in a stall, where I open the envelope with shaking hands. I should wait and do this with Mason, but it feels like a trick—as if Christian knows some terrible secret about me that even I don't.

When I unfold the paper, I'm confused. It's the bank copy of a processed check for five thousand dollars to Nic Mendez. Why did Mason's dad write a check to Nic?

But then my eyes land on the signature line. Christian didn't write this check. Mason did.

CHAPTER 37

MASON

With the exception of my parents, who I'm saving for last, I think I finished making the rounds with everyone while Bailey was in the bathroom. Now we can enjoy our dinner, dance to a couple of songs, and politely excuse ourselves for the rest of the evening.

But first I have to find her.

I wander around the party looking for her and run into Lindy.

"Did your wife go missing?" she asks, a knowing smile on her face.

I frown. "Where is she?"

She shrugs. "I don't know. Last I saw her, she was talking to your dad. Seemed like important business, so I didn't butt in."

What was she talking to my dad about? Why would she even want to talk to him?

I turn around, walking away from Lindy without another

word.

My phone buzzes with a text from Owen.

> **Owen:** *She was going to get a cab and leave, but I talked her into letting me take her. We're at the hotel bar. Don't know what's wrong, but it's bad. Did you tell her about the money?*

I don't bother telling anyone or even getting my car from the valet. I grab a cab to the hotel, my heart racing and my stomach in knots.

I find her in the bar, drinking with Owen.

"You trying to steal my girl?" I ask Owen, trying for lightness.

Bailey's jaw goes hard. "What if he is? Do you have enough money to pay off a veteran NFL player?"

"Oh, damn," Owen whispers.

Did he say something to her? Did Ron get to her? I thought she blocked that fucker's number, but he could have found her online like he did me.

She turns to Owen. "How much would he have to pay you to stay away from me? Five grand? Sixty? What does a ho like me go for these days?"

"Bailey," he says softly. "Come on."

My stomach drops. *Fuck. Fuck, fuck, fuck.* "Let's go somewhere and talk," I say quietly. I don't want to have this conversation here.

"Your dad was right," she says, pulling an envelope from her purse. "He knows just how to get rid of me."

I take the envelope from her hands and pull out the paper. It's a photocopy of a canceled check. I feel like I just took a helmet to the gut, and I want to puke.

I never told my father about what I did, but he was still on my accounts back then, and why wouldn't he monitor them? He micromanaged every other aspect of my life.

"You paid him off," Bailey says, her voice shaking. "You paid off Nic to stay away from me." She shakes her head. "Who made you God and told you that you could meddle in my life? Who did you think you were?"

I swallow. "Can we go somewhere and talk?"

"We are somewhere," she says. "Talk."

"I'm gonna get out of here." Owen looks between me and Bailey helplessly, then backs away from the table. "You both know where to find me if you need me."

"Please?" I offer her my hand, and she stands without taking it.

The silence in the elevator is suffocating, but it's nothing compared to when we get to the room, and she flinches at the sound of the door closing behind her.

"Don't you see, Bailey? You want me to be the bad guy, but it's not that simple. If he'd *loved* you? If he'd given *two shits* about being with you? He wouldn't have taken my goddamned money."

"You say that with such surety. As if you have any fucking idea what it's like to have *nothing*. You don't know. You'll never understand." Her cheeks bloom red with anger, and she balls her hands into tight fists at her sides. "You stand there all holierthan-thou about a decision you'll never have to make."

"Like I didn't have hard decisions to make? The woman I loved was dedicating her life to a criminal."

"He served his time."

"And then he got out and picked up right where he left off." Confusion flashes over her face. "He was *dealing*, Bailey."

She flinches, and I see the surprise in her expression. The shock. Like I smacked her with the truth. "That's why I wanted him away from you. I didn't want him pulling you down."

She rubs her bare arms and meets my eyes. I've broken her heart. I see it, and for the thousandth time, I wish we could start over. I'd lie to my parents about the name of my girlfriend so they couldn't look her up and bribe her. I'd get her drunk in Vegas before Nic was ever released from prison.

"You're just like your father. So sure that your money will get you anything you want. And I guess it worked for a while, didn't it? You paid Nic for me, and instead of sucking his dick, I was sucking yours."

I flinch. "It wasn't like that. I knew you didn't want me, but I didn't want him ruining your life. I'm not my father. When he convinced Lindy to give up the baby—"

"This isn't about Lindy." She squeezes her arms so tightly that I can see the red fingerprints forming. "Your dad paid me to stay away from you. Fifteen thousand dollars in exchange for my promise that I wouldn't let our relationship become anything more than physical."

I stagger backward and blink at her. "No. I asked my mom. I

. . . She promised." Did she say he offered her money, or that she took it?

"It was your dad's deal. Not hers. At the time, I thought it was so crazy that he could do something so disgusting. I didn't have a choice. I needed the money. Your dad had a choice—whether he was going to offer it or not, whether he was going to accept me as a human being or make me be part of your life in only the cheapest way possible."

"What do you *mean*, you didn't have a choice? Everybody has a choice. Nic had a choice when I gave him that check, and he didn't blink. *You* had a choice."

I turn away. Looking at her face hurts too much. I'm sinking, being sucked deeper and deeper under the surface, and the only thing that can pull me back up is if she tells me this is all some sort of awful joke and she didn't take the money for him. "Was it for Faith?" My voice cracks. "Did she need it?"

"What?"

I close my eyes. "Was Faith the reason you took the money? You were stripping to help her. Was this more of the same? Was she sick or—"

"No. I was trying to keep Nic out of trouble. He owed some bad guys money. Not taking it was like sentencing Nic to a life of crime. It was his ticket back to prison."

"Nic? You took their money for Nic?"

"I couldn't watch the father of my child fall right back in with the people who'd gotten him arrested to begin with. He was released owing them money."

"He was dealing anyway. You didn't save him."

"I didn't *know* that!" Her voice is hoarse, raw. "But you know, you're right. I had choices. Maybe I should have taken the choice behind door number two and slept with Clarence for the money instead. He promised he'd make it *real* good for me, and you never would have known. I could have spread my legs for him every night before climbing into bed with you. I could have let him fuck me until he was tired of me. I guess I didn't really give that option as much consideration as I should have."

"He wasn't worth any option." I draw in a breath, and it fucking hurts. "It'd be different if you did it for her. It would still hurt like a bitch that you never told me, that you let them manipulate you and me, but it would be different. But the money was for him, so that's not the situation we're looking at."

"I did do it for her. Don't you understand?" She wipes at her eyes with the back of her hand, as if she's angry with the tears for appearing. "I did it for him, too. It's true. But I did it for her, because one day, one way or another, she was going to know who her real parents were, and I didn't want it to be Bailey the stripper and that drug dealer Nic, who's back in prison." She reaches out and then pulls back, shaking her head. "I told you we were too different. Our worlds too different."

"Don't. Bailey, I'm hurting too, okay, but don't—"

"I can stand here and tell you I'd do something different with what I know now, but what does that even mean?" She backs toward the door. "If I had to make the same choice with the same information I had then, I'd do it again."

allowed to hate me forever."

I grimace. "I'm not sure I'm past the point where you're allowed to say anything but how much of an ass Mason is."

"That was before the ice cream. Now, we're both going to be five pounds heavier in the morning, and the payment is honesty."

I blow out a breath. I'm not sure I'm ready for honesty, but maybe it's what's been missing in my life. "Okay. Hit me."

She straightens as she draws in a long breath, her chest rising. "I loved Nic, and I really believed that one day he'd shape up. But I also knew him well enough to see that a straight life wasn't going to be easy for him. He was so angry with the world for dealing him a bum hand." She shakes her head. "But even though he was my brother and I loved him, if I'd had the money and known he was dealing again, I would have done exactly what Mason did."

"If you'd done something like that, you would have told me. And then I could have called him on being a sellout."

"Maybe," she says. She reaches out and tucks my hair behind my ear as if I'm a little girl. "I'm saying that I understand what Mason was doing. I don't have to like his choices to be able to see that his intentions were good. I hated Nic dating you. I always believed you deserved better, and he was my brother."

I lay my head in her lap and close my eyes as she plays with my hair. "All this with the money and his father? It just proves that Mason and I are too different."

"But Mason's never been a snob. Not really. Don't you remember the night you and I were catering that dinner party at Arrow's house, and Mason was hiding in the kitchen because in the dining room they were talking about the year of the wine? He can't stand that crap. He was raised with money, but it's not fair to hold that against him when money has never been everything to him."

"The worlds we come from are too different."

"But the only world he wants to live in is the one you're a part of."

"I'm not sure if that's true anymore. I'm not sure he's going to be able to forgive me for taking that money from his dad."

"I think he will." She points to my phone, which has been buzzing since I arrived, the notification LED flashing madly. "I bet he already has."

MASON

"I'm so sorry, sweetie." Mom has been slathering on the apologies since I walked in the door this morning. "You have to believe me when I say your father did what he did for you out of love."

Dad's in his office. He's chosen not to come out and take part in this conversation. *Coward.*

"I've heard this speech before, Mom. You can't make all the shit you don't like in my life disappear."

"One day you'll have a child, and you'll understand."

"I *do* have a child. Don't you remember? On my way to

college, and my girlfriend disappears to have my baby? You took it out of my hands, just like you tried to take this out of my hands. Disapproving of something in my life doesn't grant you the right to make it go away."

"What about us?" Dad asks, emerging from his den for the first time. "Maybe I didn't do it for you. Maybe I did it for *us*. I didn't work this goddamned hard to have my son throw away his life becoming the next *Teen Dad*. And I sure as fuck didn't work this hard to watch him marry a whore."

"Christian!" Mom shouts. "Enough."

I jump forward, and Mom grabs my arm. My chest puffs. "Call her that again."

"People don't change," Dad says.

I release a puff of air. "Yeah. You can say that again." I back up, because I'm afraid if I'm this close to him much longer, I'll take a swing and it'll feel fucking amazing.

I walk out of the house, straight to my car. I came here to say my piece before leaving town, but I was an idiot if I thought my father was going to admit that he was wrong. When I start the engine, Mom's standing right beside my door. She's got her arms folded and her shoulders up around her ears as if it's thirty degrees out here and not eighty.

I roll down my window and rub my forehead, where an epic headache feels like railroad ties pounding into my temples.

"What he did was wrong and unacceptable. I would have stopped him if I'd known. That's probably why he never told me about it." She takes a breath. "I can stand here and apologize until

I'm blue in the face for what your father did, but I know it means nothing unless it comes from him, so let me apologize for my part."

I stiffen. "I thought you didn't have anything to do with this."

"I didn't at first." She drops her arms and swallows. "But after you asked me on the phone, I confronted your father about it, and he admitted what he'd done. I should have told you, maybe, but I went to her instead. I asked her to keep it quiet, and she refused." Mom gives me a sad smile. "For what it's worth, she won me over in that moment, which was hard, because I knew you might not give us a second chance, but I loved her for wanting to do right by you."

I close my eyes. Bailey has always been afraid of my parents, and the twisted knots in my chest loosen a bit at the knowledge that she stood up to them.

"I hope you'll forgive your father, Mason."

"I don't need him, Mom." I shake my head. "I don't need love that's contingent on me being a certain person or living my life a certain way. That's not love."

"No, it's not, which is why when you leave here today, he'll still love you." She lets out a long breath. "I don't know if that counts for much given what he's done, but it remains true."

"You know what the hardest part about this is?" I turn away from her and grip the steering wheel. "Realizing I'm no better than him. I screwed up. She had this boyfriend, this piece-of-shit guy she followed around. I gave him money to stay away. Just like Dad would have done. I must have made him so proud when he found out."

"Mason—"

"Don't." I shake my head, because I don't want to hear her defend him again today. "We all think our reasons justify our actions. But anything we have to keep secret from someone we love is a problem. Bailey left, and I don't know if she's coming back."

"Don't wait for her." Mom reaches out and her fingertips graze my arm. "Go after her."

CHAPTER 39

BAILEY

"When are you coming back to Seaside?" Emma asks. "Keegan and I were hoping you could do our engagement pictures, and my friend Becky is pregnant and looking for someone to do artful maternity pictures."

Leave it to Emma to make me feel like my business is about more than knowing how to get men off. What sucks is I really want to do it, but I'm not sure I can handle going back to Seaside right now. "I'm not there anymore, Em."

"What? What about Mason? Please don't tell me you're still pretending you're not in love with him."

"I think we broke up."

The phone is muffled, and I hear her tell someone else, "Bailey and Mason broke up." Then she chirps, "Keegan, I wasn't done talking to her."

"What did he do?" Keegan asks. "Tell me now so I can go beat him up. You're the best thing he ever had."

I squeeze my eyes shut. I really don't want to tell my friends the truth about what I did, but it'll get back to them one way or another, and it'll be better coming from me. At least, I think it will. "His dad gave me money back in college in exchange for my promise to never let my relationship with Mason become anything serious." I wait for his outrage, but he's silent. "I shouldn't have taken it, but I needed it, so I did."

"That's shit," he says. "Bailey, I'm so sorry he did that to you."

Why does his kindness hurt so much? "I'm not the one who deserves the apology here."

"But you do." He sighs. "I grew up poor too, remember? I get it. If you needed the money and he offered it, what were you supposed to do?"

"It's not that simple." I don't want to tell him about Mason giving Nic money. It doesn't feel right. "His parents will always be his parents, and if Mason and I want to be together, we'd always have that tension. It's complicated."

Keegan exhales loudly, his exasperation echoing through the phone.

"It doesn't have to be complicated at all." Those words don't come from Keegan but from the man standing in the middle of Mia's living room.

I put my hand over my mouth.

Mason sinks to his haunches and takes the phone from my hand. "She's gonna have to call you back," he says. He smiles as

Keegan says something, then says, "Of course I did . . . Yeah . . . Shut up, Keegan, I'm working on it." He taps the screen to end the call then tosses the phone onto the couch.

Mia appears behind Mason, her purse slung over her shoulder. She nods toward the door. "I'm gonna step out for a bit. Call if you need me."

I swallow and nod but don't take my eyes from Mason as Mia walks away and the door clicks closed behind her.

"You said it's complicated, but there's nothing complicated about the way I feel for you. The other crap is messy, but it doesn't change the fact that nothing hurts as much as watching you walk away."

I want to jump into his arms, and I want to tell him to leave.

I want to listen to every word he has to say, and I want to refuse.

"I should never have offered Nic money to stay away from you." He sits in front of me on the coffee table and leans forward, his elbows on his knees. "I didn't intend to, but in the end, I saw an opportunity to keep you safe from his influence, and I took it."

"He was a son of a bitch," I say, my eyes filling with tears all over again. "He promised me he wouldn't deal anymore." I shake my head. "I think I knew and just didn't want to admit it to myself. I didn't want to believe that I'd sold my soul for nothing. I'm just as bad as Lindy. I'm worse."

"But you're not, Bailey." He shakes his head. "She didn't need the money, and she didn't just take a check. She took my *child*. You did what you believed you had to do. You were in an impossible position and you needed the money. As much as it hurts, I understand." He reaches for my hand and skims his fingertips across my knuckles, then lifts his eyes to mine. "Come home."

"I promised myself I'd never take your money, and I already have. Through your parents, through your money to Nic, through my student loans . . ."

"I don't care about the money. I only care about you, but I get it. I understand how it feels dirty to you, like I bought you." He closes his eyes, and I steal the moment to study his perfect face—the angle of his cheekbones, the firm cut of his jaw, his soft lips. "Bailey, I don't want to *buy* your love any more than you want to be bought. I want to wake up every day and know you're there because you want to be. We've been through hell to be together. People don't do this shit for money. It sucks too much."

I laugh and grab his hand. "It totally sucks."

"Can we kiss and make up yet?"

"What about your dad?"

"I don't want to kiss him," he says. I laugh, and that makes him grin, but his smile falls away as he shrugs. "Whether you're in my life or not, my father and I will have a difficult relationship. He's my father, but he's not my family."

I frown. "What makes someone your family, then?"

"Family is the foundation of your life. They're who you go home to, who you need when you have a bad day, and who you can forgive for anything." He slides a hand into my hair and looks into my eyes. "For me, that's always been you."

"And the Gators win!" the announcer calls, and Mia and I dance around Mason's living room—not just in celebration of the win but in celebration of Mason finally getting the play time he deserves. I've been back in Seaside for two weeks and this is the second game Mason's been a starter again. Rumor has it that Bill was sick of losing and finally did what he should have been doing all along—told the coaches to play whomever they thought could win the game.

Since both of our husbands are traveling this weekend, Mia flew down to spend the weekend with me. "This calls for wine," I say, heading to the kitchen before I stop myself and turn back to her. "Unless you're pregnant?"

She laughs and shakes her head. "I'm not and we aren't trying yet. But it is nice to know that if we had a surprise we would both be okay with it."

"Absolutely. I get that."

She joins me in the kitchen. While I get the wine, she pulls two glasses from the cabinet. "Both when Mom moved away and when Nic died, the loss just came so suddenly that sometimes I have to remind myself that I don't need to rush my life with Arrow, and even if I wanted to, it wouldn't bring Nic back."

My hand shakes as I pour the wine. She just gave me the opening I need, but I'm so nervous. "Do you remember the summer in high school when my sister adopted a new baby and I came down to help her?" I study Mia's face as I ask her. I feel as if I've been holding my breath all day.

"You mean when you blew off the first two weeks of school because you were having too much fun in Florida?" She nods but she's smiling. "I remember."

I bite my lip. "I wasn't just coming down to help her. I was coming down because I had to be here." I pull up a picture of Faith on my phone and hand it to Mia. "That's Faith. She turned six this summer."

Mia's eyes widen as she looks at the screen. I wonder if she sees what no one else knows to look for—Nic's kind eyes, Mia's heart-shaped hairline, a smile that is just like mine. "She's beautiful."

She doesn't suspect anything, and guilt has my heart in a vise. She *wouldn't* suspect anything because she's my best friend, and she wouldn't expect me to keep such a big secret. "She's Nic's."

Mia tears her eyes from the screen to look at me, and they're full of questions.

"She's mine and Nic's." A dozen emotions cross over Mia's face, and I hold my breath, waiting to see which will stay.

"I have a niece?"

I nod. "I'm sorry I couldn't tell you. I'm sorry I never told you. I was so scared. And Sarah really is very private. Her life fell apart when her husband left, and I think maybe part of her wondered if she had any right to Faith after that. She'd been so self-righteous about raising her, because she had this great life to give my little girl. And then that all fell apart, and she was only getting by with my help. It's not like I was trying to take Faith back, but maybe subconsciously she was always worried I might want to. And who wouldn't? This kid's amazing."

Mia's hand shakes. Her fingers hover over the screen as if she wants to touch it but is afraid Faith might disappear if she dares.

"I want you to meet her."

Her eyes lift to mine. "Really?"

"I got the okay from Sarah. She doesn't want Faith to know you're her daddy's sister—not yet—but if you're okay with just being Aunt Bailey's friend, we can go meet her today."

"Thank you, Bailey." She bites her bottom lip and tears spill onto her cheeks. "Thank you so much."

I shake my head. "What are you thanking me for? I kept this from you, and that wasn't right."

She squeezes my hand. "Thank you for giving me my brother back. In a way."

I wrap my arms around her and hug her so tightly, saying a silent prayer of thanks for having a friend like her, even if I never did anything to deserve her.

CHAPTER 40

BAILEY

"What are you doing, Mason?"

"Okay," he says. "You can open your eyes."

I'm nervous, my stomach fluttering as if it's nothing more than scraps of paper in the wind. But when I do open my eyes, I'm not even sure where we are. It's dark, and there's a fence in front of us and lights in the distance. "I don't understand."

"We're at the airport."

I look at the lights in front of us and then back to Mason and his anxious smile. "Yeah, but why?"

He swallows. "Nic used to take you to the airport on dates, right?"

"Yeah . . ."

"I'm glad I wasn't your childhood crush, because crushing on the bad boy next door made you daring. I'm glad I wasn't your first love, because loving a man everyone thought the worst of made you unapologetic. I'm grateful I wasn't your first lover, because giving Faith to your sister made you selfless. I don't want to erase Nic from your life, because I'm madly in love with the woman you are, and he's part of you."

My eyes brim with tears. *Damn. Why does he have to be so good at this?*

"I can't bring him back for you, Bailey. All these years I've been waiting for you to want me more than you want him, but almost losing you for real made me realize how stupid that was. Love isn't an elementary school game of kickball. It's not about being picked first. It's about wanting to give you everything I can. It's about wanting to experience life with you by my side. I know you don't like fancy things, which is good, because God knows if they'll ever renew my contract, and a two-year NFL career doesn't exactly make for a life of riches." Chuckling, he ducks his head. "I don't need fancy things, and I don't need you to love me more than you loved him. I just want a chance to love you and live my life with you, and to bring you as much happiness as I can. I'll take whatever love you have to give me. Less or more, bigger, smaller—love doesn't work like that, and I'm sorry I thought it did."

In my chest, my healing heart aches at its seams. "I never loved Nic more than I love you. I just loved him more publicly than I loved you. Because a girl like me is allowed to love a guy like him, and even I didn't have the audacity to love a man like you, Mason. Loving Nic wasn't scary, because I always knew he'd push me away again. And if he ever stopped pushing me away, I knew exactly what a life with him would look like. But loving you is the most terrifying thing I've ever done, because it means I have to believe in myself enough to think I deserve your love in return."

He draws in a ragged breath and shakes his head. "Jesus, Bailey, you deserve more."

I squeeze his hands. "I'm getting there, okay? But this?" I wave to the lights of the airport in the distance. "Mason, I don't need you to try to be Nic or give me what Nic would have given me. I don't *want* that. I just want you, as yourself, giving me the chance to grow, the chance to be brave enough to love you despite my mistakes."

"You have me."

"Forever?"

"And always."

EPILOGUE

BAILEY

When I wake up, there's a ring on my finger and a man in my bed. Both were there yesterday, and both were in my plans. *Thank you, Vegas.*

Behind me, Mason groans and nuzzles his face into my neck. "Is it morning already?" he asks, his hand sliding over my stomach and slinking lower.

I place my hand on top of his. "It is morning already. Feeling rough?"

"I think I might be too old for Vegas."

I laugh and twist in his arms so I can see his face. "We didn't even drink last night."

"Or sleep," he says, grinning. "Not that I'm complaining."

"It was fun, wasn't it? Everybody together again." We all flew out yesterday and met at the same hotel where we gathered for the weekend one year ago. Then, we were there for Arrow and

Mia's bachelor and bachelorette party. This time, we're doing the same for Keegan and Emma. It's so much like the last trip, but so different. This time, Mason and I actually got to spend the weekend in each other's arms instead of just wanting to.

"How's my bride this morning?" he asks, his voice low and husky.

"Tired and happy." I skim my fingertips over the stubble on his cheek. There's something about this man before he shaves that makes me purr. "Do you think our friends think we're crazy?"

"Do I care?" He kisses my neck. His hand slips between our bodies and finds its way between my legs.

"Mason, focus." The command loses power when I spread my thighs and shift my hips to give him a better angle.

"I am focused." He touches me with the flat of his palm, rocking against me before exploring with his fingers.

I shove at his shoulder so he rolls to his back. Straddling his hips, I hold his hands on either side of his head. "I asked if you think our friends think we're crazy."

"What's crazy about renewing our vows?" He tugs his hands free and cups my breasts, his thumbs skimming over my nipples.

I tilt my head to the side and rock my hips. "Maybe the part where we did it in a wedding chapel in Vegas," I say, breathless. "Or the part where we did it in the middle of the night."

He arches his hips off the bed to put pressure between my legs. "You can't claim you were drunk this time."

"I was completely sober," I whisper.

"And you can't run away from me."

I grin. “I mean, I *could* . . .”

He grabs my hips and guides me to slide over him and down his hard length. After last night’s marathon lovemaking, I woke up ready, but I still gasp, a little tender as he enters me.

“I don’t want to run away,” I tell him. “You’re not going to dodge my calls like you did the first time we got married, are you? I prefer it when you’re talking to me.”

“You like it when I talk?” He skims his fingertips across my belly and then dips to between my thighs where he finds my clit with his thumb. “Do you want me to talk about how this will never get old? Or about how good it feels to know you’re going to be in my bed every night? I’ll talk all damn day if that’s what gets you off.” My eyes float closed. “Focus, Bailey.” But his thumb keeps working, and it’s hard to think about anything but how good it feels to have him filling me up. My body winds tighter and tighter. “Do you have any idea how much I want you? How much I think about you? Any idea how beautiful you are?”

He removes his hand from between my legs, and I cry out, but then he’s rolling me to my back, switching our positions so his weight is on me—delicious and sweet. He frames my face with his hands and smiles down at me, his eyes hazy with lust.

My phone plays Mia’s ringtone, and Mason groans. “Did I seriously tell her I considered her family? Because she’s about to get blacklisted. You need to teach her what mornings in Vegas are reserved for.”

I laugh, but my laughter dissolves as he pulls my knee up and slides in deeper. “They’re waiting for us,” I murmur. “Remember, we're supposed to do breakfast."

"I'd better hurry, then," he says, clearly in no hurry at all.

THE END

Thank you for reading *In Too Deep*, the fifth book in The Blackhawk Boys series. If you'd like to receive an email when I release a new book, please sign up for my newsletter at lexiryan.com

If you enjoyed this book, please consider leaving a review. Thank you for reading. It's an honor!

IN TOO DEEP

Playlist

"I Was Made for Loving You" by Tori Kelly, feat. Ed Sheeran
"Fallingforyou" by The 1975
"L.S.D." by Jax
"Something Just Like This" by The Chainsmokers
"Issues" by Julia Michaels
"Malibu" by Miley Cyrus
"Lay Me Down" by Sam Smith
"Use Me" by The Goo Goo Dolls
"Heavy" by Linkin Park feat. Kiiara
"Skinny Love" by Birdy
"Bad Liar" by Selena Gomez
"Stay" by Zedd feat. Alessia Cara

Other Books

by LEXI RYAN

The Blackhawk Boys

Spinning Out (Arrow's story)

Rushing In (Chris's story)

Going Under (Sebastian's story)

Falling Hard (Keegan's story)

In Too Deep (Mason's story – coming September 2017)

Love Unbound

by LEXI RYAN

If you enjoy the Blackhawk Boys, you may also enjoy the books in Love Unbound, the linked series of books set in New Hope and about the characters readers have come to love.

Splintered Hearts (A Love Unbound Series)

Unbreak Me (Maggie's story)

Stolen Wishes: A Wish I May Prequel Novella (Will and Cally's prequel)

Wish I May (Will and Cally's novel)

Or read them together in the omnibus edition,

Splintered Hearts: The New Hope Trilogy

Here and Now (A Love Unbound Series)

Lost in Me (Hanna's story begins)

Fall to You (Hanna's story continues)

All for This (Hanna's story concludes)

Or read them together in the omnibus edition,

Here and Now: The Complete Series

Reckless and Real (A Love Unbound Series)

Something Wild (Liz and Sam's story begins)

Something Reckless (Liz and Sam's story continues)

Something Real (Liz and Sam's story concludes)

Or read them together in the omnibus edition,

Reckless and Real: The Complete Series

Mended Hearts (A Love Unbound Series)

Playing with Fire (Nix's story)

Holding Her Close (Janelle and Cade's story)

Other Titles

by LEXI RYAN

Hot Contemporary Romance

Text Appeal

Accidental Sex Goddess

Decadence Creek Stories and Novellas

Just One Night

Just the Way You Are

ACKNOWLEDGMENTS

I usually thank my husband first, but this time I'd like to thank the genius who thought of cold-brew coffee. I mean, the warm stuff is awesome, but I've come to the conclusion that cold brew and me are soul mates. It's there for me when the writing gets tough, and if there's one thing I know I can count on, it's that the writing *will* get tough.

In all seriousness, I can't write a book without thanking my husband. As I once heard a writer say of her partner in an acceptance speech, "I could do it without you, but I wouldn't want to." Brian understands me and my process, and he picks up the slack when getting a book revised to my standards means a weekend (or three) away from the family. Thank you for everything, Brian. Thank you for believing in me and encouraging me when I need it most. You're truly my favorite . . . next to cold brew. Let's say you're a very close second.

In addition to my rock-star husband, I'm surrounded by a family who supports me every day. To my kids, Jack and Mary, thank you for making me laugh and giving me a reason to work hard. I am so proud to be your mommy. To my mom, dad, brothers, and sisters, thank you for cheering me on—each in your own way. I'm so grateful to have been born into this crazy crew of seven kids.

I'm lucky enough to have a life full of amazing friends, too.

This book is for Stef, who gets how simple and painful and beautiful Bailey's choice was. My characters are never based on my friends, but sometimes their bravery is inspired by them. Many thanks to Mira, the bringer of laughter, the giver of pep talks, and the holder of all my (terribly boring) secrets. Thanks also to my workout friends and the entire CrossFit Terre Haute crew, especially Robin, who checks up on me when I disappear too long into the writing cave and likes to remind me that taking care of myself is important too, and my coach, Matt, who creates workouts that are so freaking hard I go more consistently just because I'm trying to avoid that *I think I'm going to die today* feeling that comes with taking time off.

To everyone who provided me feedback on this story along the way—especially Janice Owen, Lisa Kuhne, Mira Lyn Kelly, and Samantha Leighton—you're all awesome. Thanks to my nephew Kai, who humors this old lady with answers when she asks things like, "Do people still say *punked*?" Thank you to Nathan Pence, who works at the federal prison that Bailey visits in this book. Those scenes would have been completely inaccurate if it hadn't been for him. Any remaining errors are my own. As always, I owe thanks to many people for helping to make this idea in my head into something worth reading.

Thank you to the team that helped me package this book and promote it. Sarah Hansen at Okay Creations designed my beautiful cover and did a lovely job branding the series. Rhonda and Lauren, thank you for the insightful line and content edits and for being understanding when I can't meet a deadline to save my life. Thanks to Arran McNicol at Editing720 for proofreading. A shout-out to my assistant Lisa Kuhne for trying to keep me in line. (It's a losing battle, but she gives it her all.) Thank you to Give Me Books for organizing the release and to Jennifer Beach for making the gorgeous teasers. A huge thank-you to the USA Today Happily Ever After blog for featuring the cover reveal. To all of the bloggers and reviewers who help spread the word about my books, I am humbled by the time you take out of your busy lives for my stories. I can't thank you enough. You're the best.

To my agent, Dan Mandel, for believing in me and staying by my side. Thanks to you and Stefanie Diaz for getting my books into the hands of readers all over the world. Thank you for being part of my team.

And last but certainly not least, a big thank-you to my fans. I've said it before and I'll continue to say it every chance I get—you're the coolest, smartest, best readers in the world. I wouldn't get to do this job without you, and appreciate each and every one of you!

~Lexi

CONTACT

I love hearing from readers. Find me on my Facebook page at facebook.com/lexiryanauthor, follow me on Twitter and Instagram @writerlexiryan, shoot me an email at writerlexiryan@gmail.com, or find me on my website: www.lexiryan.com